Eternal Flame

by:

Jacquelyn Bishop

This book is dedicated to all of my wonderful friends here at Columbus Estates who have encouraged me so much

Thank you ALL

PROLOGUE

The fire had burned low in the hearth, its embers casting a faint glow across the stone walls of Tristan's chamber. The hour was late, yet sleep would not come.

He sat at the edge of the oak table, fingers curled around the hilt of his dagger as if expecting trouble to find him even here, in the sanctuary of his stronghold.

Outside, a cold wind howled across the battlements, rattling the shutters and carrying with it a foreboding Tristan could not shake.

That's when he heard it—the steady clatter of hooves on the cobbled courtyard below.

Tristan rose, his movements fluid, controlled. He crossed the chamber in three long strides and threw open the window.

A cloaked rider dismounted, torchlight flickering across the silver crest of the Order of the Silver Flame stitched into his tunic.

Tristan's jaw tightened.

The rider had come for him.

By the time the servant escorted the messenger into the hall, Tristan was already waiting, fully dressed, boots laced tight, sword strapped to his hip.

The cloaked figure bowed low. "My lord, forgive the hour."

Tristan's piercing blue eyes didn't waver. "Speak."

The messenger pulled a sealed scroll from inside his cloak, offering it with both hands. "A summons. From the Order."

The wax seal bore the sigil of a flame encircled by a serpent—unchanged for centuries.

Tristan broke the seal with his thumb. The parchment crinkled in his hands as his eyes swept across the lines of elegant script.

"Lord Tristan de Léon,

You are hereby summoned to appear before the High Council of the Silver Flame at first light on the seventh day. Matters of grave importance threaten the realm, and only those sworn to the Order may stand against them.

You will come alone.

For the sake of the crown and kingdom, do not fail us.

Signed, Grandmaster Sareth"

Tristan's fingers tightened around the parchment until it creased.

The Order.

The brotherhood he had once sworn allegiance to.

The same brotherhood that had nearly cost him everything.

He stared into the fire, his jaw hardening.

They would not call him unless the danger was real.

And yet…

He glanced toward the closed door of Olivia's chamber. She was here now, in his world. A part of him wanted to burn the scroll, to ride away with her and leave the Order to fight their own battles.

But he couldn't.

He never could.

Evelyne appeared in the doorway, her long blonde hair braided down her back.

"You're leaving," she said softly. Not a question.

Tristan looked at her, his expression unreadable. "It seems I have no choice."

Evelyne's gaze flicked to the scroll in his hand. "You always have a choice."

Tristan shook his head. "Not anymore."

* * *

CHAPTER ONE

The early morning light streamed through the tall windows of Ravenshire's solar, dancing across the floor in golden ribbons. The air was filled with the quiet hum of birdsong and the faint scent of wildflowers drifting in on the breeze.

Olivia leaned against the stone balcony, watching as Tristan crossed the courtyard below. His dark mantle clung to his shoulders as he swung into the saddle with easy grace, the rising sun catching the faint streaks of gold in his hair. The scroll was tucked into his cloak.

The stronghold lay silent behind him, Olivia's presence lingering like the warmth of a dying fire. As the gates creaked open and he rode into the cool morning, he whispered under his breath— "For crown and kingdom... or for her?"

The question haunted him as he disappeared.

Olivia smiled softly, but her eyes lingered a moment longer than usual.

Something was different about him lately.

* * *

When he returned from his early ride, she met him at the door with a teasing arch of her brow.

"You're restless," Olivia said. "You keep riding out before dawn, pacing the halls at night. What is it?"

Tristan's blue eyes softened as he brushed a kiss across her temple. "You've become far too perceptive, my love."

"I married you," she quipped. "I have to be."

But her light tone didn't mask her concern. She trailed him as he unfastened his riding cloak and laid it over the chair.

Tristan paused, his hand resting on the hilt of his sword. "There's something you don't yet know about me... about the oath I swore long before I ever knew you."

He retrieved a small scroll from his belt, its wax seal marked with a flickering flame—the sigil of the Order.

"This came three nights ago." His voice was low, almost reverent.

Olivia's fingers brushed the edge of the parchment. "What exactly is the Order of the Silver Flame?"

Tristan exhaled. "A brotherhood older than any kingdom. Sworn to protect what is sacred—the Heart of Elander, and other relics whose power could destroy nations."

"And you're one of them?" she whispered.

"I was. I still am."

He met her gaze, something haunted flickering in his eyes.

"I swore an oath to defend the light, even if it cost me everything. And now..." He tapped the scroll. "They're calling me to fulfill that oath again."

"After all we've survived, they summon you now?" Olivia murmured, her hand sliding over his.

8

"This may be bigger than both of us, Olivia."

She straightened, her chin lifting with quiet resolve. "Then we'll face it together. Whatever comes."

He walked over and stood near the window, the torchlight casting his sharp features in shadow. His fingers drummed lightly against the hilt of his sword—not from impatience, but from the weight of the decision he carried.

Olivia stood behind him, arms crossed, her expression already set in quiet defiance. She had heard enough to know something was wrong.

"Tristan," she said softly, though there was steel in her voice. "You're going somewhere, aren't you?"

He turned, his blue eyes meeting hers. There was hesitation there—not fear, but something deeper. "Aye." His voice was low, careful.

"Then I'm coming with you."

A faint smirk tugged at the corner of his lips. "You always say that."

"Because I mean it." Olivia stepped closer, her hands curling into fists at her sides. "If there's danger, you'll need me. The amulet chose both of us, Tristan—not just you."

His expression softened slightly, but the tension in his jaw remained. "You don't understand. This isn't about danger. It's... a summons."

"From who?"

"The Order." His voice dropped to a whisper. "They've called me to appear before them. And their message was clear, Olivia—I must come alone."

"That's ridiculous!" she snapped. "If they have questions for you, they'll have questions for me, too. I won't stay behind like some helpless—"

Tristan closed the distance between them in a stride, his hands gently but firmly grasping her shoulders.

"Livvy." His voice was soft now, but no less commanding. "You think I want to leave you behind? Every step I take without you feels wrong. But if the Order sees you, if they sense the power of the amulet in your possession before we understand their intentions..." He shook his head. "I will not risk them seeing you as a threat."

Olivia's lips trembled as she searched his face. "So what am I supposed to do? Just sit here and wait? What if something happens to you?"

Tristan smiled faintly, brushing his thumb across her cheek. "You've saved me before. And if need be... you'll save me again."

He leaned in close, his forehead resting gently against hers.

"Stay. Trust me, Olivia. I'll come back to you."

And though every fiber of her being screamed to argue, Olivia closed her eyes, pressing her hand to his chest.

"You'd better."

He kissed her softly, as if sealing a promise. Then he grabbed his cloak, swirling it around his shoulders, and walked into the shadows.

CHAPTER TWO

The air at the compound of the Order of the Silver Flame was heavy, almost suffocating. A storm threatened on the horizon, but the tension among the brotherhood inside was worse than any coming tempest.

Tristan's boots echoed sharply on the stone floor as he entered the hall.

Every pair of eyes turned to him—some with respect, others with suspicion.

At the far end of the room, a tall man with a white mantle embroidered with the sigil of the Flame stepped forward. Master Sareth, leader of the Order.

"Lord Tristan," he greeted, though his voice was tight. "You come not a moment too soon."

"What's happened?" Tristan demanded, his piercing blue eyes scanning the assembled knights.

Master Sareth's expression darkened. "The Flame flickers. One of our own has betrayed us."

A younger knight spat. "Say his name. Marlowe."

A ripple of murmurs spread through the hall.

Tristan froze, the weight of the name hitting him hard.

"Marlowe was expelled years ago," Tristan said evenly. "He should not have been allowed near the Flame again."

"And yet he came," Armand replied grimly. "He stole something sacred from the inner sanctum—the Ember of Eternity."

The room seemed to darken at the words.

"He means to destroy us, Tristan," Armand said. "And you knew him better than any of us."

Tristan's jaw tightened. Memories of fighting beside Marlowe flashed through his mind—his loyalty, his laughter, and finally... his betrayal.

"Marlowe swore vengeance the day he was cast out," said Sir Hugh, Tristan's closest friend in the Order. "Now he's keeping that vow."

Armand's voice turned urgent. "Come swiftly, or all will be ash."

Tristan's fists clenched. "Where is he?"

"He's fled to the old fort at Black Hollow," Hugh said. "It's well defended and he has... followers. Outcasts. Mercenaries. Men with nothing to lose."

Tristan's blue eyes burned with determination. "Then we'll take everything from him."

But as he turned to leave, Sareth's voice stopped him. "Tristan... beware. Marlowe knows you better than anyone. And the Ember's power is... changing him."

"If you fail—"

"I won't."

* * *

The candlelight flickered across the stone walls of the Hall of the Silver Flame, where the initiates knelt in solemn silence.

Two young men stood out among them—Tristan and Edward Marlowe.

They had entered the Order together.

Trained together.

Bled together in the crucible of tests designed to shape them into protectors of the king and guardians of the realm's most ancient secrets.

Tristan remembered how Marlowe's mind worked—sharp as a blade, ambitious as a hawk.

Marlowe always had the answers first, the plans second, and the confidence to make others follow him.

"You could lead us all one day," Tristan had once said to him with a grin.

Marlowe's smirk in return had been chilling in hindsight. "And why not? This Order needs someone who doesn't flinch at hard choices."

At first, they were inseparable. But ambition has teeth.

And Marlowe's brilliance hid a darker hunger.

When the Order denied Marlowe's request to use the amulets as weapons to enforce the king's will, something broke in him.

14

"We swore to protect the realm," Tristan had argued when Marlowe confided his anger. "Not to rule it."

"And yet we let fools sit the throne and squander its power!" Marlowe's voice had echoed in the stone chamber. "You're too blind to see it, Tristan. If the amulets can shape destiny, why should we not shape it?"

* * *

The hall of the Order of the Silver Flame was silent save for the crackle of torches along the stone walls. The air was thick with tension, betrayal coiled like a viper in the shadows.

Marlowe stood in the center of the room, his dark eyes flashing with defiance, his hands still dusted with blood.

"You fools," he snarled. "You think yourselves pure? You think your oaths make you righteous?"

The Grand Master's voice was cold and final. "You have betrayed the sacred trust of this Order. You have taken coin from our enemies. You have endangered not only us, but the very balance we swore to protect."

Marlowe laughed bitterly, though the sound lacked mirth. "And yet you'll still send men like Tristan to clean your messes."

At the edge of the circle, Tristan stiffened. His jaw clenched as he stepped forward. "Edward..."

Marlowe's gaze snapped to him. "Ah, Tristan. The perfect knight. The loyal hound."

15

"You were my brother," Tristan said quietly, pain flashing in his eyes. "Why?"

Marlowe's smirk faded, replaced by a raw, desperate rage. "Because I was tired of being nothing. I was tired of standing in your shadow."

He stepped closer, his voice dropping into a vicious whisper. "Do you know what it's like, Tristan? To be overlooked? To watch you—the golden knight—get everything while I rot in the dark?"

"This isn't you," Tristan said. "You can still turn back."

But Marlowe's hand went to his sword. "No. This is who I am now."

"Then you leave me no choice," Tristan murmured.

Steel sang as swords were drawn. The hall erupted into movement as Marlowe lunged.

The clash of steel rang out, echoing through the sacred chamber.

Tristan parried Marlowe's wild strikes, his every movement controlled, measured.

"Stand down, Edward!" Tristan shouted.

"Never!" Marlowe roared. "If I can't have this Order, I'll burn it to the ground!"

Their blades locked. Tristan's strength began to overpower Marlowe's frenzied attack.

"You're better than this," Tristan said through gritted teeth.

"No," Marlowe spat. "I'm free."

With one swift movement, Tristan disarmed him, the blade clattering to the floor.

Marlowe fell to his knees, chest heaving. "Do it," he hissed. "End it."

But Tristan hesitated. "I will not kill you. That's not justice."

The Grand Master's voice cut through the silence. "Edward Marlowe, you are hereby stripped of all rank and cast out from the Order. Your name will be struck from our rolls. You are no brother of ours."

Marlowe's scream of rage echoed as the guards dragged him away. His eyes burned with hatred as they locked on Tristan one final time.

"This isn't over," he vowed. "You'll pay for this, Tristan. You'll pay in blood."

That night, Marlowe left the Order.

He didn't just walk away—he stole one of the sacred scrolls.

To Tristan it felt like a blade through the ribs.
The brother he trusted most had become the enemy he could never forget.

* * *

The air was sharp and cold, carrying the scent of pine and earth as Tristan rode out to meet Hugh. Tristan tightened the reins on his horse, guiding it through the forest path. Ahead, the faint sound of hoofbeats quickened his pace.

Hugh emerged from the trees, cloaked in deep brown, his sharp eyes scanning their surroundings before settling on Tristan.

"You're late," Hugh said dryly, though a small smirk tugged at his lips.

"And you're impatient," Tristan replied, dismounting. "But I'm here, aren't I?"

Hugh pulled a folded piece of parchment from his cloak and handed it to Tristan. "These are Marlowe's last known movements. He's in a keep for two days north. Guarded. Paranoid. And still in possession of the scrolls."

Tristan's jaw tightened. "Then we take them back before he does more damage."

Hugh crossed his arms. "This isn't a simple theft. He's expecting trouble. And if Marlowe realizes we've been sent by the Silver Flame, he'll burn the scrolls before he lets them fall into our hands."

"Then we move quietly," Tristan said. "In and out, unseen."

Hugh raised a brow. "Since when are you quiet?"

Tristan smirked faintly. "Since now."

18

Hugh unfolded a rough sketch of Marlowe's keep.

"The scrolls are likely in the upper chamber, guarded day and night. Two watchtowers. Six men on rotation. A hidden postern gate near the southern wall—unguarded, but locked."

"We'll need to get past the guards, the dogs, and whatever traps Marlowe's set," Hugh said grimly.

Tristan's fingers brushed the hilt of his sword. "I'll handle the guards."

Hugh shook his head. "Not if I handle them first."

They exchanged a glance—two seasoned warriors, each refusing to back down.

Finally, Hugh smirked. "Fine. Let's see who's faster."

They mounted the horses and rode toward the looming silhouette of Black Hollow Fort. The ancient stonework was cracked and blackened with age, a relic of a war long past— much like his memories of Marlowe. Those memories stung like old wounds.

Tristan's mind was heavy as Valour's hooves clopped against the frosted ground. Once, Edward Marlowe had been like a brother. They had fought side by side, bled for the same cause, and laughed over tankards of ale until dawn.

But that was before the betrayal.

Before Marlowe turned to greed and shadows, and before the sacred scrolls of the Order had vanished—taken by the one man Tristan had sworn he could trust.

As they crested the last ridge, the fort came into full view. A sprawling ruin of moss-covered stone, jagged towers like broken teeth against the gray sky. The iron gate hung crooked on its hinges, creaking with every gust of wind.

The moon hung low, casting a pale silver light over the sprawling fort. The outer walls loomed ahead like a sleeping beast, lanterns flickering at intervals where the guards patrolled lazily, unaware of the two figures crouched in the shadows of the nearby woods.

Tristan pressed his back against the rough bark of an oak, his eyes scanning the battlements.

"The north wall," he whispered. "That's their weakest point. Only two men on patrol."

Hugh grinned, adjusting the dagger at his belt.

"Two men, eh? Easy enough—if you don't mind getting your hands dirty."

"We do this my way," Tristan said sharply. "No bodies unless there's no choice."

Hugh rolled his eyes. "You're no fun."

Moving like shadows, they crept across the open stretch of grass toward the north wall. The faint crunch of their boots on frostbitten earth was masked by the distant howl of a wolf.

Hugh pulled a length of rope from his pack, fixing a grappling hook to the end. He twirled it once, twice, and sent it flying.

Clink.

It caught on the stonework, and both men froze.

A guard coughed from above but didn't look down.

Tristan exhaled. "Go."

They scaled the wall swiftly, pulling themselves up hand over hand until they reached the parapet.

Two guards. One dozing, the other staring out over the dark forest.

Tristan moved like a predator, silent and deadly. He pressed a hand over the first man's mouth and dragged him down, striking the back of his head with the pommel of his sword.

Hugh slipped behind the second, a dagger flashing briefly in the moonlight before the guard slumped unconscious.

"No bodies, eh?" Hugh whispered with a smirk. "Just a nap."

Tristan shot him a look. "Quiet."

They dropped down into the courtyard, keeping to the shadows.

The scent of smoke and roasting meat filled the air— some poor soul on the night shift was cooking his supper.

Tristan whispered, "We get what we came for, and we're gone. No heroics."

"Speak for yourself," Hugh muttered.

They slipped through a narrow door into the barracks. Voices drifted from the other side—cards, laughter. The men inside were distracted.

Tristan pointed to the far end of the corridor. "That room. That's where the map said the scrolls will be."

They moved quickly, avoiding creaky floorboards, until they reached the door.

Locked.

Hugh grinned. "Finally, something fun."

He knelt, pulling a small pouch of tools from his belt. Within seconds, the lock clicked open.

"We're in," he whispered.

Inside, they found the sealed scrolls Tristan had been ordered to retrieve.

"Go," Tristan urged.

But as they turned back toward the courtyard, a torch flared to life.

"Who goes there?"

A sentry.

Tristan cursed under his breath. "Run."

They sprinted across the open space as the shout of alarm went up.

"Intruders!"

Arrows hissed past them as they scrambled up the rope. Tristan reached the top, hauling Hugh up just as a guard's sword slashed at his boots.

"Cut the rope!" Hugh barked.

Tristan sliced through it with one stroke, sending the grappling hook tumbling down into the fort.

They dropped to the forest floor and vanished into the trees, their breath misting in the cold air as shouts echoed behind them.

Hugh let out a breathless laugh. "You know, for a knight, you make a damn fine thief."

Tristan smirked. "And you talk too much."

* * *

The night was thick with mist as Tristan and Hugh rode silently through the dense forest, the sound of their horses' hooves muffled by the damp earth. The moon hung low, casting silver light through the trees, and ahead, a faint glow flickered—the sacred fires of the Order of the Silver Flame.

"Do you trust them?" Hugh asked quietly, his voice low as if the forest itself might overhear.

Tristan's jaw tightened as he adjusted the leather satchel across his chest, the ancient scrolls within bound tightly. "I don't have a choice," he murmured. "The scrolls don't belong to me. They were entrusted to my family to protect, not to hoard."

Hugh glanced at him sidelong. "And yet, they're the same Order that cast out your father for refusing to use their power for war."

"And I will not repeat his mistake," Tristan said firmly, his blue eyes flashing in the moonlight. "If these scrolls truly hold the knowledge to control the amulets, then they cannot fall into the wrong hands—not Marlowe's, not the king's, not even ours."

As they reached a clearing, an ancient stone archway loomed ahead, half-swallowed by ivy. Beyond it, the flicker of torches revealed hooded figures in long robes of blue and silver—the brothers and sisters of the Order.

Tristan dismounted, feeling the weight of history pressing down on him. Hugh followed, a hand resting on the hilt of his sword, eyes scanning the shadows.

A tall figure stepped forward, his hood falling back to reveal a stern face etched with lines of wisdom and age. His gray eyes burned with an inner fire.

"Lord Tristan," the man said, voice calm but carrying power. "You bring us what was lost."

Tristan inclined his head. "I bring back what my family swore to protect."

He unfastened the satchel carefully, holding it out. "The scrolls of the Silver Flame. May their wisdom serve only the pure of heart."

The elder took them reverently. "And the Heart of Elander?"

Tristan's jaw tightened slightly. "Still safe. For now."

As the brothers and sisters of the Order stepped forward to take the scrolls into their sanctum, the elder's eyes narrowed on Tristan.

"You carry more than duty, Tristan de Léon. The amulet's power has marked you. You and the woman who bears its twin are entwined in its fate."

Tristan stiffened. "What do you mean?"

The elder's voice lowered. "The amulets feed on devotion... and sacrifice. To wield their full strength, you may be asked to give everything."

Hugh muttered under his breath. "That sounds ominous."

Tristan's hands curled into fists. "If that time comes, I'll face it."

The elder's gaze softened ever so slightly. "Pray it does not come too soon."

As Tristan and Hugh mounted their horses to leave, the sacred flames behind them flickered higher, as if sensing the weight of what had been returned.

"Well," Hugh said as they rode into the night. "That wasn't unsettling at all."

Tristan smirked faintly. "It's the Order. They speak in riddles even when they're pleased."

Hugh chuckled. "Let's just hope Olivia never hears that part about sacrifice."

Tristan's expression darkened slightly. "She's already given too much."

And with that, they spurred their horses forward, vanishing into the mist.

CHAPTER THREE

The castle gates loomed ahead as Tristan rode through the misty morning, Ravenshire's stone towers breaking through the low clouds like sentinels of old.

The road was quiet, the steady rhythm of hooves striking the dirt the only sound as Valour carried him home.

Ravenshire was home—it was his.

Here, he was not just Lord Tristan, the king's favored knight or the subject of court whispers.

Here, he was the master of his land, the protector of his people.

* * *

The Great Hall of Ravenshire was alive with golden firelight, the long table crowded with platters of roasted meats, fresh bread, and Old Martha's famous spiced stew that filled the air with a savory aroma. The crackle of the hearth blended with the hum of cheerful voices, creating a warmth that reached deeper than the flames themselves.

At the head of the table, Tristan sat back in his chair, a rare smile tugging at his lips. He watched as Olivia laughed at one of Aldric's dry jokes, her fingers curled lightly around a goblet of wine.

"Eat, my lord! You're too thin," Old Martha scolded as she plunked another thick slice of bread onto Tristan's plate.

27

"And you, Lady Olivia—don't you dare let him share that with you. I made plenty."

Olivia grinned. "You're spoiling us, Martha."

"Spoiling you? Nonsense," Martha huffed, though her eyes twinkled. "You've been working yourselves ragged. Sit. Eat. Laugh. That's an order."

Aldric leaned forward, smirking at Evelyne. "You know, if Tristan keeps smiling like that, the entire court might faint in shock."

"Hush," Evelyne said with a laugh. "It's good for him to look human once in a while."

Gideon swirled his wine lazily, his smirk devilish. "Human? He's practically glowing with contentment. Olivia, what have you been giving him?"

Olivia's cheeks warmed, but she shot back playfully, "Perhaps I've been teaching him how to enjoy himself."

Tristan arched a brow at her, a hint of mischief in his blue eyes. "Careful, my lady. That almost sounded like a challenge."

A young squire, invited to dine with them that night, chimed in timidly, "Lord Tristan, is it true you once took down three men in the lists before breakfast?"

Tristan shook his head with a wry smile. "Not before breakfast. After. Never fight on an empty stomach."

The table erupted in laughter.

As the evening went on, Olivia leaned closer to Tristan, her voice low so only he could hear.

"You know, there's still a bottle of Martha's plum wine in the kitchens."

Tristan's lips curved into a grin. "Is that so? Do you suppose we could get to it without being caught?"

Olivia's eyes sparkled. "Not if you keep grinning like that."

"Then we'll have to be quick."

* * *

The halls of the keep were hushed, the flickering torchlight casting soft shadows against the stone walls. Dinner had long since ended, and the stronghold was finally quiet. Even Evelyne and Aldric had retired early, leaving Tristan and Olivia blessedly alone.

The chaos of the day melted away into the soft crackle of the fire in their room. Olivia sat curled on a fur blanket by the hearth, her knees drawn to her chest as she watched Tristan remove his sword belt and set it gently aside.

"You never let it leave your sight," she murmured.

Tristan looked over his shoulder at her, a faint smile tugging at his lips. "It has kept me alive too many times to grow careless now."

His blue eyes softened with a rare warmth. He crossed the room in a few long strides and offered her his hand.

"Come with me. No questions."

She hesitated only briefly before slipping her fingers into his. "You're trouble, Lord Tristan."

"Always," he murmured, pressing a kiss to her knuckles. "But tonight, the good kind."

They slipped out through the side hall, Tristan leading her into the quiet courtyard. The night air was crisp, and the stars scattered across the sky like diamonds on black velvet. The moonlight painted everything in a pale silver glow.

"It's beautiful," Olivia whispered, gazing upward.

Tristan didn't answer—not with words. He was watching her, the way her hair caught the light, the curve of her lips as she smiled.

"Not half as beautiful as you," he said finally, his voice low and rough.

Olivia flushed, lowering her eyes. "You'll make me forget how dangerous you can be when you talk like that."

Tristan stepped closer, tipping her chin up with his fingers. "Good. Then I'm doing my job."

He kissed her—soft and slow at first, as though savoring every second. But when she responded, her hands sliding up into his hair, the kiss deepened, turning urgent. He pulled her closer until she was pressed to the hard planes of his chest.

When they broke apart, his forehead rested against hers. "You undo me, Olivia." He pulled her into his arms, and kissed her again—long, slow, and deep—while the stars and the silence of the castle wrapped them in their own little world. Their kiss was soft at first, tentative, as if testing the fire between them—then it deepened, becoming urgent, consuming.

Tristan's fingers tangled in her hair, tipping her head back as his lips moved against hers. Olivia clutched at his shoulders, feeling the strength beneath her hands, the warmth of him pressing her closer.

When they finally pulled back, Tristan's breath was ragged.

"If you don't stop looking at me like that," he growled, his forehead resting against hers, "I'll forget every oath I've ever sworn."

Olivia smiled faintly, her own breathing uneven. "Maybe I want you to."

And with that, he kissed her again—harder this time, his hands roaming as though committing every inch of her to memory.

They didn't make it back to their chambers.

Instead, they stumbled into the empty library, the scent of parchment and candle wax filling the air as Tristan pressed her back against the door, his mouth tracing a path down her neck.

"Tell me to stop," he murmured, his voice husky.

"Don't you dare," Olivia breathed, tugging him closer.

The library was quiet, save for the soft crackle of a dying fire in the hearth. Moonlight streamed through the tall windows, casting silver light across the endless rows of books.

Tristan backed Olivia gently against the shelves, his eyes dark with hunger as they bore into hers.

"We shouldn't..." Olivia whispered, though her hands were already clutching at the front of his tunic.

"Tell me to stop, and I will." Tristan's voice was low, ragged, but there was no mistaking the challenge in his tone.

She didn't.

His mouth was on hers before she could take another breath, the kiss consuming—wild and desperate—as though they'd been holding back for far too long.

Their teeth clashed, tongues tangling, and Olivia gasped into him as his hands cupped her face, then slid down her neck to her shoulders.

Her fingers dug into his broad chest, dragging him closer as heat flared between them.

"You drive me mad," Tristan murmured against her lips, one hand sliding down her spine to press her hips flush against his.

Books shifted and toppled from the shelves as he lifted her onto the table, knocking over a pile of parchment. He pressed her back gently, staring down at her with eyes that burned like a storm.

"I can't be careful with you," he rasped, his thumb brushing across her lips. "Not tonight."

"Then don't," she breathed, her voice trembling.

Clothing was discarded in frantic motions, hands roaming, fingers fumbling at ties and buttons. Olivia's gown pooled around her hips as Tristan's calloused hands explored her bare skin.

He pressed hot kisses along her jaw, down her throat, savoring every soft sound she made. "You're mine," he murmured into her ear. "Every breath... every inch of you."

When he entered her, it was slow at first—achingly deliberate—his forehead resting against hers as their breaths mingled in the stillness of the library.

"Tristan..." her voice was a soft cry, her fingers tangling in his hair.

"I've waited for this—" his words caught as she arched beneath him, urging him deeper, harder. "God, Olivia..."

The rhythm between them grew frantic, urgent. Every thrust sent her heart racing, her moans filling the quiet space as he claimed her with every movement.

Their lips met again—kissing, biting, breathing each other in.

"You're everything," Tristan growled, his voice breaking as his control began to slip. "Everything I never thought I could have."

"Then take it," she whispered fiercely. "Take me."

He obeyed.

When it was over, Tristan cradled her against his chest as they lay tangled on the floor, the firelight flickering over their flushed, sweat-slicked skin.

"You've ruined me," he murmured, pressing a kiss to her temple. "I can't let you go now."

"Good," Olivia whispered back, her fingers tracing lazy circles over his chest. "Because I'm not letting you go either."

CHAPTER FOUR

The morning air carried a chill through the stone corridors of Ravenshire, but inside the Great Hall, there was a different kind of tension—one that hummed in Tristan's veins the moment the messenger arrived.

"Lord Tristan de Léon," the rider announced, bowing low as he handed over a sealed parchment. "You are summoned to court by order of His Majesty."

The red wax bore the king's sigil—three roaring lions. The seal was unbroken, but the weight of it already pressed heavily on Tristan's shoulders.

He cracked the seal, his eyes scanning the formal summons.

"He commands my presence... and requests Olivia, Evelyne, Aldric and Gideon join me."

"All of us?" Evelyne asked sharply, stepping into the room.

"Everyone," Tristan confirmed grimly. "It's no request— it's an order."

Olivia frowned. "Why would he summon all of us?"

Tristan's jaw clenched. "Perhaps because he doesn't trust me to return alone."

Evelyne crossed her arms. "Or because Marlowe has whispered enough poison into his ear to make him curious about Olivia."

Aldric spoke from where he leaned against the doorframe. "And curious kings are dangerous kings."

Tristan exhaled. "All the more reason for us to be cautious."

* * *

The castle stirred with quiet urgency as they prepared to leave.

Olivia packed what few belongings she had, her fingers brushing over the amulet at her throat. It felt heavier than usual, as though it knew what awaited her in the capital.

"Are we walking into a trap?" she asked Tristan as he tightened the straps on his sword.

He paused, meeting her gaze. "Possibly."

Olivia exhaled slowly. "Then why go?"

His voice softened, though his jaw remained tight. "Because refusing would make us guilty in the king's eyes— even if we are not."

That night, Tristan found Olivia in the library, staring into the flicker of the candlelight.

"We'll face this together," he said quietly, stepping closer.

She looked up at him, her eyes filled with worry. "And if Marlowe tries to turn the king against us?"

Tristan's hand brushed her cheek. "Then I'll remind His Majesty why he trusted me once. And if that fails..."

His blue eyes darkened. "I'll fight for you, Olivia. Even against a king."

* * *

At dawn, the gates of Ravenshire creaked open. Tristan, Olivia, Evelyne, Aldric, Gideon and their small retinue rode out, the hooves of their horses clattering against the cold stone bridge.

The journey to the capital would take three days.

Three days before they discovered why the king had called them... and what new dangers awaited at court.

The sun was warm overhead, and the air smelled faintly of crushed grass as the group rode along the winding path toward the king's court.

Tristan and Olivia rode side by side, his serious expression softening whenever she leaned closer to whisper a teasing remark.

"You're staring again," Olivia said with a smirk, pretending to adjust the reins.

"I am not," Tristan replied flatly, but there was a flicker of amusement in his blue eyes.

"Oh no?" Olivia teased. "Is it the horizon that has you frowning like that, or are you thinking of ways to beat me in sparring again?"

Aldric snorted behind them. "If you're still sparring with him, my lady, you've more bravery than most."

Evelyne smirked. "Or more foolishness."

Gideon, riding slightly ahead, turned in his saddle. "Careful. Lord Tristan might pout if you beat him, Olivia."

Tristan shot him a warning glare. "Do you want to ride the rest of the way with a dagger sticking out of your back, Cross?"

Gideon grinned. "Depends. Would I look more fearsome, or would it ruin my good doublet?"

That evening, they stopped at a small roadside inn for the night.

Tristan had insisted they keep their presence quiet, but Olivia and Evelyne had other ideas.

While Aldric and Gideon discussed patrols outside and Tristan sharpened his blade, the two women slipped into the inn's cellar.

"You're sure this is a good idea?" Evelyne whispered.

"No," Olivia said with a grin, "but that's what makes it fun."

They returned moments later with a small cask of wine.

"You're going to get us all hanged," Tristan growled as he watched them pour goblets around the fire.

"Oh hush," Evelyne said, passing him a cup. "You need it more than anyone."

Gideon raised his glass. "To the knight who doesn't know how to smile. And the lady who makes him try."

Tristan scowled, but Olivia caught the corner of his mouth twitching upward. Just barely.

* * *

The forest was eerily quiet, the only sound the soft crunch of leaves beneath Tristan's horse. He moved with caution, hand resting lightly on the hilt of his sword, his instincts prickling.

"Something isn't right," he muttered under his breath.

Behind him, Aldric, muscles taut, scanned the tree line. Gideon lingered to the side, eyes sharp, every step silent despite the crunch of fallen leaves underfoot.

Evelyne and Olivia trailed behind. Evelyne whispered, "Why does it feel like we're being watched?"

"Because we are," Tristan muttered over his shoulder. "Stay close to that tree. And don't make a sound."

Without warning, the silence shattered—the twang of bowstrings and the hiss of arrows cut through the air.

"Down!" Tristan bellowed. shoving Aldric aside as three arrows buried themselves into the trunk of a nearby oak.

"Ambush!" Aldric yelled, drawing his sword.

From the shadows of the trees, Marlowe's men surged forward—rough, armed mercenaries with hunger and cruelty in their eyes.

Gideon drew twin daggers, grinned wickedly. "Ah, finally. I was getting bored."

Steel sang as Tristan drew his blade, the bright metal flashing in the dappled sunlight. "Shields up! Form a line!"

The clash of steel rang out as the three men met the attackers head-on.

Evelyne pulled Olivia behind a tree.

Tristan and Marlowe's lieutenant clashed in the clearing, steel ringing in sharp bursts.

"Where's Marlowe?" Tristan growled as he parried a strike. "Where is your coward master?"

The soldier spat blood and grinned. "Closer than you think."

Tristan's blade flashing in the dappled sunlight as he cut through two of Marlowe's men in quick succession.

Aldric fought beside him with raw strength, swinging his blade with precision born of countless battles.

Gideon danced in and out of reach, his twin daggers flashing as he cut tendons and slit throats, moving like a shadow with deadly intent.

"You bastards picked the wrong knight to ambush," Aldric growled, kicking one of the mercenary's square in the chest.

"And the wrong thief," Gideon added with a wicked grin, spinning one of the men into the path of his comrade's blade.

Evelyne and Olivia pressed themselves against the trunk of a massive oak.

"Stay quiet," Evelyne whispered, clutching the small dagger she carried for protection. "Don't draw attention to us."

But it was too late.

One of Marlowe's men broke from the fray and charged toward them, sword drawn, his expression twisted with malice.

"Got you, pretty little mice," he snarled.

Evelyne raised her blade, but before she could strike, Olivia stepped forward. Her pulse thundered in her ears, but she held her ground.

The man lunged—but Olivia ducked low, grabbing a fallen branch and swinging it hard into his ribs.

He grunted, stumbling sideways, and she seized her chance— slamming the branch into his face with enough force to send him crashing into the dirt.

The man groaned, dazed. Olivia snatched Evelyne's dropped dagger and pressed the blade to his throat.

"Move again and I swear I'll make sure you regret it," Olivia hissed, her voice shaking but fierce.

The man froze, eyes wide. He hadn't expected this from her.

Evelyne stared, stunned. "Olivia…"

But there was no time for more words—

* * *

"Tristan de Léon," Marlowe drawled. "I had hoped for a more… private meeting." Edward Marlowe, his smirk sharper than a dagger, stepped out of the shadows.

Tristan's eyes narrowed. "Marlowe. You'll regret stepping out of the shadows."

"On the contrary," Marlowe said, drawing his own blade. "This is where the fun begins."

The air was filled with the ring of swords and the cries of combat.

Tristan fought like a man possessed.

Every move was precise, deadly. He cut down one man, then pivoted to deflect a strike aimed for Aldric.

But his true focus was on Marlowe. Their eyes locked.

"You've chosen the wrong side," Tristan growled, advancing.

"I've chosen the winning side," Marlowe shot back, lunging forward.

Their blades met with a clang that reverberated through the clearing. Sparks flew as they clashed again and again, each strike more brutal than the last.

Tristan's muscles burned, his breath coming in sharp bursts, but he pressed on. He couldn't afford to falter.

With a roar, Tristan unleashed a flurry of strikes, forcing Marlowe onto the defensive.

As they circled one another, Marlowe's foot caught on a tree root. Tristan seized the moment. He disarmed Marlowe with a swift strike, sending his sword flying into the underbrush.

Tristan's blade pressed against Marlowe's throat.

"Yield," Tristan growled, his voice low and dangerous.

But Marlowe only smiled. "Do it. Kill me. Prove to her what kind of man you really are."

Tristan's grip tightened on his sword... then he pulled back. "You're not worth it."

Marlowe staggered to his feet, clutching at his bruised throat.

"This isn't over," he spat, retreating into the trees with the remnants of his men.

Tristan exhaled sharply, sheathing his sword. "No. It's just beginning."

Aldric wiped his blade on the grass. "Bloody cowards. Not even proper soldiers."

Gideon crouched to retrieve one of his daggers from a corpse, glancing toward Olivia and Evelyne. "Seems the ladies held their own."

Tristan turned sharply, his cloak flaring with movement. "What happened?"

Olivia, her breathing uneven, her hand still gripping the bloody dagger tightly. "He came for us. I—I stopped him," she said, her voice trembling, but steady enough to meet his gaze.

Tristan's eyes hardened for a heartbeat as he scanned her from head to toe for injury.

When he saw none, his expression softened—anger giving was to a protective calm.

He stepped closer, his voice low but laced with intensity. "You did what you had to do."

He reached out, his hand wrapping gently around hers, prying the blade from her grip. "Listen to me." His voice was soft now, steady and reassuring. "You're safe. You did the right thing. You were brave."

* * *

The small group rode in close formation, the sound of hooves muffled against the damp earth as the castle's towers rose in the distance. Tristan and Olivia led the way, while Evelyne, Aldric, and Gideon followed just behind, voices low but lively.

Tristan's warhorse moved with confident strides, his dark mane rippling like a banner in the wind. Tristan sat tall in the saddle, one hand resting easily on the reins, the other never straying too far from the sword at his side. His eyes swept the path ahead, alert for any danger.

Olivia's horse, a spirited chestnut mare gifted to her by Tristan, seemed to sense her uncertainty. But Olivia kept her posture steady, her hands tight on the reins. She had been riding with Tristan long enough to start learning the rhythm of the animal beneath her.

"You're holding your reins too tight," Tristan said, glancing at her with a faint smirk. "You'll make her nervous."

Olivia frowned. "I'm nervous."

"She can feel it," he replied smoothly. "Relax your shoulders. Trust her."

"It's not the horse I'm worried about," Olivia muttered under her breath.

"No?" Tristan arched a brow, clearly amused. "Are you worried about me, then?"

"I'm worried about the man who might still try to kill us before we even get to the castle."

Tristan's smirk faded slightly, his expression sharpening as he scanned the forest edges. "He won't try again."

Olivia's chest tightened at the cold certainty in his voice, but she also felt a flicker of warmth. "You sound so sure."

"I am."

As they reached a gentle incline, Tristan slowed his horse until he was riding just behind her. "Your posture's improved," he remarked.

"Was it that bad before?" Olivia asked, half-offended.

"Terrible," Tristan said with mock seriousness. "I've seen children in the village ride with more grace."

She shot him a glare over her shoulder. "Careful, Sir Knight. I could still run you off the road."

"If you could control that horse well enough to pull it off, I might be impressed."

Olivia huffed. "Don't tempt me."

"You know, Tristan," Evelyne said, "it's been a long time since I've been to court. I'd forgotten how exhausting it is just thinking about smiling at people I despise."

"It's more than smiling this time. Marlowe will be ready. I can feel it," Aldric said.

Gideon smirked. "So serious, Aldric. You'll give yourself wrinkles. It's not all doom and treachery, you know. There's fine wine. And scandal. And plenty of bored nobles ripe for mischief."

Olivia glanced back. "Mischief? That sounds like your specialty, Gideon."

Gideon grinned "You wound me, my lady. I'm entirely innocent."

"Innocent? That's rich, coming from a man who was nearly hanged for stealing the Duke of Arclay's horse," Tristan said dryly.

Gideon shrugged "I was borrowing it. Temporarily."

Evelyne smiled "Borrowing a duke's horse at midnight is hardly temporary, Gideon."

As the group fell into comfortable chatter, Tristan slowed his horse slightly so that Olivia's mount drew alongside his.

Tristan leaned closer. "You're quiet. Thinking about the court?"

Olivia nodded "It's... a lot. The stares. The whispers. I'm not sure I'm ready for it."

Tristan's voice was soft but firm. "Let them whisper. They're cowards hiding behind silk and jewels."

Olivia smiled faintly. "Easy for you to say. You're the intimidating knight."

Tristan grinned "Ah, but you've seen me at my worst—covered in mud after sparring with you."

Olivia teased, "You're just upset I nearly bested you."

Tristan laughed. "Nearly being the key word."

Gideon leaned toward Evelyne and Aldric. "I say after all this talk of courtly doom, we sneak into the castle kitchens later and liberate a bottle of wine."

Aldric rolled his eyes. "And risk getting caught like a pair of wayward squires? No, thank you."

Evelyne said with a sly smile, "Oh, come now, Aldric. When was the last time you did something reckless?"

Aldric said gruffly, "Staying alive isn't reckless. It's practical."

Gideon grinned. "Practical is boring. You're coming with me."

Evelyne (to Olivia): "You'd come too, wouldn't you?"

Olivia laughed. "I feel like this is a trap."

"If you're caught, I'll have to rescue you from the kitchens. Again," Tristan said with mock seriousness.

"You make it sound like you'd enjoy the excuse."

Tristan smirked. "Perhaps I would."

Hours later, as the sun began its descent toward the horizon, the silhouette of the royal castle emerged in the distance—its high towers and stone walls rising like sentinels against the fading sky.

Olivia exhaled slowly. "We're really doing this."

Tristan gave a single, solemn nod. "We are."

"And when we get there?" she asked quietly. "Will the king welcome us?"

Tristan's jaw tightened. "He will. Or he'll try to tear us apart."

Olivia met his gaze, seeing the steel resolve in his eyes.

"Then let him try," she whispered.

Tristan's smirk returned, faint but reassuring. "That's my girl."

The sound of hooves echoed off the stone walls as Tristan, Olivia and the others rode through the castle gates.

The courtyard was alive with movement—stable boys rushing to take the reins, servants carrying baskets of food and bolts of cloth, and nobles pausing mid-conversation to turn and stare.

All eyes were on them.

Tristan's black and silver cloak stirred faintly in the breeze as he dismounted, his posture radiating quiet power. He extended a hand to Olivia, helping her from the saddle.

She took it, her fingers trembling slightly though she kept her chin lifted. It felt like stepping into the lion's den.

"That's Lord Tristan de Léon," one courtier whispered, half in awe, half in suspicion.

"And the woman? Who is she?" another asked, eyes narrowing.

"They say she has him under some kind of spell..."

"A witch, no doubt. How else could she hold his attention?"

"She's not even noble-born."

"The king won't tolerate this."

"Perhaps she'll be gone by morning..."

Olivia caught fragments of their words, but Tristan's hand at her back was steady, guiding her forward.

"Ignore them," he murmured softly, low enough only she could hear.

But she could feel the weight of their judgment, their curiosity cutting sharper than any blade.

The Great Hall was no better. As they entered, nobles lined the walls, their rich fabrics and jeweled collars glittering in the firelight. They all stopped to watch the pair.

The king's advisor, a gaunt man with a hawk-like nose, stepped forward.

"Lord Tristan," he said coolly. "The king awaits you in his chambers." His gaze flicked briefly to Olivia, narrowing ever so slightly. "And... your companion."

The throne room was heavy with silence as Tristan and Olivia stepped forward.

The massive wooden doors groaned as they shut behind him, leaving them standing alone on the polished stone floor. At the far end, the king sat in his high-backed chair, the golden lion crest of his house gleaming in the torchlight. The scent of burning cedar filled the air.

Every step they took echoed in the Hall. To his left, nobles and courtiers lined the walls, whispering in hushed voices. He could feel their eyes on him—some curious, others openly hostile.   The king's eyes followed Tristan as he approached.

"Lord Tristan de Léon," the king's voice boomed, cutting through the murmurs. "Do you know why I summoned you here?"

Tristan stood before the throne, his posture straight, his expression calm—but inwardly, his thoughts churned. He bowed low. "To answer for my actions, Your Majesty."

"Indeed," the king replied, his tone sharp. "You have served me well, Lord Tristan. But there are whispers in my court. Whispers of disloyalty. Treachery. Treason. Of a knight who places his own desires above his king."

Tristan's jaw tightened. "My loyalty to you and this realm has never wavered."

"Has it not?" the king pressed, rising from his throne. "And yet, you bring a woman of mysterious origin into my court. You defend her against my own councilors. You defy my expectations at every turn."

Tristan's gaze didn't falter. "I have fought for this kingdom. I have bled for it. And I will not apologize for protecting the innocent from vipers within these walls."

The nobles gasped. One or two even stepped back.

But the king's expression darkened. "You dare speak so boldly?"

Tristan drew himself up to his full height. "I speak boldly because I know the truth."

The king's hand gripped the arm of his throne. "Do you?"

Tristan's voice softened but carried a dangerous edge. "There are snakes at your feet, Your Majesty. And they whisper lies to poison your judgment. I will not stand idle while they destroy what you have built."

The king's piercing gaze held him in place for what felt like an eternity.

At last, the king exhaled slowly and sat back down. "You speak with conviction, Lord Tristan. But words are wind."

He gestured toward the courtiers. "Prove to me that you are not blinded by love. That you are still the knight I once trusted."

Tristan inclined his head. "How shall I prove it, Your Majesty?"

The king's lips curled into a thin smile. "You will take on a mission for me. Dangerous. Uncertain. And you will succeed... or not return at all."

The Hall erupted into murmurs again.

The king leaned back in his throne, fingers drumming lightly on the armrest. "There are stirrings of rebellion in the western reaches. Bandits, traitors, and whispers of men who once swore fealty to me now meeting in secret." His voice was calm, but beneath the smooth tone lay a steel edge that promised there would be no arguing.

The room went still at the king's words.

His voice was calm, but beneath the smooth tone lay a steel edge that promised there would be no arguing. His gaze sharpened on Tristan. "I am sending you as my envoy to the western outposts. I need someone I trust to uncover the truth... and if necessary..." The king's eyes gleamed coldly. "Extinguish the threat before it spreads."

Tristan bowed his head. "As you command, Your Majesty."

But inwardly, his stomach tightened. This was no mere diplomatic mission

The king's lips curved into a cold smile. "You will succeed. Because you have no choice. It is settled. Lord Tristan, you will depart within the week."

* * *

"Tristan..." Olivia's throat ached. She wanted to argue, to beg him to refuse, but she knew better.

"Don't look at me like that," he murmured, brushing a loose curl from her face. "I've faced worse odds before."

"I don't like it," she said softly.

A flicker of pain crossed his eyes. "Which is why I have to succeed."

* * *

Tristan rode alone at dawn, his cloak billowing behind him, the cold air biting at his skin. Every step of his horse's hooves echoed like a countdown. He could feel the weight of his sword at his hip. If the whispers were true, he would need it soon.

And yet, through the danger, one thought kept pulling at him. Olivia.

"I have to come back to her," he muttered under his breath. "No matter what it takes."

When Tristan rode to the king's western outpost, he expected to deal with minor unrest, But he was met with a scene that chilled him to the bone.

The gates hung slightly ajar, creaking in the wind. No sentries stood watch. The smell of smoke and blood lingered in the air.

Tristan dismounted, his boots crunching over scattered debris.

Inside the outpost walls, he found signs of a struggle—overturned barrels, shattered shields, and bloodstains on the dirt.

Tristan knelt beside a fallen soldier, fingers brushing over the torn insignia on his tunic. "The king's men didn't stand a chance."

As he searched further, he found an empty strongbox where the outpost's weapons and supplies should have been. A torn banner, bearing the mark of a rival faction—a crest that Marlowe's men were rumored to use in secret. A surviving soldier, half-conscious, who whispered a warning:

"They... they knew we were coming. Someone betrayed us... from within."

Tristan's jaw tightened. "Marlowe."

The air in the outpost was heavy with the scent of blood and smoke.

Tristan knelt beside the wounded soldier, his gloved hand gripping the man's shoulder. The soldier's face was pale, slick with sweat, his breaths shallow and ragged.

"Hold on," Tristan urged, his voice low but firm. "Tell me—who betrayed us? Did you see?"

The soldier's lips trembled. "N-no... I didn't see... but they were waiting. They knew everything. Even our numbers... our route..."

Tristan's jaw clenched. His mind was already racing. This wasn't a simple ambush. Someone within the king's camp had leaked their plans.

The soldier's head lolled back. "I tried... to warn..."

"Save your strength," Tristan said, but he knew it was too late.

The man exhaled his last breath.

Tristan stood slowly, his eyes narrowing. "A traitor in our midst," he muttered under his breath. "This isn't over."

* * *

Tristan stood tall, his blue eyes scanning the line of wounded soldiers sitting on rough benches. Some were bandaged hastily, others pale from blood loss, but all alive—alive enough to speak.

"I need every detail," Tristan said, his voice low but carrying authority. "No matter how small, no matter how strange."

The soldiers shifted uneasily, exchanging glances.

One man coughed and spoke first. "Sir... before the ambush, I saw one of the king's men—Sir Kaelen—break away from formation. He said he was scouting ahead, but..."

Tristan's jaw tightened. "But?"

"He never came back."

Another soldier spoke up, his voice trembling. "Sir Kaelen wasn't the only one. I swear I saw him speaking to two strangers near the tree line before the first volley hit us."

Tristan's eyes narrowed. "Strangers?"

The soldier nodded. "They wore no crest. Moved like shadows. I thought I imagined it until the arrows started flying."

Tristan exhaled slowly, his mind racing. Kaelen. Tree line. Shadows. This wasn't just an ambush.

"Who else noticed anything?" he demanded, his voice sharp now.

A younger soldier hesitated before speaking. "Sir... when the retreat was sounded, some of the king's men... they didn't follow orders. It was like they wanted us cut down."

Tristan's hands clenched into fists. Betrayal.

The flap of the commander's tent whipped open with a snap, letting in a gust of cold air as Tristan stormed inside. His boots thudded against the packed earth, every step radiating controlled fury.

The commander looked up from a map, startled. "Lord Tristan—"

"You gave the orders," Tristan cut him off, his voice low and edged with steel. "Who else knew?"

The air in the tent grew heavy.

The other officers froze, glancing between them. No one dared speak.

The commander's lips pressed into a thin line. "Careful, Lord Tristan. This isn't the time—"

"The time?" Tristan slammed his palm down on the table, rattling the ink bottles and scattering the carefully placed markers. "You sent us into a trap. Men are dead because of you."

The commander's jaw tightened. "I did what was necessary—"

"Necessary?" Tristan's voice rose, his blue eyes blazing. "Necessary is holding the line. Necessary is fighting the enemy. Sending my men into an ambush to cover your mistake is not necessary."

A deadly silence filled the tent.

"Who else knew?" Tristan demanded again, his tone dropping to a dangerous whisper. "Or should I assume this betrayal goes deeper than your incompetence?"

The commander's face flushed, but he didn't answer.

Tristan leaned in close, his voice like ice. "If you ever sacrifice my men again to save yourself, I will drag you from this tent and let the army decide your fate."

The commander swallowed hard. "You forget yourself, Lord Tristan—"

"No," Tristan interrupted sharply, straightening to his full height. "You forget who I am." Tristan's authority crackled in the air like lightning in a storm.

He took one slow step forward, his blue eyes narrowing dangerously. "You sit in this tent giving orders while men die because of your cowardice."

The commander's face flushed, a mix of fear and indignation. "You will not speak to me that way—"

Tristan slammed his gloved hand on the map table, the sound like a thunderclap.

"I'll speak to you any way I damn well please," he growled. "I have bled in the mud for this army. I have carried men off the field on my own back. Do not presume to lecture me about sacrifice when your boots have never touched the front lines."

The tent fell silent, every soldier present frozen, watching the exchange.

58

The commander faltered, sweat beading on his brow. "This is treasonous talk—"

Tristan's voice dropped to a deadly calm. "No. This is loyalty to the men who fight while you cower behind parchment and wine."

Tristan straightened to his full imposing height, his cloak shifting around his broad shoulders. "You will not question my command again. Because if you do, I will drag you into that battlefield myself and let the enemy decide your worth."

The commander swallowed hard and looked away.

"Am I understood?" Tristan demanded, his voice as sharp as drawn steel.

"Y-yes, my lord."

Tristan's gaze lingered a moment longer before he turned on his heel, the tension in the tent releasing like a bowstring snapping.

* * *

The kingdom was nearly pacified, but one rebel band still resisted, striking from hidden strongholds in the forested hills.

The king's command was clear: "End this, Tristan. Crush them, bring me their leader's head." Tristan gathered men—a hand-picked force of skilled soldiers—and prepared for his mission. As they tracked the rebels deeper into the mountains, Tristan began to sense the danger.

The first pale light of dawn crept across the horizon, casting the world in shades of gray and gold. The air was heavy with tension, the kind that comes just before a strike. As dawn broke over the rebel camp, Tristan and his men surrounded it.

Tristan crouched low in the underbrush at the edge of the clearing, his piercing blue eyes fixed on the flickering glow of the rebel campfires.

Around him, his men waited silently, their weapons ready. The stillness was broken only by the distant crackle of fire and the faint clinking of armor as someone shifted their weight.

"Positions," Tristan murmured, his voice low but commanding.

His second-in-command nodded and gestured to the others. Half the men melted into the trees to flank the camp, while the rest stayed close, ready to surge forward at Tristan's signal.

Tristan's hand rested on the hilt of his sword. He could feel the cool leather grip beneath his fingers, the familiar weight anchoring him in the moment.

"There are sentries—two by the eastern fire," someone whispered, who had returned only moments ago from scouting the perimeter.

"Did they see you?" Tristan asked without looking at him.

"Please. They couldn't see a bear charging them in daylight," he scoffed.

Tristan allowed a faint smile. "Good. When I move, you circle behind the tents. Cut off their retreat."

"And if they surrender?" someone asked.

Tristan's expression hardened. "Then we take them alive. If they fight..."

"No mercy." one of the men finished grimly.

Tristan gave a sharp whistle—the signal.

In an instant, chaos erupted.

His men surged forward, blades flashing in the dawn light. Arrows hissed through the air, finding their marks.

Screams rang out as the rebels scrambled from their tents, weapons clutched in fumbling hands.

Tristan was a storm of steel, cutting down two men before they even raised their swords.

"Hold the line!" he roared to his men. "Don't let them break!"

A rebel lunged at him with a crude axe, but Tristan sidestepped and slammed the hilt of his sword into the man's temple, dropping him like a sack of grain.

The air was thick with smoke and shouting, but Tristan moved with deadly precision, his presence cutting through the panic like a blade.

The air was heavy with smoke and the sharp tang of steel. In the ruined village square, Tristan stood tall, his hand resting lightly on the hilt of his sword. Opposite him, the rebel leader—a burly man with a scar running down his jaw— watched him with narrowed eyes. Around them, men on both sides held their breath, waiting for the first move.

The rebel leader grinned. "So, the king sends his loyal hound to do his bidding. Tell me, Lord Tristan, how does it feel to fight for a master who cares nothing for the blood on your hands?"

Tristan's voice was low and steady. "Better than betraying my oath and slaughtering innocents for coin."

The rebel leader's smirk faltered.

"You call them innocents?" the rebel leader snarled. "These peasants starve while you feast in your stone halls. We fight for freedom."

Tristan stepped forward. "You fight for your own power. Don't mask greed as justice. You've burned villages, taken women, killed children. That is not freedom—it's tyranny."

The rebel's hand hovered near his axe. "And what will you do, knight? Cut me down? Will that bring back your precious honor?"

Tristan's fingers curled tightly around his sword hilt. His voice was calm, but his eyes blazed. "Surrender. Call off your men, and I'll spare your life. Keep fighting, and your blood will stain this square."

The tension snapped like a drawn bowstring.

The rebel leader gritted his teeth. "I'll die before I kneel to your king."

Tristan drew his blade slowly. "So be it."

The rebel leader let out a roar and charged. Steel clashed against steel as their men erupted into chaos around them, but the square belonged to Tristan and the rebel leader now, their duel the center of it all.

The clang of steel rang out one final time as Tristan disarmed the rebel leader with a swift upward strike, sending the man's sword clattering across the dirt. The rebels, routed and broken, had fled or surrendered—but their leader still stood, breathing hard, bloodied and furious.

Tristan stepped forward, blade lowered but firm, his presence like a thundercloud ready to break.

The rebel spat at his feet. "You fight for a crown that would crush you."

Tristan tilted his head, calm and cold. "And you fight for nothing but your own ambition, dressed in lies."

The man sneered. "You don't understand what it means to be free."

"I do," Tristan said softly, but every word cut sharper than any sword. "It means carrying the weight of honor, not casting it aside when it no longer suits you."

The rebel lunged with his last ounce of strength—only to have Tristan drive his sword through his chest in one clean motion.

As the man crumpled to his knees, choking, Tristan stepped closer, voice low and final: "Your rebellion ends here—not with glory, but with the silence of a coward who mistook chaos for courage."

And with that, the rebel leader collapsed. Behind him, his men dropped their weapons.

The battle was over.

And Tristan de Léon stood victorious—not just in strength, but in conviction.

The rebel camp lay in ruins—tents smoldering, weapons scattered, and the survivors kneeling with their hands bound.

Tristan nodded, his mind already racing ahead. This was only one rebel camp. There would be more. And somewhere out there, Marlowe was still moving his pieces across the board.

"We ride for the castle at first light," Tristan said.

* * *

The air was thick with fog that night, the fortress walls looming like silent sentinels in the moonlight.

Kaelen crouched in the shadows of the outer bailey, his dagger glinting faintly under the pale glow. His heart thundered—not from fear, but from anticipation. This was his chance.

Tristan had returned victorious from the western campaign, and the king planned to honor him with land and title. It was intolerable.

Kaelen's orders were simple: Strike quickly. Make it look like a skirmish in the streets. Then disappear before the city guard could react.

He had watched Tristan from afar, studying the knight's movements like a hawk. He knew Tristan preferred to walk alone at night, visiting the men injured in the field hospital.

"Soft-hearted fool," Kaelen had muttered under his breath. "He'll never see it coming."

Kaelen moved silently across the courtyard, slipping past a sentry.

There—Tristan's silhouette emerged from the infirmary, the knight carrying a basket of bread to the gate guards.

Kaelen's grip tightened on his dagger. This was it.

He lunged from the shadows—but Tristan spun around with lightning reflexes, his sword flashing in the moonlight.

Steel met steel as Kaelen's dagger was knocked from his hand.

"Coward!" Tristan growled, his blue eyes blazing with fury. "You'd strike from the shadows instead of facing me like a man?"

Kaelen staggered back, panic flooding his veins. He hadn't expected Tristan to be so fast.

"Wait! I—I was paid—"

But Tristan advanced, knocking Kaelen to the ground and planting a boot on his chest.

"Paid by whom?" Tristan demanded, his sword tip pressing against Kaelen's throat.

Kaelen trembled, his resolve crumbling. "Marlowe... it was Marlowe! He... he promised me gold, a place in the court—"

Tristan's lips curled into a cold smile. "Then you've gambled poorly."

"Please!" Kaelen begged. "Spare me!"

Tristan's sword held steady for a long moment before he stepped back.

"Run," he said quietly. "And pray I never see your face again."

Kaelen fled into the night, but his failure cost him everything.

CHAPTER FIVE

The sound of hooves echoed through the stone courtyard as Tristan rode through the castle gates, his dark cloak snapping in the wind. The smell of blood and smoke still clung to his armor after days on the field.

At Tristan's side, a burlap sack hung from his saddle. The shape within left little to the imagination.

The gates creaked closed behind them as servants and soldiers alike stopped to stare. Whispers spread like wildfire.

"Is it true? Did he defeat them?"

"He has the rebel leader's head."

"God help us all."

Tristan dismounted with quiet efficiency, his boots striking the cobblestones as he approached the steps to the keep.

A guard stepped forward nervously. "Lord Tristan... the king awaits you in the Great Hall."

Tristan gave a sharp nod, then tossed the sack onto the stones with a wet thud. "Take it to him," Tristan said, his voice low but commanding.

The guard hesitated, staring at the blood seeping through the sack.

"Do it," Tristan snapped.

Two guards quickly lifted the sack and carried it toward the Hall, their faces pale.

From a high balcony, Olivia stood watching as Tristan strode across the courtyard.

Her heart twisted at the sight of him. His armor was dented, streaked with blood and soot. His blue eyes, piercing as ever, seemed harder somehow.

"He's done it," Evelyne murmured beside her. "The rebellion will falter without their leader."

Olivia bit her lip. "And yet... he looks like he's lost something."

* * *

The sack was unceremoniously dumped at the base of the throne.

The king leaned forward, eyes narrowing as a guard unfastened the ties.

The rebel leader's head rolled out, lifeless eyes staring into nothing. A hush fell over the court.

"You have done well, Tristan," the king said slowly. "The rebellion is over."

Tristan inclined his head but said nothing.

The king's voice hardened. "But at what cost?"

Tristan's jaw flexed. "At whatever cost was necessary to end their treachery, sire."

The king studied him for a long moment before nodding. "Go. Rest. You've earned it."

* * *

Tristan had barely made it back to his chamber, his steps heavy, his body marked with fresh cuts and bruises beneath his tunic. He removed his armor piece by piece, exhaustion weighing on him like iron chains.

There was a knock. "It's me." Olivia's voice. Soft. Hesitant.

"Come in."

She rushed to him, her hands reaching for his shoulders her eyes scanning him from head to toe. "You're hurt."

Tristan smirked faintly, shaking his head, trying to steady himself. "It's nothing. I've been worse."

But she could see the strain in his eyes, the way his jaw tightened as though holding back the pain.

"Sit," she ordered softly, guiding him to the edge of the bed.

He didn't argue. Not this time.

She gently peeled his tunic away, revealing angry red welts and a deep gash across his ribs.

Her breath hitched at the sight. "This isn't nothing, Tristan."

He smirked faintly. "It looks worse than it is."

"Don't do that." Her hands trembled as she fetched a basin of warm water and a clean cloth. "Don't pretend you're made of stone."

Tristan watched her as she worked, dabbing carefully at the blood. She glanced up at him, her expression softening.

"Don't make light of it," she murmured. Her fingers brushed a bruise blooming across his ribs.

"You shouldn't see me like this," he said softly.

"I've seen you much worse."

Tristan caught her hand in his. "I brought peace for the kingdom... but at what cost to myself?"

For a moment, neither spoke. The only sound was the crackle of the fire and her quiet, deliberate movements as she cleaned and bandaged his wounds.

"You frightened me," Olivia whispered finally.

Tristan caught her wrist gently, his thumb brushing her pulse. "I'm still here."

"You can't promise you'll always come back," she said, her voice trembling now.

His blue eyes softened. "No," he admitted. "But I can promise I'll fight until my last breath to return to you."

And before she could respond, he pulled her closer, his forehead resting against hers. "I'm yours, Olivia. In every way that matters."

Her hand cupped his cheek, and she whispered back, "And I'm yours, Tristan."

Tristan pressed a soft kiss to her hand and pulled her into the bed. "Tonight, I want to hold you."

He slid into bed beside her, gathering her into his arms. She fit perfectly there, her head resting against his chest, his fingers gently stroking her hair. His arms tightened slightly around her, and she felt his lips press to the crown of her head. "Then let the world wait."

They both drifted into sleep entwined, safe, and utterly at home in each other's presence

CHAPTER SIX

The massive oak doors creaked open as Edward Marlowe stepped into the Great Hall. The polished stone floors reflected the torchlight, and the nobles turned, whispering as they watched him cross the chamber.

Marlowe's presence was like a shadow falling over the room.

He was tall and lean, his dark hair streaked with silver at the temples, and his piercing gray eyes swept the Hall with a predator's calm. He wore the king's colors—a sign of supposed loyalty—but on his hand, he still wore the sigil ring of the Order of the Silver Flame.

From his position near the throne, Tristan stiffened. He recognized Marlowe immediately.

"So," Tristan muttered under his breath, his jaw tight. "The viper crawls back into the garden."

"Why is he here?" Olivia asked.

Tristan's voice was low and sharp. "Because he's good at pretending he isn't what he is."

The king rose from his throne, arms outstretched. "Sir Edward Marlowe," he declared, his voice carrying through the Hall. "A son of the Order returns to us, repentant and seeking redemption."

Tristan's fists clenched.

Marlowe bowed low, his expression smooth as polished steel. "Your Majesty, I live only to serve the crown. My past mistakes weigh heavy on me, and I would see them undone by my service."

The king nodded approvingly. "Then you shall have that chance."

After the king dismissed the court, Tristan strode across the Hall, his boots echoing on the stone.

"Marlowe."

Edward turned slowly, his gray eyes narrowing as they met Tristan's icy blue stare.

"Ah. Lord Tristan de Léon."

Tristan stopped a mere foot away, his hand resting lightly on the hilt of his sword. "You shouldn't be here."

Marlowe smirked. "And yet, here I am."

"I know what you are," Tristan growled. "A liar. A snake. And if you so much as look at Olivia—"

"You'll do what?" Marlowe asked softly, his smile widening. "Kill me? Here in the king's Hall?"

Tristan's jaw tightened. "Don't test me."

Marlowe leaned in slightly. "Don't worry, Tristan. I'm not here for your... lady. I'm here for something much bigger."

Before Tristan could respond, Marlowe brushed past him with a smirk. "But do keep your sword sharp, old friend. You may yet need it."

Sir Edward Marlowe was already plotting in the court's candlelit halls. Marlowe knew Tristan's growing influence threatened his own ambitions. So he started small—spreading whispers.

"Sir Tristan was once loyal, yes... but have you not heard? He returned from his last campaign a changed man."

"They say he keeps a foreign witch at his side."

"Would you trust a knight so easily swayed by a woman?"

The rumors slithered through the court like smoke, curling into the ears of lords and ladies.

Marlowe's goal wasn't to strike outright—Not yet. It was to sow doubt. To turn the king's favor brittle.

And if Tristan faltered, even for a moment... Marlowe would be ready to strike.

* * *

The clang of swords rang out in the crisp morning air.

Tristan and Sir Marlow circled one another in the training yard, boots grinding into the dirt as they tested each other's guard.

It had begun as a sparring match—a simple test of skill.

But now?

Now it felt like a battle.

"Come now, Tristan," Marlow sneered as his blade clashed hard against Tristan's. "Is court life so softening that you've lost your edge?"

Tristan's jaw tightened. "Keep talking, Marlow. It'll be your only advantage."

The men watching murmured, shifting uncomfortably. This wasn't like the usual sparring bouts—the air was thick with tension.

Marlow struck hard, a vicious swing that Tristan barely deflected.

The blades screeched as they locked, and Marlow leaned in.

"Tell me, how long before your little lady tires of playing noble? You think she'll still want you when you've lost your title?"

Tristan's blue eyes flared with cold fury.

"You speak one more word of her, and this won't be a sparring match."

Marlow smirked. "Hit a nerve, did I?"

Tristan twisted, breaking the blade lock, and drove Marlow back with a series of rapid strikes.

The men watching exchanged nervous glances—this wasn't training anymore.

Steel sparked. Tristan's strikes were relentless, his movements precise and punishing.

Marlow stumbled back, his smirk faltering as he realized— Tristan wasn't holding back anymore.

"Yield," Tristan growled.

Marlow spat in the dirt. "Never."

Tristan's next strike sent Marlow's sword flying from his hand. The blade clattered to the ground, and Tristan's sword was at Marlow's throat in a heartbeat.

"I said. Yield."

Marlow's chest heaved. His pride burned hotter than the blade's edge. But finally, he muttered, "I yield."

"Enough!" Evelyne's voice cut through the yard as she strode toward them. "This was supposed to be practice," she said sharply, glaring at both men. "Not a grudge match."

Tristan exhaled slowly, his grip on his sword loosening. But his eyes never left Marlow.

"You should know better," Evelyne hissed at Marlow. "You baited him, didn't you?"

Marlow scowled, retrieving his fallen blade. "You'd do well to watch your brother, my lady. He's not as composed as he pretends."

Tristan's jaw flexed. "And you'd do well to leave before I forget Evelyne's presence here."

Marlow spat again, then stormed off.

Later, Olivia found Tristan in the courtyard, wiping down his blade.

"You didn't have to prove anything to him," she said softly.

Tristan glanced at her, his expression softening. "I wasn't proving anything to him." He sheathed the sword. "I was reminding him what happens when a man pushes too far."

Olivia raised a brow. "And what happens if I push you too far?"

Tristan smirked, stepping closer. "You're the only one allowed to."

* * *

The king's private chamber was lit only by the flicker of candlelight, the heavy scent of wax and parchment filling the air. He sat behind a massive oak desk, quill in hand as he signed decrees, his face lined with the weight of rulership.

The doors creaked open, and Marlowe stepped in unannounced.

"Your Majesty," he said, voice smooth but carrying a current of urgency.

The king looked up sharply. "This had better be important, Sir Marlowe."

Marlowe bowed deeply. "It concerns your safety—and the safety of the realm."

Marlowe approached, his dark cloak whispering against the stone floor. "It is the woman... Olivia."

The king's brow furrowed. "What of her?"

"She is no mere woman, Your Majesty," Marlowe said with a measured tone. "I have reason to believe she practices witchcraft."

The king's face hardened. "Be careful, Marlowe. Those are grave words."

"Grave, yes. But necessary." Marlowe stepped closer, lowering his voice. "Have you not seen it yourself? The strange energy that seems to follow her? The unnatural influence she holds over Lord Tristan? He would defy even you for her."

The king's jaw tightened, his mind replaying the events of the past weeks—the rumors, the way Tristan had shielded Olivia, even against court custom.

Marlowe pressed on. "And the amulet she carries—my men have whispered of its glow. Magic, Your Majesty. Dark magic."

"Do you have proof?" the king demanded, his voice like a blade.

Marlowe's lips curved into a cold smile. "Allow me to provide it. Grant me leave to search her chambers, to interrogate her. I will expose her for what she truly is."

The king leaned back in his chair, staring at the dancing candle flames. He had trusted Tristan for years, valued him like a son. But the court had grown restless. Whispers spread like wildfire.

If Olivia truly was a witch...

The king exhaled sharply. "Bring her to the hall at first light. I will question her myself."

Marlowe bowed low, hiding his triumphant smirk. "As you command."

CHAPTER SEVEN

The room was quiet except for the crackle of the low fire and the soft sound of Tristan's steady breathing. Olivia lay curled at his side, her head resting on his chest, lulled to sleep by the rise and fall of his chest.

The heavy thud of boots woke Tristan instantly.

The door slammed open. Wood splintered against the wall, and torchlight flooded the chamber.

"By order of the king!" a voice bellowed. Armed guards barreled into the chamber, swords drawn.

"What is the meaning of this?" Tristan roared, leaping from the bed.

His hand reached for the sword leaning against the wall, but two guards grabbed his arms, holding him back.

"Stand down, Lord Tristan!" the captain barked. "We are here for the woman."

"You'll not touch her!" Tristan growled, his voice a lethal snarl. He struggled against their grip, his muscles straining.

"By the king's command, she is to be brought before the court. Now."

Two more guards yanked Olivia from the bed, dragging her to her feet.

"Tristan!" she cried, her voice shaking. Her hair tumbled loose around her face as she tried to pull free. "What's happening?!"

"Don't fight them," Tristan shouted. His voice was hard but his eyes burned with helpless fury. "I'll come for you, Olivia. I swear it."

"Hold him!" the captain ordered. "Take her!"

As Tristan fought like a caged animal against the guards holding him back, Olivia was pulled toward the door, her bare feet scraping across the cold stone floor.

"Tristan!" she screamed again. "Don't let them take me!"

But they dragged her down the corridor.

With brute strength, Tristan twisted out of the guard's grasp. One guard went flying into the table, splintering it. Tristan's fist connected with another's jaw, dropping him cold.

He grabbed for his trousers, pulling them on quickly, then snatched his sword from its scabbard.

He grabbed Olivia's robe that was draped over the chair and stormed from the room, shirtless and barefoot, his eyes burning.

Moments later, Olivia was thrown to her knees in the center of the Great Hall. Torches flared along the walls, casting long shadows. She covered her breasts.

The king sat at the far end, his face carved from stone.

"Lady Olivia," he said coldly, "you are brought before this court to answer accusations."

"Accusations?" Olivia gasped. "What accusations?!"

Marlowe stepped forward from the shadows, his smirk gleaming in the torchlight. "Witchcraft," he said softly. "The lady has ensnared Lord Tristan's mind. And now she must answer for it."

The great oak doors slammed open with a deafening crack, sending a hush rippling through the Hall.

All eyes turned as Lord Tristan stormed in, his bare feet striking the stone floor with the force of his anger. His blue eyes burned with barely contained fury.

He didn't hesitate. Didn't slow.

Every noble in the room shrank back as Tristan strode straight for Olivia, who stood in front of the king.

Before anyone could speak, Tristan's strong arms swept around her protectively, pulling her to his chest, covering her with the robe.

"What is happening here?" he demanded, his voice like steel cracking across the Hall.

The chatter died instantly. The firelight flickered against Tristan's face, highlighting the sharp lines of anger etched into his expression.

"My king," Marlowe said, bowing deeply. "It grieves me to bring such tidings."

Tristan's jaw clenched. "This is madness."

Marlowe smirked. "Is it? I have witnesses."

A trembling maid was brought forward, clutching a handkerchief to her chest. Her cheeks were pale, her eyes wide.

"I... I didn't mean to spill the wine," she stammered. "But Lady Olivia... she whispered strange words, and later that night, I was struck down with fever!"

Tristan's voice cut through the hall like steel. "A fever is not witchcraft. This is baseless."

But Marlowe wasn't done.

"What of the candle, then?" he pressed. "It flared as she passed—several saw it. And the injured sparrow healed in her hand! These are no mere coincidences."

Another servant stepped forward nervously. "I saw it, my lord. The bird... it flew away as though reborn."

At Marlowe's command, guards entered Olivia's chamber. Moments later, they returned, holding a bundle of strange objects.

"Bones. Runes. Dried herbs," the guard reported grimly.

Marlowe raised his voice triumphantly. "Witch's charms, my king!"

The hall erupted in horrified whispers.

Tristan's voice was like thunder. "This is a lie. These were planted."

Marlowe's smirk widened. "Were they? Or are you too blinded by her spell to see the truth?"

All eyes turned to Olivia.

Her chin lifted, her voice steady despite the weight of the accusation. "I have done nothing but stand at Lord Tristan's side. You fear me because you do not understand me."

Marlowe sneered. "We fear you because you are unnatural."

The king's gaze darkened. "Enough. This will be investigated. Take her to the dungeon."

"No!" Tristan yelled.

The Great Hall fell into stunned silence.

Tristan stood, his arms wrapped protectively around Olivia, his broad frame shielding her from the accusing stares of the court. His blue eyes burned with fury, his jaw tight as he faced the king.

"Your Majesty," he said through gritted teeth, "you cannot—"

"Enough!" the king's voice thundered, cutting through Tristan's protest. "The accusations are grave. Until the truth is known, the woman will be held in the dungeons."

"No." Tristan's voice was low, deadly. He pulled Olivia tighter against him. "You will not take her from me."

Guards moved forward, hesitation in their steps. They knew Tristan's reputation. One wrong move, and blood would be spilled in the king's hall.

"Tristan—" Evelyne's sharp voice cut through the tension. She was at his side in an instant, her hand gripping his arm. "If you resist, they'll accuse you of treason!"

"Let them!" Tristan roared, his voice raw with rage.

Aldric stepped forward, grabbing Tristan's other arm. "Think! You can't protect her from a cell!"

"You don't understand," Tristan growled, his body coiled like a predator about to strike. "If they take her, she may not survive this."

Gideon appeared behind him, moving with quiet precision. "You're no good to her dead, my friend. Let them think they've won—for now."

The guards reached for Olivia, and Tristan's grip on her tightened. "Don't you dare touch her!"

"Tristan," Olivia whispered, her fingers brushing his jaw. Her eyes were wide with fear but steady. "Please... don't fight them. I'll be all right."

"No, you won't," he rasped. "I swore to protect you. I won't let them take you."

But Evelyne, Aldric, and Gideon held him fast.

"Brother," Evelyne whispered fiercely, her own eyes wet. "You'll lose everything if you don't let her go—for now."

85

The guards stepped forward. One pried her from Tristan's arms while another yanked her wrists behind her back.

"No!" Tristan roared, straining against Aldric's grip. "Don't touch her!"

Olivia was dragged across the cold stone floor, her eyes locked on Tristan's. "Tristan!" she cried.

"Olivia!" His voice cracked as he fought against the hands holding him back. "I'll come for you! Do you hear me? I'll come for you!"

"I know!" she shouted back, her voice breaking. "I know you will!"

The doors slammed shut behind her.

And Tristan fell to his knees, his body shaking with rage. "I'll kill him for this," he whispered.

* * *

The stone wall was cold against Olivia's back as she sat huddled in the corner of the small, damp cell. Shadows crept along the walls, cast by the single torch flickering faintly outside her barred door.

Her wrists ached from where they had been bound earlier, though the ropes had been removed when the king deemed her "no threat."

But she felt like a threat.

To herself.

To Tristan.

Every sound in the corridor beyond made her flinch—the scuff of boots, the metallic clink of armor, the muffled laughter of guards. Each step might bring Marlowe.

And yet... she almost wished it would. The waiting was worse than anything.

She stared at the amulet still hanging from her neck, its silver surface cold to the touch. At times it felt like it pulsed faintly, as if trying to speak to her.

"Do something," she whispered to herself, her voice hoarse. "Think, Olivia. You've been through worse than this."

Had she?

No.

Not like this.

Her thoughts turned to Tristan. A sharp pang of guilt cut through her chest. She had been the distraction.

"It's my fault," she murmured, burying her face in her knees.

But then she remembered the way Tristan had looked at her—his piercing blue eyes alight with determination even in the midst of chaos.

"No," she said more firmly this time, raising her head. "He's coming for me. He has to."

The sound of boots echoed again, louder this time. She held her breath, her fingers curling tightly around the amulet.

87

The key to her return.

The key to Tristan's survival.

"Open it," came Marlowe's voice, smooth as silk and twice as dangerous.

The guard's keys rattled. The lock clanked.

The door creaked open, and Marlowe stepped in.

"Ah, my little mouse," he said with a mocking smile. "Let's talk, shall we?"

Olivia forced herself to meet his gaze. "What do you want from me, Marlowe?"

He raised a brow, stepping closer until the hem of his coat brushed her knees. "What do I want? The better question is, what does Tristan want with you?"

Her jaw tightened. "That's none of your concern."

"On the contrary, my dear," he murmured, crouching to meet her eye level, "it's very much my concern. Tristan is reckless where you are involved. Dangerous. And for what? A woman who fell into his path?"

Olivia's voice sharpened. "He cares for me. Something you wouldn't understand."

Marlowe's smirk deepened. "Oh, I understand perfectly. But caring... caring makes men weak. Caring leads knights like Tristan to fall on their swords."

He reached out suddenly, brushing a stray lock of her hair from her face. She flinched but held her ground.

"You've caused quite a stir, Olivia," Marlow whispered. "The court fears you. The king suspects you. And Tristan..." He chuckled darkly. "Tristan would burn the world for you. But tell me, if he burns, would you burn with him?"

Olivia's fingers tightened in her lap. "I'd rather burn than ever side with you."

Marlowe's smirk turned cold. "That can be arranged."

He leaned closer, his voice dropping to a whisper. "When the pyre is built and they chain you to the stake, let's see how much fire your heart truly holds."

Olivia's chest tightened, but she didn't let her fear show. "When Tristan comes for me, you'll be the one in the fire."

Marlowe's laughter echoed through the cell. "You really believe he'll come for you?"

"I don't just believe," Olivia said softly. "I know."

Marlowe stood up. "Tristan has challenged me to a duel to the death. If he wins you live and walk free. If I win you will burn."

He turned and strode out, the door slamming shut behind him.

* * *

The torches along the dungeon walls flickered weakly, their light barely reaching the cold stone floor. The air was damp, heavy with the scent of mildew and fear.

Olivia sat on the narrow bench in her cell, her arms wrapped tightly around herself. She had tried to be strong, but now, in the silence, her resolve felt like it was cracking.

And then— the sound of boots on stone. Slow. Steady. Familiar.

Her head lifted up just as Tristan appeared in the dim light, his black cloak brushing the floor, his sword strapped firmly at his side.

"Tristan," she whispered.

He stepped closer, wrapping his hands around the iron bars of her cell. His blue eyes locked onto hers—intense, fierce, yet soft with emotion.

"It's set," he said quietly, his voice low so no one else would hear. "The duel will take place at first light."

Olivia's breath hitched. "So soon?"

Tristan's jaw tightened. "Marlowe forced the king's hand. He wants it to end quickly."

"You can't—" she started, but he shook his head, cutting her off.

"I can," he said firmly. "And I will. You are not going to die here, Olivia."

She gripped the bars, leaning forward until their foreheads nearly touched. "What if you—"

"No." His hand came up, cupping the side of her face through the bars. "Don't say it. I will not fall to that man. Do you hear me?"

Tears pricked her eyes, but she nodded. "I hear you."

"Good." He exhaled sharply, his thumb brushing against her cheek. "Then you'll be ready to leave this place tomorrow."

The clank of iron echoed as the guards approached, their boots scraping across the cold stone floor.

Tristan stood in front of Olivia's cell, his hands wrapped tightly around hers through the bars. The dim torchlight caught the flicker of desperation in his eyes.

"Time's up, Lord Tristan," one of the guards grunted.

Tristan didn't move. His thumb brushed over Olivia's knuckles, memorizing the feel of her hands as if he might never get to touch her again.

"Look at me," he said softly, his voice low but commanding.

Olivia raised her tear-brimmed eyes to meet his.

"You are stronger than this cell. Stronger than their lies," he murmured. "And I swear on my life, Olivia—I will not let them take you from me."

"You don't know what they'll do," she whispered, her voice trembling.

"They'll do nothing," Tristan growled. "Because I won't allow it."

The guards shifted uncomfortably behind him.

"Lord Tristan, we must escort you out—now."

Tristan's jaw tightened, but he leaned closer, his forehead pressing against the bars.

"When this is over, I'll come for you." His voice softened, almost breaking. "And nothing—not kings, not traitors, not even the devil himself—will keep me away."

"Promise me," Olivia whispered, clutching his hands tighter.

"I promise."

One of the guards stepped forward. "Lord—"

Tristan turned abruptly, towering over them, his eyes blazing like a storm. "Touch her, and you'll answer to me."

The guards hesitated, glancing at one another nervously.

Tristan turned back to Olivia one last time.

"Hold on for me." His voice was rough, but his eyes softened as he spoke. "Just hold on."

And then he let go, his fingers lingering for a heartbeat too long before stepping back as the guards moved in.

He didn't look back as they led him out—but his vow hung in the cold air like susurrus of a blade drawn.

* * *

The stone walls were cold. So cold they seemed to seep into her bones.

The small window above her was barred, moonlight filtering through like pale fingers grasping for her soul. The faint sounds of the banquet upstairs had faded long ago, replaced now by distant footsteps and the occasional rattle of chains.

She pulled her knees to her chest, clutching the amulet in her hand so tightly that the edge pressed into her skin. It was warm. Too warm. Like it knew her fear.

At first, she prayed. Not in the way she once did, as a child—soft and trusting—but in a desperate whisper, words tumbling from her lips.

"Please... don't let him die for me. Don't let him throw his life away."

Then came the tears. She tried to fight them back, but they came anyway, streaking down her cheeks as she sobbed.

The weight of it all crushed her chest.

If Tristan lost...

If Marlowe won...

She would burn.

And Tristan would die trying to save her.

But then something in her shifted. Her tears slowed. Her jaw clenched. She would not meet her end sobbing in the dark like a frightened girl.

"No," she whispered fiercely, clutching the amulet. "I won't let this be the end."

She drew in a deep breath, forcing her fear down.

If this was her fate, she would face it with her head high.

But deep down, a voice whispered, "Tristan won't let it come to that."

And for the first time in hours, Olivia believed it.

CHAPTER EIGHT

The cold air of dawn hung heavy over the castle. Mist curled in the streets of the square, clinging to the stones like ghostly fingers. The sky was a pale gray, the sun not yet risen.

The sound of boots echoed as guards dragged Olivia through the narrow streets, their hands like iron on her arms as she stumbled forward.

Her robe, now torn and dirtied, trailed behind her. Her hair hung loose around her face, tangled and damp with morning dew.

In the square, a crowd was already gathering, some hungry for blood and spectacle—a sea of faces, some curious, some to be entertained.

Peasants, nobles, and soldiers stood in silence, their breath puffing in the chill air as they waited. A pyre had been built in the center—a crude wooden stake loomed ahead, its wooden beams darkened by past fires. A pile of faggots surrounded its base, dry and ready to burn.

Olivia's heart pounded in her chest as she fought to keep her head high, though her legs trembled beneath her.

At the front stood Marlowe, his arms folded, lips curled in satisfaction.

"Bring the witch forward," he commanded. "Chain her."

Two men stepped forward and bound her wrists tightly behind her, the cold bite of iron cut into her skin. She felt the heavy chains tighten around her waist, locking her to the stake. The sharp scent of smoke lingered in the air from the torches held by the executioners.

Marlowe stepped forward from the crowd, his lips curling into a cruel smile. "A fitting place for a witch, wouldn't you say?"

Olivia met his gaze, defiance blazing in her eyes despite the fear twisting her stomach. "This is madness!" she spat. "I am no witch!" She gritted her teeth, refusing to give him the satisfaction of seeing her break.

Marlowe's smile faltered for a moment, but he quickly recovered. "Burning you will end this farce. And Tristan? He will watch you die."

Her blood ran cold

The crowd murmured uneasily. Some shifted their weight, unsure if they should be here. Others whispered about the foreign woman and her strange ways.

The square was silent except for the crackle of torches and the low murmur of the gathered crowd. Above, the gray sky seemed to press down, heavy and suffocating, as if the heavens themselves were holding their breath.

Olivia stood chained to the stake, her eyes wide with fear as the executioner stepped forward to read the proclamation.

"By the order of His Majesty, King Henry V, Lord Tristan de Léon and Sir Edward Marlowe shall fight to the death. If Lord Tristan is victorious, the woman accused of witchcraft shall be spared. If he falls..."

The man's voice faltered for a moment as he glanced at Olivia. "Then she shall burn at the stake."

A ripple of unease moved through the crowd. This was no friendly sparring match. This was life and death.

Tristan stepped forward, every inch the warrior, his sword already unsheathed, gleaming like liquid fire in the torchlight. His piercing blue eyes locked on Marlowe, cold and unyielding.

"This ends here," Tristan growled.

Marlowe smirked, his own blade flashing as he drew it. "It ends with you, de Léon. And with her screams."

Tristan's blue eyes were ice, his jaw tight as he stepped forward. "You've run out of lies, Marlowe. Now you'll answer with your blade."

Marlowe smirked, circling him. "You should've stayed in the shadows, Tristan. Now you'll die in the light."

The king and his men watched tensely from the edges of the square.

The two men circled, boots crunching against the stone. The crowd held its breath as the first clash of steel rang out—a sharp, grating sound that echoed across the square.

Marlowe struck first, his blade a silver blur in the torchlight. Tristan parried hard, the clash of steel echoing like a cannon shot.

They exchanged blows, each strike faster and heavier than the last. Sparks showered the stones as their swords scraped and locked, neither man giving an inch.

Tristan broke the deadlock with a vicious shove, sending Marlowe stumbling back. He advanced, his footwork quick and deadly precise.

"You've betrayed your king, your men, and your honor, and now you're trying to kill an innocent woman!" Tristan growled, swinging low and forcing Marlowe to leap aside. "Why?"

"Honor's for fools," Marlowe hissed, launching a savage counterattack. "Power is all that matters! As for the woman—"

Tristan struck, his blade slicing toward Marlowe's shoulder. "You'll have no power where you're going!" he snarled.

But Marlowe parried, twisting his blade and driving forward with brutal force.

The fight was vicious, primal. Sparks flew as sword met sword.

Marlowe's blade slashed across Tristan's shoulder, tearing cloth and drawing blood. Tristan didn't flinch. He pressed forward, each strike fueled by one thought alone: Olivia.

"You're slower than I remember," Marlowe hissed, shoving him back.

Tristan's lips curled into a snarl. "And you're still a coward."

He feinted left and struck right, his blade slicing across Marlowe's arm. Blood welled, dripping onto the stone.

Marlowe roared and lunged forward, slamming his shoulder into Tristan's chest and knocking him to the ground.

His sword came down in a vicious arc—

But Tristan rolled, narrowly avoiding the killing blow, stone scraping his hands raw.

He kicked Marlowe's knee, sending the man stumbling, and scrambled back to his feet.

Their swords clashed again, over and over, the sound like rolling thunder.

Marlowe was relentless, his strikes heavy and punishing, but Tristan was faster, more precise.

Marlowe swung hard, but Tristan sidestepped at the last second. He stepped into the next strike, slamming his elbow into Marlowe's face.

Bone crunched. Blood sprayed. Marlowe staggered, but he didn't fall.

With a roar, Marlowe swung wildly, his blade slicing the air.

Tristan ducked the blow, rolled, and came up behind him—driving his boot into Marlowe's back and sending him sprawling into the dirt.

"Yield," Tristan barked, his sword at Marlowe's neck.

"Never!" Marlowe spat, kicking out and knocking Tristan off balance.

The two men crashed together, fists flying as their swords fell to the ground.

Tristan drove his knee into Marlowe's ribs with brutal force. Marlowe punched him square in the jaw, splitting his lip.

Both men scrambled for their weapons. Tristan reached his first.

Marlowe lunged recklessly, his face twisted in hatred. "Die!" he screamed.

But Tristan pivoted sharply, sidestepped the thrust. With a roar, Tristan slammed his pommel into Marlowe's jaw, stunning him.

And then—with one fluid motion—Tristan drove his blade straight through Marlowe's chest.

The square went silent as Marlowe gasped, eyes wide, blood bubbling on his lips. Blood bloomed across this tunic.

"For Olivia," Tristan whispered coldly.

With a final shove, he pulled his blade free. Marlowe crumpled to the stone with a hollow thud, his sword clattering from his lifeless hand.

The square was silent.

Tristan stood over Marlowe's body, chest heaving, blood dripping from his blade.

"It's done," he murmured, his eyes dark with exhaustion and fury.

Tristan didn't wait for the king's order. He strode across the square, his bloodied sword still in hand.

The executioner froze as Tristan reached the stake. With one swing, he shattered Olivia's chains.

He caught her in his arms, holding her tight. "It's over," he whispered. "You're safe."

"I thought—" she whispered.

"Don't think," he murmured, pressing his forehead to hers.

The king rose slowly, his voice carrying across the stunned courtyard.

"Lord Tristan de Léon... you have proven your honor and strength before the crown."

"And the woman?" a courtier dared to ask.

The king's gaze swept over Olivia. "She is no witch. She is under the protection of Lord Tristan and the crown itself."

The crowd murmured, some in awe, others in anger.

But Tristan didn't care.

He had won.

CHAPTER NINE

After the intensity of court life and the venomous whispers, Tristan, Olivia and the others retreated to the safety of Ravenshire.

As their horses trotted through the familiar gates, Olivia felt a sense of relief wash over her. The air smelled of pine and hearth smoke, and the sound of distant laughter from the garrison gave the stone walls a sense of life she'd missed.

"We're home," Evelyne said softly, a smile tugging at her lips. "And still in one piece."

The sound of hooves echoed in the courtyard as Tristan, Olivia, Evelyne, and their weary retinue finally rode through the gates of the stronghold.

The sun had dipped low behind the hills, casting the castle in warm amber light. Dust clung to their boots and cloaks after days on the road.

Old Martha was the first to appear, bustling out of the Great Hall with a wide smile.

"Lord Tristan! Lady Olivia! Evelyne! Praise heaven you've returned safe!" she exclaimed, wiping her flour-dusted hands on her apron before rushing forward.

Olivia slid from her horse, her legs aching with relief, but she was smiling. "We're glad to be back, Martha."

Tristan dismounted with practiced ease, handing Valour's reins to a waiting groom. His blue eyes softened as he looked over the familiar stones of his home. "It's good to see this place again," he murmured.

Other servants and retainers gathered in the courtyard, some carrying lanterns to light the twilight, others coming simply to see their lord and lady return.

The grooms stepped forward briskly, leading the tired horses away to the stables. Valour snorted, tossing his mane as if proud to have carried his rider through yet another dangerous journey.

Tristan rubbed the stallion's neck affectionately. "Good lad," he murmured before giving him over.

Evelyne swung down gracefully from her mare and caught Martha in a quick hug. "We've much to tell you," she said with a small grin, though her voice hinted at the weight of all they had endured.

"I'll have the hearth blazing and warm food ready in no time," Martha promised. "The kitchens are stocked well, and I've a fresh loaf cooling as we speak."

Olivia laughed softly. "That sounds like heaven."

"And a bath," Evelyne added pointedly. "I think we all smell like road dust and horse."

Tristan smirked. "You said that as though I don't always smell like horse."

"It's worse than usual," Evelyne teased back.

As they all laughed, Tristan reached for Olivia's hand, giving it a gentle squeeze. "Come on," he said quietly. "Let's go inside. You're home now."

* * *

The air in the Great Hall was warm and inviting as Tristan and Olivia stepped through the heavy oak doors. The crackle of the fire in the hearth chased away the autumn chill, and the scent of freshly baked bread and roasted herbs wafted from the kitchen.

Old Martha bustled out from the kitchen, her round face breaking into a grin the moment she spotted them.

"Welcome back, we've missed you!" she exclaimed, wiping her flour-dusted hands on her apron. "Lord Tristan, Lady Olivia, you've both come back to us in one piece. About time too."

Olivia smiled, feeling the tension in her shoulders ease. "Martha, we've missed you."

"Hmph," Martha sniffed, though her eyes softened. "And I've missed you, my lady. Now sit yourselves down before you collapse in a heap. You look half-starved."

Tristan smiled. "We've had worse welcomes."

"And you'll have a proper one here, I'll see to it." Martha gestured to the long table by the fire. "Go on, sit. I'll not have my lord and lady standing about like servants."

Within moments, Martha set down a steaming bowl of thick stew, fragrant with herbs and chunks of tender venison.

104

Warm loaves of bread, golden and crusty, appeared next, followed by a small wheel of cheese and fresh apples from the orchard.

"Eat," Martha commanded, hands on her hips. "There's more where that came from. And don't you dare leave a crumb."

Olivia let out a soft laugh. "We'll try not to."

Tristan tore a piece of bread, dipping it into the stew. "You've outdone yourself again, Martha."

"Of course, I have," she said briskly, though her cheeks flushed at the praise. "You think I'd let the master of the house waste away?"

The Great Hall of the castle was alive with the clinking of goblets and the low murmur of voices as the evening meal was served. Candles flickered along the length of the table, casting golden light on the faces of the knights, and a few watchful servants lingering at the edges of the room.

At the high table, Tristan sat beside Olivia, his posture relaxed but his eyes scanning the room for every smile and raised glass.

To Olivia's other side sat Evelyne, poised and regal in her deep blue gown, her sharp eyes didn't miss a thing.

Across from them, Aldric and Gideon were already deep into a discussion—though by the smirk on Gideon's face, it was more banter than strategy.

Servants moved swiftly between the tables, setting down platters of roasted pheasant, bowls of spiced root vegetables, and baskets of crusty bread. The air was rich with the scent of herbs, garlic, and dripping fat.

Aldric tore into a hunk of bread, his gruff voice cutting through the chatter.

"This is the first time in days I've eaten something that wasn't charred over an open flame."

Gideon smirked, swirling his wine. "That's because you cook like a soldier, not a chef."

"And you cook like a thief—stealing someone else's meal." Aldric shot back dryly.

Gideon raised his goblet. "Why waste energy cooking when I can charm a lovely kitchen maid into bringing me supper?"

Olivia tried to stifle a laugh, but Evelyne didn't bother hiding her amused snort. "You're shameless, Gideon."

"Shameless, yes," Gideon replied smoothly. "But effective."

Tristan leaned toward Olivia as he reached for a small tart on her plate. "You've hardly touched your food."

"I'm still learning to keep my appetite when half the court is staring at me."

His lips curved into the faintest smile. "Let them stare." He took a bite.

"Easy for you to say," she muttered. "You've worn that armor of confidence for years. I'm still fitting into mine."

Tristan's smile softened. "It suits you already."

Olivia felt her cheeks warm and quickly took a sip of wine to mask it.

As they ate, Olivia glanced at Tristan. "It feels strange to be back. Like the world has been holding its breath for us."

He gave her a small smile. "It has. And now it exhales."

She laughed softly. "That's poetic for you."

Tristan leaned back in his chair, the firelight flickering across his face. "I'm allowed one poetic moment. Don't expect many more."

"We'll see," she teased.

He smirked, then reached for his goblet of wine. "We're home, Olivia."

CHAPTER TEN

The air was crisp and cool, the sun already slipping behind the hills as twilight bathed Ravenshire in shadows. Orange and amber leaves carpeted the courtyard, crunching softly beneath the boots of the castle's inhabitants as they bustled about. Preparations for the Samhain feast were well underway—long trestle tables in the Great Hall had been laden with roasted meats, spiced apples, bread shaped like twisted knots, and honeyed nuts.

At the gates, lanterns carved from turnips glowed with eerie faces, their flickering lights warding off any spirits said to wander on this sacred night when the veil between worlds was thinnest.

Olivia stood beside Evelyne, watching as children in makeshift costumes ran through the courtyard laughing, some dressed as spirits, others as woodland beasts. She smiled softly. "It reminds me of Halloween back home."

"Hollow what?" Evelyne asked, tilting her head in curiosity.

"A holiday like this," Olivia said. "But with far more sugar and fewer ghost stories that feel like they might actually be real."

Tristan approached then, dressed in a deep charcoal tunic embroidered with silver thistles. His sword hung at his hip, but his demeanor was relaxed. "You speak of ghosts," he said, eyeing the jack-o'-lantern turnips, "yet you wear no charm to keep them away?"

Olivia lifted the amulet from around her neck, its faint glow catching the light. "I have this."

He gave a low chuckle. "Fair enough."

As the evening darkened, the people of Ravenshire gathered inside the Great Hall. A roaring fire warmed the stone walls, casting dancing shadows. At the head of the table, Tristan raised his goblet. "To Samhain—let the harvest rest, let the old year pass, and may the new one brings peace."

A chorus of "To Samhain!" echoed.

Gideon stood by the hearth, watching those gathered. "Ah, you want a story, do you?" he said, flashing his crooked grin, the firelight dancing in his eyes. "Well then, let me tell you about the cursed bell of Bracken Hollow. Have you ever heard it toll? No? That's because those who do don't live to talk about it."

He leaned in, voice low and conspiratorial, as everyone around the fire leaned closer.

"Bracken Hollow was a tiny hamlet—long since abandoned—nestled between the edge of Wyrmwood Forest and a moss-covered hill where an old chapel stood. The villagers had built it centuries ago, stone by stone, and at its peak they hung a bell. A mighty thing, forged from black iron and silver ore, they said. Beautiful sound, too—clear as the morning sky. But cursed? Aye."

He took a slow sip of his drink, letting the tension hang.

"They say the bell only rang on its own. No rope. No hand. Just... tolling. And every time it did, someone died. No warning. No mercy. Just a long, echoing clang, and by dawn, another soul would be cold in their bed. Always someone who had a secret. A lie. Blood on their hands."

Jon, one of the stable hands and ever the skeptic, crossed his arms and gave Gideon a sideways look. "A bell that rings on its own? Likely the wind, or some rusted old rope creaking."

Someone near the fire muttered, "A death bell."

But Mae, Jon's wife, leaned in closer, her eyes gleaming with a mix of curiosity and unease. "They say the bell tolls for lost souls—those who were never laid to rest." She glanced toward the hearth where the flames danced like spirits. "I believe there's truth in old stories."

Gideon nodded solemnly. "Aye, but worse. The last time it rang was thirty years ago. A taxman from the capital had come sniffing around. Greedy sort. He laughed at the stories, mocked the chapel, even climbed up the bell tower. That night—clang—the villagers found him with his throat slit, lying face down on the chapel steps. No footprints. No weapon. Just the bell, still gently swaying."

"What happened to the village?" someone asked.

"They say the villagers fled. Burned the chapel to the ground—but the bell wouldn't melt. Wouldn't break. It still hangs there, rusted and untouched, part of a stone archway,

110

door frame, still stands. A metal bracket juts from the masonry, and the bell dangles from a rusting chain, eerily surrounded by ivy and moss, with the rest of the chapel reduced to scorched rubble. And every few years, some fool dares to go looking for it."

He paused dramatically. "I went once."

Everyone froze.

The children were enthralled, clinging to every word. One of them asked, "Did you ever hear it ring yourself, Master Gideon?"

Gideon's grin widened. "Once. I was passing through Bracken Hollow just after dusk. No wind. No footsteps. And then—clear as anything—the bell rang once. I didn't wait for it to ring again. Got as far as the chapel gates. Fog rolled in. Horses refused to go any farther. Heard something—metal against stone. Like chains dragging. I turned back. Fast." He grinned again, but it didn't reach his eyes this time. "Never go to Bracken Hollow. Not unless you want the bell to toll for you."

That sent a shiver through the room, and even Jon couldn't entirely hide the way his expression shifted.

Tristan, standing near the fire with Olivia, arched a brow. "You're lucky the ghosts didn't follow you home."

Gideon smirked. "Who says they didn't?"

The hall erupted in laughter—but the story lingered like a shadow well into the night.

111

Later, music filled the hall. A fiddler played a lively reel as dancers twirled. Olivia found herself drawn into the merriment, her gown brushing the rush-strewn floor as she laughed and spun. Tristan eventually pulled her aside.

"Come with me," he said in a low voice, mischief sparkling in his eyes.

"Where?"

"The kitchens. There's still wine hidden in the back. The good kind."

Evelyne, catching the gleam in their eyes, gave a knowing look but said nothing as they slipped away.

In the kitchens, they found a quiet alcove and an unopened cask. Olivia leaned against the table as Tristan struggled with the stopper, finally yanking it free.

She took a sip from the ladle and laughed. "That's strong."

"And stolen," he said proudly. "Which makes it better."

"I still don't understand how you can steal from yourself."

They stayed there a while, the firelight from the hearth flickering around them. Outside, the wind howled through the eaves, a reminder of the spirits said to walk on Samhain night.

They returned to the Great Hall just before the final candle was extinguished for the evening. Samhain had always been a night for stories, for reverence—and now, for mischief, laughter, and quiet moments that would live long in memory.

* * *

After Samhain, the pace of life at Ravenshire quickened. With winter's breath creeping ever closer, it was time to bring in the last of the crops. Root vegetables—turnips, carrots, and parsnips—were pulled from the earth. Cabbages were cut, apples gathered and stored in straw, and herbs hung to dry in the kitchen rafters.

The stone walls echoed with soft chatter and the rhythmic clatter of knives on cutting boards. Baskets of carrots, parsnips, onions, and turnips sat heaped on the large wooden table. Olivia, sleeves rolled up and hands dusty with earth, leaned over a basket beside Evelyne and Old Martha.

"We've had a good yield this season," Evelyne said, peering at the fat turnip in her hand. "This one looks like it could feed a soldier by itself."

Martha snorted, "And likely give him gas for a fortnight. Wash it well, dear."

Olivia laughed as she scrubbed a carrot. "So... what's the best way to keep all this from spoiling?"

"Ah, that depends," Martha said. "For the root vegetables, like these here, we layer them in barrels of sand. Cool and dry, that's the key. Down in the cellar they go."

Evelyne nodded. "Keeps them fresh through the frost. We'll bury the carrots and turnips first. Onions get braided and hung, and the rest we'll pickle."

"Pickle?" Olivia asked.

With a knowing smile Martha said, "Aye, vinegar, salt, spices—preserve near anything if you know the tricks. Come, I'll show you."

She led them to a row of large clay crocks near the hearth. Olivia watched as Martha tossed sliced cucumbers and pearl onions into one, then poured over a steaming brine of vinegar, garlic, and dill. "Let them sit a few days, and you'll have something crisp and sharp enough to wake a dead man's appetite."

Olivia wrinkled her nose and grinned. "I'm not sure that's who we're feeding."

"Tristan eats like he is one of the dead when he's brooding. A good pickle might revive him," Evelyne teased.

Olivia chuckled, "Maybe I'll sneak some into his stew."

They shared a laugh as they worked. Outside the window, a breeze rustled the drying herbs strung above the hearth, and the scent of rosemary and thyme filled the room. In this small, simple act of storing the harvest, they found both purpose and peace.

Clay ovens and hearths burned day and night as Olivia worked alongside the women to preserve what they could. They salted meats, dried fruits, and filled jars with pickled vegetables. Large wheels of cheese were waxed and tucked away, while grains and flour were measured, stored, and sealed from damp. Olivia marveled at the precision of it all— the rhythm of survival honed by generations.

The air was rich with the scent of herbs and smoke, of brine and vinegar and hard-earned warmth. Olivia rolled up her sleeves, hands busy salting strips of meat as baskets of apples and onions were passed down the long wooden table.

"Pass me that crock, will you, love?" called Mistress Elen, a broad-shouldered woman with flour on her cheek and a laugh like rolling thunder.

Olivia handed it over, brushing back a strand of hair. "How do you make all this look so easy?"

"Years of doing it by torchlight, with hungry mouths to feed," Elen chuckled. "You've got a good hand for it, though. City folk usually drop the jar before it's full."

"I'm not sure I even qualify as 'city folk' anymore," Olivia said with a small laugh. "Not with all the dirt under my nails."

A younger girl named Brenna slid a jar of pickled carrots toward her. "What's it like where you're from?" she asked, wide-eyed. "Do you really have glass windows and machines that talk?"

Elen swatted her with a dish towel. "Don't pester, child."

Olivia smiled. "No, it's all right. Yes, we do. But we also forget to slow down and do things like this. There's something satisfying about it."

"Aye," said another woman, Maeryn, as she layered apples into a drying rack. "This work binds us. Through winter and war, feast and famine. Every jar is a promise."

115

"That's beautiful," Olivia murmured.

Elen looked up from her crock of green beans. "You've got a poet's ear and a healer's hands. No wonder Sir Tristan watches you like he does."

Olivia flushed and nearly dropped her jar. "He does not."

Brenna giggled. "Oh, he does. Even the stable boys talk about it."

Maeryn leaned in with a wink. "Don't worry, love. There's no better place to be in love than beside a hearth, between brine and bread."

They all laughed, and Olivia joined in, the warmth of their camaraderie sinking deeper than the firelight. For a moment, the looming threat of war and magic, betrayal and ancient power, faded into the clink of jars and the scent of rosemary.

* * *

Martinmas marked the grim but vital chore of butchering livestock. It was the last chance before the deep cold to cull animals that would not survive the lean months.

The air was sharp with the scent of frost and woodsmoke. A low mist curled along the ground as the sun struggled to rise over the trees. In the courtyard behind the castle, men had already gathered near the pens, sharpening knives and muttering low. The animals sensed it—restlessness stirred in the herds.

Tristan approached from the far end, his cloak dusted with frost, Olivia at his side, wrapped warmly in a fur-lined mantle. The crackle of a nearby fire mixed with the lowing of cattle and the bleating of uneasy sheep.

"Martinmas," Tristan said grimly, scanning the pens. "The feast of Saint Martin—and the season's last mercy for those who won't survive winter."

"It's necessary," Olivia said quietly, watching one of the older steers paw at the frozen ground. "But it still feels cruel."

He nodded. "Aye. But come February, every salted ham and smoked side of beef will be a blessing."

From across the yard, Aldric called out, "We're culling the three oldest from the herd. They'll not fatten further, and their joints are failing."

Tristan motioned to him. "I'll lend a hand with the second. The brindled ox."

Aldric raised a brow. "The beast that nearly crushed Edward last spring?"

Tristan smirked. "He'll go down easier than Malric did."

That earned a few chuckles. Even Gideon, perched on a fence rail with a mug of something steaming, let out a low laugh. "Let's hope the ox doesn't ask for a duel first."

Olivia gave Tristan a look. "Should I be worried you enjoy this part too much?"

He raised his hands in mock defense. "I'm simply doing my duty to the larder."

117

Evelyne emerged from the main hall, her apron already smeared with flour. "If you're done jesting, I'll need someone to help me with the blood sausages. And Tristan, don't forget— your promise to carry that half hog to the smokehouse."

"Yes, my lady cook," Tristan replied, bowing dramatically.

Evelyne smirked. "Keep jesting and I'll have you rendering fat till dusk."

Tristan leaned toward Olivia as he grabbed a rope halter. "Save me," he murmured. "Or at least bring me a cup of wine when I'm elbow-deep in offal."

"I'll consider it," she replied, teasing. "If you bring me back a haunch for the stew pot."

They moved to their work—necessary, somber, but part of the rhythm of life at Ravenshire. The air rang with the clang of iron, the calls of men, and the distant toll of the chapel bell. Winter was near, but the castle stood ready.

At dawn, smoke rose from the stone outbuildings as pigs were slaughtered and hung. Nothing was wasted—hams were salted, intestines cleaned for sausages, and fat rendered for cooking. Olivia, though initially horrified, assisted where she could, helping make blood pudding with the kitchen maids and stuffing sausages while trying not to gag. Tristan checked on the smokehouse, ensuring the precious meat would last through winter.

By evening, Ravenshire Hall blazed with torchlight and cheer. Tables groaned beneath roasted meats, loaves of warm

118

bread, wheels of cheese, and spiced cider. Boughs of autumn leaves and bundles of wheat adorned the rafters. The castle bustled with music—fiddles, lutes, and drums—and a scent of rosemary and cloves filled the air.

Tristan entered wearing a deep green tunic embroidered in silver. Olivia, in a gown of deep cranberry trimmed in gold, turned more than a few heads. Evelyne's eyes sparkled as she noticed the way Tristan looked only at Olivia.

Servants brought platters of honey-roasted pork, squab stuffed with herbs, and fresh apples baked in sugared crusts.

A minstrel stood and recited a poem in tribute to the harvest, and then a toast was raised in Tristan's name for the strong leadership he had shown since returning from court.

Once the meal had been cleared, the tables were pushed back and musicians began to play. Tristan extended a hand toward Olivia, his voice soft. "Will you dance with me, my lady?"

She smiled and took it. "Always."

As they moved through the steps, twirling across the rush-strewn floor, Olivia laughed breathlessly. "Do you remember when you nearly dropped me learning this?"

"I remember," he murmured, leaning in. "I remember thinking I never wanted to let you go."

Not far off, Gideon leaned against a column, watching the couple. His eyes flicked toward the crowd—and toward a dark-cloaked figure slipping from the hall.

119

But for this one night, under the warmth of firelight and song, Tristan and Olivia danced as though nothing else mattered—safe in the echo of joy, mischief, and love.

* * *

Martinmas was also a time when hired servants might be dismissed or rehired for the new year. Coins exchanged hands, and feasts were held for those staying on.

The chill of late autumn drifted through the stone halls of Ravenshire, carrying with it the scent of roast goose and spiced apples. Servants bustled about preparing for the Martinmas feast, a celebration not only of St. Martin but of endings and beginnings. Contracts were renewed, wages were paid, and those not retained packed their bundles and prepared to move on before winter set in.

Coins clinked as Tristan personally handed out silver to his retainers, renewing oaths of loyalty with a firm clasp of arms and a nod of respect. Those who chose to move on were honored too, their service recognized with warm words and farewell bread.

In the Great Hall, long tables were adorned with fresh greenery and candles. Evelyne supervised the seating arrangements while Olivia helped the cook place sweet tarts beside roasted fowl and steaming vegetables. The fire roared, casting golden light across banners bearing the stag and flame.

Later, as laughter filled the hall and minstrels tuned their lutes, Tristan caught Olivia sneaking an extra honeycake from the serving tray. She grinned up at him, mischief in her eyes.

"You're stealing from your own table," he murmured with mock sternness.

"I'm tasting it to make sure it's safe for the lord of the manor," she replied with a wink.

They ended up sneaking down to the cellars again, this time to steal a skin of mulled wine, and toasted to the year ahead beneath the flickering torchlight.

* * *

The dead were honored with candlelight and quiet prayers. The chapel was draped in black and violet, incense curling into the rafters. Bells tolled low and mournful through the valley.

Villagers left small loaves called "soul cakes" on graves and doorsteps, and Olivia joined Evelyne and others to light candles for loved ones lost. That night, the Great Hall was hushed. Stories of ancestors and tragic knights were whispered by firelight, and even Gideon was unusually somber.

The glow of candlelight danced across the solemn faces gathered in the Great Hall. The fire crackled gently as its warmth pushed against the chilly air. Olivia sat beside Evelyne near the hearth, a soft woolen shawl draped around her shoulders. Across from them, Gideon leaned back in his chair, his normally irreverent expression subdued.

"I remember," Evelyne said softly, holding her candle close, "my mother would bake soul cakes with cloves and rosemary. She said the scent would guide spirits home."

"I've never seen anything like this," Olivia whispered. "It's beautiful. Peaceful."

"Peaceful until the wind howls," Gideon muttered, glancing toward the tall windows. "Then you remember just how many souls still wander."

Tristan, seated beside Olivia, reached for her hand beneath the table and gave it a gentle squeeze. "You need not fear the restless dead, Olivia. It is the living who pose the greatest danger."

A wry smile tugged at Gideon's lips. "Now that's a cheerful thought."

Across the hall, an elder knight with silver hair spoke in a gravelly voice. "When I was a squire, I saw the Black Hound of Bracken Hollow on Samhain night. They say it guards the chapel ruins where the old bell tower once stood."

"A bell that hasn't rung in thirty years," said another, his voice thick with wine. "And won't, unless a soul lost unjustly calls it."

"I heard it once," a younger stable hand piped up. "Years ago. Just before my uncle passed."

Evelyne crossed herself instinctively. "That bell was forged in sacred flame. It only rings when justice is wronged— or vengeance is near."

Gideon leaned closer to the fire, his eyes reflecting its flicker. "Or when someone's telling tales to keep the young ones awake all night."

Laughter rippled gently through the group, easing the weight of the moment. Olivia looked around, seeing how grief was not buried here, but remembered—spoken aloud and honored with warmth and shared memory.

Tristan raised his goblet in a quiet toast. "To those we've lost—and to the hope that we carry them with us."

All around the circle, others lifted their cups, murmuring, "To the lost."

And for a moment, even the silence felt sacred.

* * *

As November faded, the mood turned solemn. Advent marked a season of spiritual preparation, with daily prayers, fasting, and reflection. The feasting stopped, replaced by simple meals. No weddings were held, and the merriment of Samhain gave way to contemplation.

As November faded, the mood within Ravenshire turned solemn. Advent marked a season of spiritual preparation—daily prayers, quiet reflection, and fasting replaced the feasting of weeks past. The laughter of Samhain had dwindled into soft hymns and candlelight.

Each evening, as the bells tolled Vespers, a new candle was lit in the chapel, symbolizing hope and the approaching birth of Christ. Olivia found comfort in the quiet ritual, and

Tristan stood beside her during the services, his presence steady and warm.

One night, as the candle was lit and the congregation began to sing, Olivia leaned slightly toward him.

"It's peaceful here," she whispered.

Tristan glanced down at her, his voice low. "It quiets the battles within."

She turned her eyes to the flame. "I never thought I'd find peace in a place like this... in a time like this."

He gently brushed her hand with his fingers. "Peace is not bound by time. Sometimes, it finds you where you least expect."

The priest's voice rose in prayer, and they both bowed their heads.

As the people filed out, Tristan stood before the chapel altar, head bowed, sword laid before him in reverence. Candles flickered, casting warm light across the carved nativity.

Olivia watched from the doorway. He looked peaceful, solemn—every bit the knight devoted not only to her, but to something greater.

He whispered a prayer: "For light in darkness. For mercy. For the strength to protect what I love."

She joined him, taking his hand, and they knelt together in silence, the sacred hush wrapping around them like a benediction.

Later, as they stepped out into the cold night air, Olivia pulled her shawl tighter.

"Your people... they believe in something greater," she murmured.

"So do you," Tristan said. "Even if you don't yet know its name."

She smiled faintly. "Maybe I'm starting to."

He held out his arm, and she took it. As they walked slowly back toward the keep, their steps fell into an easy rhythm—quiet but full of understanding.

"You've changed me, Olivia," he said softly, just above the wind. "I never thought I'd believe in anything beyond sword and duty."

She looked up at him, her breath misting. "And you've given me something I never thought I'd find... a place to belong."

Though Advent was a time of restraint, some feast days were still observed. On St. Andrew's Day, the Scots and border folk in service at Ravenshire shared tales and played music. A roasted goose was served, and even Olivia found herself tapping her foot to the fiddle.

On the eve of St. Nicholas's Day, the Great Hall of Ravenshire was filled with a gentle buzz of anticipation. Children whispered excitedly, peaking at the hearth where their shoes had been placed in neat rows. Small gifts—dried fruit, carved toys, and sweets—were placed in shoes by the hearth. Olivia helped make them with the steward's wife, Agnes, wrapping dried pears in linen and tucking brightly colored ribbons around bundles of nuts.

"She'll never forget this," Agnes said, watching a wide-eyed little girl tiptoe near the hearth and scurry back giggling. Olivia smiled, the warmth of the scene softening the ache of so many uncertainties. "Neither will I," she murmured.

Later that night, after the fires had died to a warm glow, Tristan walked the quiet halls alone. He carried a single silver coin—an old one, worn with age but polished to a bright shine. He paused outside Olivia's door, glanced once around, and slipped it silently into her shoe beside the hearth.

He said nothing of it the next morning, even as Olivia lifted the coin from her shoe with a puzzled look. Evelyne, catching her smile, said nothing but raised an eyebrow knowingly.

As the castle stirred with merriment, Olivia tucked the coin away in the small pocket inside her gown. When she next saw Tristan—grinning as he oversaw a pair of squires trying to outdo each other with wooden swords—she said casually, "Strange. Someone left a silver coin in my shoe."

He didn't look at her. "Sounds like you've caught the eye of St. Nicholas himself."

"Oh? Then I shall keep my boots polished from now on."

His lips twitched, but he gave her a sidelong glance full of silent affection. "See that you do."

Snow blanketed the hills beyond the castle, the towers dusted in frost. Inside the Great Hall, warmth radiated from a roaring hearth, shadows dancing on the stone walls. Holly and ivy were woven into garlands across the archways, while fragrant bundles of rosemary and dried orange hung above doorways for good luck.

Evenings by the fire Olivia sat cross-legged beside the hearth, mending, while Evelyne spun flax into thread. Old Martha recounted eerie stories of spirits that walk between worlds during the long nights, and the youngest servant girls clung to each other, eyes wide.

A troupe of traveling players arrived from the north. They performed a haunting ballad and a comedic farce. Olivia laughed with Tristan in the corner, her shoulder brushing his—just enough to make him glance at her with a half-smile and tease her later that night.

The hearths blazed with warm firelight, casting flickering shadows against the ancient stone walls. Laughter filled the air as children darted between guests wearing crowns of holly and ivy, and tables overflowed with roasted meats, spiced cider, and sweet apple tarts.

Evelyne stepped outside the bustling Great Hall for a breath of cool night air when something rustled in the shadows behind her.

"Who goes there?" she called, half-smiling, expecting one of the castle boys playing tricks.

But a low, eerie voice drifted through the dark corridor. "It's still winter..." it moaned theatrically, "and the veil's not quite closed..."

Evelyne whirled, heart skipping, as a cloaked figure emerged from the shadows, draped in white linen and dragging a length of chain behind him. His voice deepened dramatically. "You dare walk alone, lady? The spirits hunger for the living—"

With an eye-roll and zero hesitation, Evelyne grabbed the closest object—a rolled-up wool stocking hanging by the laundry line—and smacked the ghost full in the face.

"Gideon Cross," she growled, as the ghost dropped the chain and doubled over laughing, "you miserable, spooky toad."

Gideon peeled back the linen with a grin, revealing his tousled dark hair and mischievous green eyes. "You must admit, I had you going for a moment."

"I admit no such thing," Evelyne said, suppressing a smile. "You're lucky I didn't fetch a lantern and burn your sheet."

From the far end of the corridor, Olivia and Tristan poked their heads out. "Is that Gideon I hear being throttled?" Tristan asked, raising an amused brow.

Olivia giggled. "He was pretending to be a ghost again, wasn't he?"

Evelyne crossed her arms. "I'm putting salt across the threshold and barring him from entering."

Gideon, straightening with a dramatic bow, added, "And yet you'd miss me if I vanished into the mist forever, wouldn't you?"

"Only because you owe me a bottle of plum wine," she replied crisply, stalking back inside with her chin high.

Tristan shook his head, chuckling. "One of these days, Cross, she really will put a hex on you."

"I live for danger," Gideon called, dusting off his sheet and tossing it aside. "And dramatic entrances."

* * *

As Christmas neared the kitchens buzzed with warmth and the scent of cinnamon, nutmeg, and cloves. Olivia helped the cook knead spiced dough. She was terrible at it—covered in flour—but she enjoyed herself.

She stood at a long wooden table, sleeves rolled up, hands deep in a mound of sticky spiced dough. White flour dusted her cheeks, nose, and even a streak through her hair. Beside her, a stout cook named Cecily watched with hands on her hips, trying not to smirk.

"Ye're kneadin' it like it's a squabbling child, not a loaf of bread, my lady."

Olivia laughed. "That's exactly how it feels! It keeps fighting back.

"Better hope the fruitcake doesn't bite when it's done!" one of the kitchen boys quipped.

Olivia made a face as the sticky dough clung stubbornly to her fingers. "At this rate, I'll be wearing more of it than we'll bake."

"She's already half cake!" another kitchen boy laughed from across the room.

The laughter grew. One of the older kitchen boys handed Olivia a finished fruitcake, freshly glazed and still warm. Curious, she took a bite.

"Whoa! That's... that's a whole army of spices marching across my tongue." Olivia sputtered.

"Too much for your modern stomach?" the first boy said.

"It's like Christmas and a thunderstorm had a baby. But I love it," Olivia giggled.

Cecily chuckled, "That's the brandy, dear."

Just then, the kitchen door creaked open and Tristan peeked in, drawn by the commotion. He took one look at Olivia—covered in flour, laughing with the staff—and leaned against the doorframe, smiling. "I leave you alone for one hour and you start a rebellion in the bakery."

"Help me and I'll promote you to assistant rebel baker," Olivia beamed.

He crossed the floor, took her hand—and promptly got dough smeared across his palm.

"Lovely. Now we match."

"Careful, Lord Tristan. She'll have you making pastries by sunset," the second boy said.

"And she's got good instincts. Reckon she could run the place in a week!" Cecily told him.

Tristan looked at Olivia with mock seriousness." You plan to conquer my castle with flour and fruitcake?"

Olivia grinned. "One slice at a time."

They laughed together, warm in the scent of baking, the crackling hearth, and the company of people who, like Olivia, had started to see her not just as a stranger, but as one of their own.

* * *

It was Christmas Eve. Snow clung to the stone windowsills, and the scent of spiced wine and roasting meat filled the Great Hall. Garlands of evergreen, holly, and rosemary were strung along the rafters, and torches flickered against the old stone walls. All awaited the moment when the great Yule Log would be brought in.

A horn sounded from the courtyard.

The doors swung wide, letting in a rush of frosted air— and six strong men entered, dragging the enormous oak log on a wooden sled lined with pine boughs. The log was adorned with ribbons and sprigs of mistletoe, its bark glistening with frost, its size nearly as long as a horse.

Cheers rose from the gathered household as the men pulled it through the hall and placed it with great care into the massive hearth at the center of the room.

Tristan stepped forward, cloaked in a dark fur-trimmed mantle, a small bundle of seasoned wood cradled in his arm. Olivia stood beside him, her cheeks pink from the cold, watching the solemn beauty of the moment unfold.

Tristan raised his voice, steady and warm. "This is the Yule Log," he said, gazing out at the gathering crowd. "It is more than firewood—it is tradition. A ward against evil. A blessing upon this household. And a symbol of light's return, as the sun lengthens its journey across the sky after the winter solstice."

He held up a smaller, darkened piece of wood wrapped in linen. "This is a fragment of last year's log, preserved for this very night. By lighting this year's fire with last year's flame, we carry forward protection, prosperity, and memory. It is sacred—and festive."

Tristan knelt and placed the fragment gently against the base of the new log. He took a taper from the torch behind him, its flame steady and bright. With reverent hands, he lit the edge of the old wood, and the fire caught quickly, crackling and curling through the fresh pine boughs.

The hall burst into cheers and applause as the flames leapt up. Warmth flooded the space, and the shadows danced along the ceiling.

Tables groaned with food—roast goose, honeyed carrots, fresh bread, and golden pies. Mulled wine and ale flowed freely. Children laughed near the corners of the hall. Old songs were sung. Tales of brave knights, clever foxes, and mischievous spirits were shared by the hearth.

Tristan returned to Olivia's side, his voice soft now. "It will burn through Twelfth Night," he said. "So long as the flame holds, so too does the blessing."

She looked up at him, the firelight dancing in his eyes. "It's beautiful," she whispered. "And ancient. I love that it's both."

He smiled. "Like Ravenshire itself."

And together, beneath the glow of the Yule fire, they joined friends and family in the oldest kind of magic—a warm heart, a blazing hearth, and the promise of light returning.

In the smaller banquet hall, everyone dined on roast goose, sweet winter vegetables, and spiced apples. The dancing began after, lively reels and slower waltzes. Tristan danced with Olivia under the glow of torchlight. He leaned close and murmured something that made her laugh.

That night, as snow fell outside and the embers glowed low, Olivia's amulet pulsed faintly. She stepped onto the balcony alone. The stars shimmered overhead, and for a moment, she thought she saw something move in the mist beyond the trees.

Snow had begun to fall softly outside the stone walls of Ravenshire, dusting the courtyard in white. Inside the Great

Hall, the hearth blazed with warmth, throwing golden light across the carved timbers and hanging garlands of evergreen and berries. Most of the castle had retired early after the winter's feast, leaving Tristan and Olivia alone near the fire, nestled on a cushioned bench beside a low table.

Olivia clutched a woolen bundle tied with a simple red ribbon. She watched Tristan from the corner of her eye as he sipped mulled wine, his tunic slightly undone at the throat, his hair still damps from the snow. A shadow of a smile tugged at his mouth.

"You've been staring at me for some time now, Lady Olivia de Léon," he said without looking at her. "Should I be alarmed?"

She grinned and nudged the bundle into his hands. "No. But you should open that."

Tristan looked down at the gift, then slowly untied the ribbon. Inside was a pair of gloves, hand-stitched from fine, dark leather and lined with warm rabbit fur. But what caught his eye was the embroidery on the cuffs—his initials, stitched beside a tiny sword.

"They're not much," she said quickly, "but I thought your hands might like something warmer than gauntlets."

Tristan studied the gloves, then looked at her, his voice low and sincere. "I've never received anything like this."

"Never?"

He shook his head. "Not since I was a boy. Gifts were more political than personal."

"Well, this one's from the heart," she said softly.

Tristan set the gloves aside and reached under the bench. From beneath his cloak, he drew a slim bundle wrapped in linen. "Then I must do better than gauntlets and battle steel."

He handed it to her.

Olivia unwrapped the cloth carefully—and gasped.

It was a book. An old one, bound in worn red leather. The pages were yellowed, but the cover bore the mark of a healer's crest—the very same emblem she'd told him about once in passing, from a medieval tapestry she'd seen in a museum. Inside, written in fine, slanted hand, were herbal remedies, illustrations of plants, and notes from a long-forgotten apothecary.

"I found it in the castle's oldest wing," he said quietly. "Thought it might suit someone who keeps saving my life."

She stared at the book, her heart full. "Tristan... this is incredible."

His fingers brushed her cheek. "You are."

They sat together, wrapped in firelight and silence, exchanging no more words, only smiles. Outside, the snow fell thicker, but inside Ravenshire, all was warm.

The firelight flickered across Olivia's face, painting her skin in hues of gold and rose. Tristan studied her in the silence that followed. The mischievous light in her eyes had softened, and something gentler had replaced it.

He set the bottle aside.

"Olivia," he said quietly. "These moments... when you laugh, when we're like this, I almost forget the danger we live with."

She turned toward him. "Then let's forget it. Just for tonight."

Their eyes held each other for a long moment before he leaned forward, brushing a strand of hair from her cheek. His hand lingered there, rough palm against soft skin. Then, slowly, his lips met hers.

The kiss was not hurried or desperate, but deep and full of longing. The kind of kiss that said: I see you. I want only you.

The fire crackled behind them as he drew her closer, her fingers curling in the fabric of his tunic.

At last, he broke the kiss and leaned his forehead against hers.

"Tell me this is not a dream," he murmured.

She smiled. "If it is, I never want to wake up."

* * *

The Great Hall flickered with firelight as the final hours of the year waned. Boughs of holly, evergreen, and mistletoe draped the stone archways. A boar roasted on the spit, and mead flowed freely. Children slept in tucked corners while the grown folk gathered near the hearth, watching the high candle that marked the stroke of midnight.

Tristan stood beside Olivia near the blazing fire, his arm around her waist. Gideon leaned near, sipping mulled wine, while Evelyne leaned her head on Aldric's shoulder and hummed a soft tune under her breath. The air was warm with hope and tradition.

As the castle bell tolled midnight, a hush fell.

Tristan stepped toward the great door to announce the start of First Foot. "According to the old ways," he said, smiling broadly, "the first soul to cross the threshold brings the year's fate."

"I've seen Gideon cheat this ritual two years in a row," Aldric muttered under his breath, making Evelyne smirk.

But tonight, the door creaked open before any of them moved.

A tall figure stepped into the torchlight. Snow dusted his cloak. His boots echoed against the stone floor as he crossed the threshold uninvited.

It was Kaelen.

Dark-haired, finely dressed, and carrying a bundle in his arms—bread, silver, and a piece of coal—he looked every bit the traditional bearer of luck. But something in his presence made the warmth in the Hall falter.

Olivia stiffened. Tristan's hand moved toward the hilt of his sword.

"My lords," Kaelen said smoothly, bowing just enough to be respectful. "Forgive the intrusion. I thought it only right to pay respects... and offer blessings for the year to come."

"Kaelen," Tristan said, his voice flat. "You were not expected."

"Ah, but fate has a way of choosing its own messengers, does it not?" Kaelen handed the gifts to Tristan, who accepted them with visible hesitation.

No one spoke. The room held its breath.

Then Kaelen's eyes landed on Olivia. "May the coming year bring revelation... and reward."

He turned and strode toward the Hall's far door, disappearing without another word.

Gideon whistled low. "Well. If that's how the year begins..."

"We'll double the watch tonight," Tristan muttered.

Olivia glanced toward the empty doorway, unease settling over her. The old superstition said the first foot shaped the fortune of the household.

And Kaelen had just walked through the door.

CHAPTER ELEVEN

The candlelight in Tristan's chamber flickered low, the embers in the hearth glowing faintly as the castle lay quiet under the weight of midnight. Moonlight filtered through the window, casting pale light over Tristan and Olivia. She sat curled on the edge of the bed, still laughing softly from their earlier sparring match, while Tristan leaned against the window, sipping from a goblet of wine.

"You're faster than I expected," Tristan teased, smirking. "But still far too easy to disarm."

Olivia rolled her eyes, tossing a pillow at him. "Only because you cheat."

Tristan chuckled, catching the pillow easily. "You wound me, my lady. A knight never cheats."

But their quiet banter was cut short by a frantic pounding at the door.

Tristan stiffened instantly, setting his goblet aside. "Who comes at this hour?"

Olivia stirred, glancing toward the door as as more knocks broke the stillness. Tristan's hand rested on the hilt of his sword as he opened the door cautiously.

A man servant stood there looking unsure. Hugh pushed past him and stumbled inside. Hugh's face was pale, his breathing uneven as he struggled to get the words out.

"There's a rumor," he said hoarsely. "It's stirring the Order—turning them against you. It claims you've broken faith, that you've... that you've betrayed your oath."

Olivia froze. "Betrayed his oath?" she whispered. "That's absurd—"

Tristan's hand came up, steady but firm, resting against her arm to keep her still. His eyes locked on Hugh, the flicker of an old warrior's instinct rising behind them.

"What else?" Tristan demanded. His voice was sharp now—commanding.

Hugh swallowed hard. "The Grand Master... he's calling for the oaths to be renewed. Every knight, every brother of the Order. He says those who refuse stand with you—and are traitors."

Tristan's jaw tightened, his lips pressing into a hard line.

Olivia stepped closer to him, her voice urgent but low. "This is a trap. Someone is trying to force you into the open."

Tristan's fingers flexed at his side. "If I do not go, they will claim I am guilty."

Hugh shook his head, almost desperate. "If you do go, they might not let you leave alive."

The room went quiet, the only sound Olivia's breath catching in her chest.

Tristan's expression didn't change, but his tone deepened into something Olivia recognized from the battlefield—controlled, calm, and deadly.

"Then I will make sure that does not happen. I must prove myself."

Olivia exclaimed, rushing forward, but Tristan held her back gently, his eyes blazing with a deadly calm. "We leave now."

Olivia grabbed his arm. "Tristan—"

He turned to her, his voice firm. "If the Order falls, the Heart of Elander falls with it. And if that happens..." He didn't finish the thought. He didn't have to.

Olivia swallowed hard. "Then I'm coming with you."

Tristan shook his head. "No."

"Yes," she shot back, her eyes flashing. "You'll need me. You know it."

The firelight in the chamber flickered across Tristan's face as he strapped on his sword belt, the leather creaking softly with every movement. Olivia stood nearby, her arms crossed tightly, her eyes blazing with frustration.

"You can't keep me here," she said sharply. "I've come this far, Tristan. I've fought—don't you dare leave me behind now."

Tristan stilled, his hand pausing on the buckle. He turned, blue eyes locking on hers, his voice low and steady.

"And because you've come this far, Olivia, I will not risk you now."

Olivia stepped closer, her hands curling into fists at her sides. "Risk me? I've proven myself to you, to Evelyne, to Aldric and Gideon! Why is this different?"

Tristan's jaw tightened. His voice was calm but iron-edged. "Because the Order of the Silver Flame is not like anything you've faced before. They're not bandits, or Marlowe's dogs, or traitors in the court. They are sworn to guard ancient powers—powers even they do not understand."

She shook her head, hurt flashing in her eyes. "You're treating me like a child."

He took her hand suddenly, pressing it flat against his chest. His heart thudded strong beneath her palm.

"I am treating you like you are the most precious thing in my life."

Olivia swallowed hard. Her defiance faltered under the weight of his words. "Tristan—"

"No." His hands gripped her shoulders gently but firmly. "You're brave, Olivia. Fierce. But this is not your burden to bear. The Order would see you as an outsider."

"What?" she demanded. "What would they do?"

Tristan's expression hardened and he shook his head. "I don't know but I don't want to find out."

The room seemed to grow smaller, the air tighter.

"I can't lose you," he said finally, his voice quieter now but no less determined. "Not to them. Not to anyone."

Olivia's throat tightened, the fire in her gaze flickering between anger and a painful longing. She wanted to argue, but the intensity in his eyes silenced her.

"Promise me," Tristan said, his forehead lowering to hers. "Promise me you'll stay."

She hesitated, then whispered, "I promise."

* * *

Moonlight spilled over the stronghold walls, casting the courtyard in a silver glow. Valour pawed the ground impatiently, sensing his master's tension.

Hugh tightened the straps on his own horse's saddle, glancing at Tristan with a grim expression. "We've no time to waste, Tristan. The Order won't last long if the Heart is turned against us."

Tristan gave a sharp nod. "Aye. But there's one thing I must do first."

He found Olivia in the Great Hall. She looked up as he approached, her green eyes searching his face.

"You're leaving," she said softly. Not a question. A knowing.

Tristan stopped in front of her, his jaw tight. She stepped closer, her hand brushing his. Tristan's hand curled around hers, strong but trembling slightly. "I don't know how long I'll be gone."

"Just come back," Olivia said fiercely.

He pulled her into his arms, burying his face in her hair. "You're my reason for coming back."

When he pulled back, he took her face gently in his hands, his blue eyes blazing with emotion. "Stay within the walls. Trust no one but Evelyne, Aldric and Gideon. Promise me."

"I promise," Olivia whispered, though her throat tightened at the words.

Tristan pressed a lingering kiss to her lips, the taste of her seared into his memory. "I'll fight my way through hell itself to return to you."

Hugh called from the courtyard. "Tristan!"

Tristan turned and went out across the courtyard. He swung up onto Valour, the great stallion tossing his dark mane.

"Keep her safe, Aldric. On your life."

Aldric gave a firm nod from the steps. "Godspeed, Tristan."

And then, with one last glance at Olivia, Tristan spurred Valour into motion, riding out through the gates with Hugh at his side.

The sound of hooves faded into the forest as Olivia stood alone, clutching the amulet tight against her heart.

* * *

The cavernous hall of the Order was lit only by the glow of enchanted torches, their silver flames flickering against the marble walls. At the center, the sacred crystal—the Heart of Elander—hovered in its cradle of ruined steel, pulsing faintly as though aware of the tension in the air.

Tristan stood among the knights in their ceremonial cloaks, the sigil of the Silver Flame emblazoned on their shoulders. At his side, he and Sir Hugh exchanged wary glances. Something felt... wrong.

The Great Hall of the Order was silent but for the echo of boots on the stone floor. Candles flickered in their sconces, throwing long, wavering shadows across the banners of the knightly brotherhood.

The Grand Master sat upon his raised seat at the far end, his face carved from stone, eyes like cold steel as they locked on Tristan.

"Sir Tristan de Léon," his voice boomed, carrying through the hall. "Step forward."

Tristan strode into the circle, his expression calm but his heart pounding like a drumbeat in his chest. Behind him, nobles and knights whispered—some curious, others hungry for scandal.

As he reached the center, Kaelen emerged from the crowd.

Kaelen strode forward, his boots striking the polished floor with deliberate steps. His cloak billowed slightly, his smirk sharp and venomous.

"Grand Master," Kaelen began, bowing with mock respect, "this man stands here draped in honor, but the truth of his treachery festers beneath."

The crowd stirred.

"He has betrayed his sacred oath to the Order. He has allowed a woman of... questionable origin to sway him from his duties. He fraternizes with her, protects her—even when it puts the kingdom at risk!"

Tristan's jaw tightened, but he said nothing. Not yet.

"And worse," Kaelen pressed on, his voice rising, "there are whispers he seeks to use the amulet's power for himself. Power that rightfully belongs to the Order!"

Gasps rang through the hall.

The Grand Master's brow furrowed. "These are grave accusations, Kaelen. Do you bring proof?"

Kaelen smiled coldly. "Proof? I am the proof." Kaelen's smirk grew wider—too wide. "In fact, my lords... I have taken steps to ensure the Order's strength. To seize the power Tristan covets for myself."

The hall erupted in shouts as Kaelen flung back his cloak, revealing the black obsidian and tarnished silver amulet glowing faintly at his chest.

"With this power, I will lead the Order—not Tristan. Not the Grand Master. Me."

Tristan's voice cut like a blade through the chaos. "You fool. You don't even understand what you've unleashed."

146

The amulet at Kaelen's neck pulsed violently, a deep hum filling the hall as an unseen wind swept through the chamber.

"Kaelen," the Grandmaster said, his voice echoing in the hall, "you've been summoned to renew your oath. Step forward."

Kaelen's lips curled into a faint smirk. "An oath?" he echoed softly. "What use are oaths to men bound by fear?"

A chill rippled through the hall.

"What are you saying?" Tristan demanded, stepping forward.

Kaelen's smirk sharpened. "I've watched this Order rot from within—men whispering of duty, of honor, while clutching their precious relic like cowards."

"Enough!" the Grandmaster barked. "Stand down, Kaelen. You do not know what you're saying."

"Oh, but I do." Kaelen drew his blade in one swift motion. The sound of steel rang like thunder in the quiet hall. "I know exactly what I'm doing."

The Heart of Elander flared brightly, the runes around it pulsing in protest.

Knights lunged for Kaelen, but he was faster—preternaturally so.

A flash of movement, and two men fell at his feet. Blood pooled beneath their cloaks.

"Kaelen, stop this madness!" Tristan shouted, his own sword raised.

"Madness?" Kaelen's eyes glinted coldly. "No, Tristan. This is clarity. The Heart does not belong to the weak."

With a powerful leap, Kaelen vaulted onto the dais. His hand shot out toward the Heart. The air around it screamed as the protective wards flared—then shattered under a surge of dark power.

"The Heart answers to strength alone!" Kaelen roared.

As his fingers closed around the crystal, a shockwave of energy exploded outward, sending Tristan and the others sprawling.

Light and shadow warred in the chamber as Kaelen absorbed the Heart's power, the runes along the walls cracking and bleeding silver fire.

Tristan struggled to his feet, blood trickling down his temple. "Kaelen! Don't do this—this power will consume you."

Kaelen turned, his eyes glowing an unholy silver. "Then let it consume me. Better that than serving fools who fear to use it."

Hugh's voice broke through the chaos. "Kaelen, you swore an oath to us!"

"And now I break it."

With a snarl, Kaelen unleashed a wave of energy that sent everyone crashing to the ground. The earth split, stone crumbled, and flames licked the night sky as if the heavens themselves were angry.

Tristan was up in an instant to meet Kaelen's blade in a shower of sparks, steel ringing against steel as the two men clashed.

"You were my brother, Kaelen!" Tristan growled, driving him back step by step.

"And you were a fool to trust me!" Kaelen spat, his blade crackling with stolen power.

As the fight raged, Kaelen's remaining allies—a handful of turncoat knights—lit the hall with fire.

"Tristan! We have to get out!" Hugh's voice echoed over the roar of flames.

Kaelen smirked as he leapt backward, the Heart clutched in his hand.

"The Order is finished. The age of the Silver Flame is over."

And with that, he vanished into the inferno.

The survivors pulled themselves from the wreckage, coughing on smoke.

The Grandmaster was dead. Half the Order had fallen.

And the Heart of Elander—their greatest treasure—was gone.

Tristan stared at the scorched dais where Kaelen had stood, his fist tightening around his sword. The smell of smoke and ash clung to everything.

The air was thick with smoke and ash as Tristan and Hugh picked their way through the crumbled halls of the stronghold. The once-proud fortress now lay in ruins—walls blackened by fire, the scent of blood and burnt timber clinging to every stone.

Tristan's jaw tightened as he stepped over a shattered beam. "We'll search every chamber. There may still be more survivors."

"God's blood," Hugh muttered, his voice tight with grief. "It's all gone."

They moved through the ruins carefully, calling out. The hours that followed were a blur of digging through rubble, binding wounds, and carrying the wounded to safety.

"Find everyone you can," Tristan ordered.

Hugh, his tunic torn and face smeared with soot, nodded grimly. "Aye, and we'll give the dead their peace."

Around them, the stronghold's courtyard was chaos— half the eastern wing engulfed in flames, survivors scrambling to escape as shouts of alarm echoed off the stone walls.

Tristan's voice cut through the panic like steel. "Buckets—form a line from the well! Hugh, take ten men and clear the courtyard of debris! Get everyone out of the eastern wing!"

Hugh nodded, wiping soot from his face. "Aye, sir! You heard him—move!"

Men rushed to obey, forming a chain to haul water from the well as others dragged burning timbers away from the collapsing walls.

"We need more hands!" someone shouted. Tristan turned sharply. "Then find them! No one else dies tonight—not if we can prevent it!"

As the roof above the kitchens groaned and split apart, Tristan sprinted through the smoke-choked doorway, sword in hand—not for battle this time, but to hack through fallen beams blocking the way.

He found two women and an elderly man huddled near the hearth. "This way!" he barked, his voice hoarse.

One woman shook her head, clutching the old man's arm. "He can't walk—"

"Then I'll carry him," Tristan snapped, sweeping the frail man into his arms. "Follow me. Now!"

They emerged into the courtyard seconds before the kitchen roof caved in behind them, sending sparks shooting into the night.

By dawn, the flames were out.

The courtyard was littered with charred wood and blackened stone, but the people were alive.

Hugh clapped Tristan on the shoulder, his own tunic scorched and torn. "You kept us together, Tristan. If not for you—"

Tristan shook his head. "If not for all of us. This was no single man's victory."

He glanced over the weary faces of survivors, their soot-streaked cheeks and hollow eyes. "But it's not over. We rebuild."

Tristan and Hugh stood among the ashes of the once-proud stronghold of the Order of the Silver Flame.

The air was thick with smoke and the acrid scent of burning parchment and oil. Charred beams creaked overhead, and scattered across the floor were the bodies of men and women who once guarded the kingdom's deepest secrets.

At the heart of it all, Kaelen was gone—and so was the Heart of Elander.

Tristan stood motionless for a moment, fists clenched at his sides. His piercing blue eyes scanned the devastation with a hollow, searing fury. "Damn him," Tristan growled, his voice low but sharp as a drawn blade. Hugh laid a hand on his shoulder, his face grim. "We'll get it back."

But Tristan shook his head. "Kaelen won't run. He's too bold for that." He stepped over a fallen pillar, his boots crunching glass and bone beneath them. "He wants me to follow. This was his invitation."

Hugh knelt to examine one of the fallen. "The Order... they're nearly wiped out. The Heart in Kaelen's hands is bad enough, but without the Order..." Tristan sheathed his sword, his jaw tight. "Then we rebuild. We find survivors. and we hunt Kaelen to the ends of the earth."

"And when we find him?" Hugh asked. "We kill him," Tristan replied coldly. "And take back what's ours."

The air was thick with smoke and ash as Tristan and Hugh picked their way through the crumbled halls of the stronghold. The once-proud fortress now lay in ruins—walls blackened by fire, the scent of blood and burnt timber clinging to every stone. They found they found more survivors huddled in the chapel— soot-covered, their eyes wide with fear.

"We hid when the attack came... they never searched here."

Tristan knelt beside her. "You're safe now." His blue eyes softened as he spoke. "Can you walk?"

She nodded weakly. "Aye... but not all of us."

 Hugh stepped forward. "Then we carry the ones who can't."

The survivors who were still strong enough began to rise, their faces set with determination despite their exhaustion. Together, they helped Tristan and Hugh bind wounds, lift debris, and search for others buried beneath the rubble.

Tristan worked tirelessly, his hands steady as he tied a splint around a broken leg. "Stay still," he said gently.

Hugh brought water to a man with burns across his arms. "Drink slow," he urged. "We'll get you out of here."

The survivors worked alongside them, gathering makeshift stretchers and tearing fabric for bandages.

"We'll take the wounded first," Tristan said. "Then return for the rest."

* * *

By mid-morning, the keep's gates swung open as they returned with wagons laden with the injured, their faces smudged with soot, their eyes hollow. The courtyard of Ravenshire became a makeshift hospice. Olivia worked tirelessly, her hands stained with blood as she stitched wounds and whispered comfort. Tristan moved among the Order's knights, quietly offering his strength where words failed.

When the wounded had been moved to safety, Tristan and Hugh returned to care for the dead.

They worked in silence, faces grim, their boots echoing in the hollowed ruins.

Each body was treated with reverence—laid gently on blankets, covered from head to toe.

"They deserve better than this," Hugh murmured.

Tristan's voice was low. "We'll give them the honor they're due. Even if the bastards who did this won't."

154

By the time the sun began to set, a small group of survivors—still strong enough to fight—gathered around Tristan and Hugh.

"We'll help," one man said firmly.

Tristan looked at each of them, seeing the spark of resolve in their weary faces.

He said, "First, we burn the dead... and prepare for what's coming."

**.

Tristan stood with the survivors in the ruins of the Order's Great Hall. The air was heavy with ash and sorrow. Smoke curled into the gray sky, carrying the scent of burned wood and loss over the fields. The scent of pine and cold earth lingered in the air as the priest moved solemnly down the line, murmuring prayers for the dead.

As the priest's final words echoed in the cold air, a silence settled over the Hall.

Tristan stood at the head of the gathering, clad in black and silver, his jaw tight, his eyes shadowed with sorrow. He felt the weight of every man who had fallen. This was his burden to carry.

They built a pyre for the dead.

The men stood in a solemn semicircle around the pyre, their faces grim.

At the center stood Tristan, black cloak billowing slightly in the cold wind. His jaw was tight, his eyes fixed on the flames.

The pyre crackled, sparks flying upward like desperate prayers.

Aldric approached him quietly. "It's time."

Tristan nodded once. His gloved hand brushed the hilt of his sword as if to anchor himself. This moment wasn't about him—it was about the men they had lost, the future they now carried.

As flames consumed the bodies, Tristan raised his voice, clear and commanding. "We stand in the ashes of those who gave their lives for us. Their courage will not be forgotten."

He turned slowly to face the men gathered, his voice deepening with conviction. "But the fight is not yet over. Enemies stir in the shadows. Betrayal lingers in these halls. And so we swear—" He drew his sword with a sharp hiss of steel. The firelight danced across the blade. "Before these flames, before their memory, and before the gods who witness all..."

He sank to one knee. "I, Tristan de Léon, pledge my sword, my blood, and my body to this cause. I will defend the innocent, protect the loyal, and crush those who seek to undo us. On my honor, I swear it."

He turned to the ragged survivors. "Swear to me now— you will not let this light die."

One by one, they dropped to their knees. They knelt at Tristan's feet, heads bowed, voices steady:

"We swear it. To you, my lord."

"To the Heart. To the Silver Flame."

"I pledge my sword to you, my lord."

"I am yours to command."

"For Ravenshire. For our fallen."

Even Aldric, the ever-loyal knight, dropped to one knee. "You've earned this, Tristan. We stand with you—always."

Evelyne stepped forward, her emerald cloak catching in the wind. Her voice was steady, though her eyes burned with tears. "By my brother's side, I have seen what true honor means. I pledge my wisdom and strength to this cause. If I falter, let these flames consume me as well."

She touched the hilt of her dagger to the flames before stepping back.

Gideon stepped forward, a grimness in his green eyes. "I'm no knight. No one would mistake me for one. But for you, Tristan... I'll fight." He placed his hand over his heart. "And for her." His eyes flicked briefly toward Olivia. "I swear, by all that's left in me, I'll see this through."

Olivia felt the weight of a hundred gazes as she stepped forward. The fire's heat licked her face. She took a deep breath and spoke softly, but her words carried over the crackling flames. "I am not of this time... but you have become my people. And Tristan—" Her voice broke slightly, but she

157

steadied herself. "I swear I will stand beside you, in this world and the next. Whatever comes, I will not leave you."

Tristan's hand found hers, squeezing tightly. Olivia stood at his side, her hand in his. She could feel the tension in him—the rage, the grief, and the quiet determination that still burned beneath it all.

Together, the group spoke: "We swear it. By flame and by steel, by blood and by bone. Let the world burn before we break our vow."

The flames roared higher, as if answering their oaths. Sparks shot into the night sky like stars being born.

Gideon, leaning against a stone pillar with his arms crossed, gave a lopsided grin. "You do have a way of inspiring loyalty, don't you?"

Tristan's expression softened, though his eyes still held that unyielding steel. "We rebuild. Together."

Hugh watched with quiet pride as Tristan stood taller, the firelight dancing in his blue eyes.

The Order was no more.

But in that moment, a new brotherhood was born.

And Tristan—he became their leader.

CHAPTER TWELVE

The stronghold of the Order of the Silver Flame lay in ruins, its banners burned, its sacred halls desecrated. The Heart of Elander—the artifact that sustained their power and unity—was gone—stolen by Kaelen and his turncoat followers.

Once a proud and secretive brotherhood, the Order had been nearly wiped out during Kaelen's massacre—a brutal betrayal that left only a few survivors scattered and in hiding.

Tristan now carried the responsibility of restoring the Order and reclaiming the Heart.

But Kaelen's betrayal had dispersed the faithful, and Tristan needed to summon allies, rally warriors, and forge new bonds to stand a chance.

In the quiet of his stronghold's war room, Tristan stood before the flickering hearth, his hand clenched tightly around the hilt of his sword.

"The Heart of Elander must be recovered," he said, his deep voice carrying the weight of purpose. "And the Order of the Silver Flame restored, or this kingdom will burn from within."

Olivia stepped closer, the firelight catching on her hair. "We can do it together."

Tristan turned sharply, his blue eyes dark with worry. "No."

"Yes." Her voice didn't waver. "I'm not staying behind while you risk everything. The amulet chose me too. Whatever danger lies ahead, we face it as one. I swore an oath to stand by you."

His jaw tightened. "You could die."

"So, could you." She stepped closer, her hand resting on his arm. "But if I stay behind, and you fall, I'll never forgive myself."

Tristan's resolve cracked, and he exhaled sharply. "Stubborn woman."

"Knightly brute." Her lips curved in a soft smile.

Finally, Tristan nodded. "Fine. But you follow my lead."

"I'll consider it."

"Olivia—"

"Fine," she teased. "Your lead. For now."

He chuckled low in his chest. "God help me."

Evelyne stood tall as ever, already strapping her blade to her hip. "I told you I wouldn't let my brother die stupidly. If this is what we must do, then let's get to it."

Aldric, leaning against the stone wall, crossed his arms. "You've got a death wish, Tristan."

Tristan smirked. "So, do you."

Aldric rolled his eyes. "Fair. I'm in."

Gideon Cross lounged in the shadows, tossing a dagger in one hand. "Ah, a noble quest to recover a lost artifact and face certain doom? You had me at 'wine and horses provided.'"

"You're only coming for the gold, aren't you?" Olivia asked dryly.

Gideon grinned. "Gold? No. Chaos? Definitely."

Tristan spread a map across the table, its edges weighed down with daggers and candlesticks. His hand traced the inked hills and valleys. He leaned over a map spread across the table in his study, Olivia at his side.

"We cannot do this alone," he said, his voice low. "There are still those loyal to the Order, hiding in the shadows. If they live, we need them now."

Olivia touched the edge of the map. "How many do you think survived?"

Tristan's jaw tightened. "Fewer than we need, but more than Kaelen expects."

Evelyne spoke quietly, her expression wary. "If you call on them, you expose yourself. Kaelen will know you are building strength."

"Let him know," Tristan growled. "Let him feel what it is to be hunted."

Olivia placed her hand on his arm. "Then we find them. We bring them back. And we fight together."

"Kaelen's forces are growing. He's not just a rogue knight anymore—he's building a kingdom of his own."

Olivia watched him, her brow furrowed. "How many will follow him?"

Tristan exhaled sharply. "Too many. And yet... not all are loyal. Some follow because they fear him, not because they believe."

Evelyne, standing nearby, crossed her arms. "Then find those men first. Turn his own force against him."

"We'll need allies," Tristan says grimly. "Every lord and free company we can convince."

"And you'll need an army," Aldric added, stepping forward. "Before Kaelen comes for us."

Tristan's blue eyes harden. "Then let's build one."

* * *

"The first step will be to travel to the old sanctuary in the northern woods, where rumors said a handful of the Order's knights still lingered in secret."

Gideon appeared in the doorway, smirking. "Ah, so we're gathering ghost stories now? Lovely. Who doesn't enjoy a suicide mission?"

Tristan shot him a look. "You're coming."

"Naturally." Gideon leaned against the doorframe. "Someone has to keep you from getting yourself killed."

Aldric strapped his sword to his side. "If there are loyalists, they'll rally to you. But only if they believe you're still one of them."

Tristan's gaze hardened. "They'll believe."

The journey to the sanctuary had been long and treacherous. The forest grew thicker as they rode, the ancient trees looming overhead like silent sentinels. The air was heavy with the scent of earth and moss, and even the birds seemed hesitant to break the stillness.

Tristan rode at the front, his hand tight on the reins. Olivia rode just behind him, her cloak pulled close against the chill.

When they finally broke through the tree line, the old sanctuary came into view—stone walls crumbling in places, ivy twisting over weathered arches. It had once been a place of refuge and strength. Now, it was battered and weary, just like the people within.

As Tristan, Olivia and the others approached, the gates creaked open. A handful of men peered out cautiously—faces marked with soot and weariness, eyes wide with both fear and hope.

"Lord Tristan..." A grizzled old man stepped forward, leaning on a staff. "We thought you were dead."

Tristan dismounted in one smooth motion, his eyes scanning the crowd.

"No," he said simply. "But I am here now."

He strode to the center of the courtyard, his cloak flaring slightly as he moved. The survivors pressed closer, drawn to him like moths to flame.

"Listen to me," Tristan began, his voice carrying easily across the ruined courtyard. "I know you've lost much. Your homes. Your kin. Your faith in the Order."

He glanced at Olivia briefly, then back to the crowd. "But I swear to you—this fight is not over. Kaelen believes he has broken us. He hasn't."

The people murmured, their eyes brightening slightly.

"We are still here," Tristan continued. "And as long as we draw breath, we have a chance. But I cannot do it alone. I need your strength. Your courage. Will you stand with me?"

For a moment, silence hung in the air. Then a young man stepped forward, fists clenched.

"I'll fight," he said hoarsely. "For my brother. For my family."

An older woman followed, resting a hand on his shoulder. "And I'll tend the wounded."

One by one, others began to nod, murmuring their agreement.

Tristan exhaled slowly, relief flickering across his face.

"Good," he said quietly. "Then we begin."

As the survivors dispersed to prepare, Olivia stepped closer to Tristan, her voice low.

"You're a natural at this."

Tristan gave her a wry smile. "I don't feel like one."

"But they trust you."

164

His eyes softened slightly. "Do you?"

Olivia met his gaze steadily. "Always."

For the first time in days, Tristan allowed himself a small, genuine smile.

* * *

After the chaos and loss, they had endured, Tristan knew one truth above all else: they couldn't remain defenseless.

In the muddy courtyard of the keep, the survivors gathered. Farmers, merchants, young men who had never lifted a sword and older men with scars from battles long past. Women, too, stood among them—faces hardened by grief but eyes burning with determination.

Tristan stood at the front, his hands clasped behind his back, his blue eyes scanning the group.

"If you wish to survive the next storm," he said, his voice low but steady, "then you must be ready to fight for yourselves, for your families, for the future."

Tristan took the strongest men aside, showing them how to grip a sword properly, how to block, and how to stay balanced in a fight. His movements were sharp, fluid, every strike precise.

"Do not waste strength," he told them, demonstrating. "Every movement must have purpose."

Aldric worked alongside him, correcting stances and barking orders when someone faltered. "If you can't hold a sword steady, then learn to hold a shield. We'll need those too."

Olivia gathered the women and older boys.

She taught them how to use daggers, staves, and even stones as weapons. Her movements were graceful yet fierce—a reminder that skill often outweighed brute strength.

"You don't have to overpower them," she said, her voice calm yet commanding. "You only have to outthink them."

Several women watched her demonstration with wide eyes.

"Strike here," Olivia instructed, tapping the vulnerable point just beneath a man's arm. "And here." She pointed to the hollow of a man's throat.

Evelyne moved among the group, her voice softer but no less firm. "Do not hesitate. Fear will not save you."

Gideon leaned lazily against a wall at first, smirking as he watched Tristan drill the men into exhaustion.

But then he stepped forward, his grin turning sharp.

"Strength and honor are fine things," Gideon said, his green eyes gleaming. "But survival often requires... other skills."

He taught those willing to listen how to move silently, how to disarm a man with sleight of hand, and even how to throw a dagger with deadly accuracy.

"A fair fight?" Gideon chuckled. "You'll live longer if you stop believing in them."

As the sun began to set, the sound of clashing swords, shouting, and laughter filled the air.

Tristan, Olivia, Aldric, Evelyne, and Gideon moved among the survivors—guiding, correcting, and encouraging.

The once-broken villagers were now standing straighter, gripping their weapons tighter, the spark of determination flickering in their eyes.

* * *

After a long day of practice in the training yard, Tristan gathered his men and household into the Great Hall. The air still smelled faintly of sweat and steel, but the mood was light, their spirits lifted as they entered the warm glow of the candlelit chamber.

"Tonight, we eat as brothers and sisters," Tristan said, his voice carrying through the room. "No drills, no politics, no burdens. Just food, drink, and laughter."

Old Martha, the stern yet beloved head of the kitchens, had outdone herself.

The long wooden tables were laden with roasted venison dripping with herbs, fresh loaves of bread still warm from the ovens, wheels of sharp cheese, and bowls of spiced apples. Clay pitchers of ale and deep red wine were passed down the line as everyone took their seats.

"Don't eat like you're still in the yard!" Martha scolded good-naturedly as two young squires reached for the bread at the same time. "Mind your manners, or you'll be washing pots 'til dawn!"

The hall erupted in laughter.

As the food and drink flowed, so too did the stories. Knights who were usually stiff-backed and solemn began sharing tales from their youth—of failed hunting trips, awkward courtly dances, and childhood mischief.

Evelyne sat at Olivia's side, grinning as she watched Tristan try (and fail) to keep a straight face while recounting a story about Gideon.

"And then," Tristan said, smirking, "our so-called 'rogue' got stuck—headfirst—trying to crawl through a bakery window. Took three men to pull him out."

Gideon groaned and raised his goblet. "It was a very small window. And the bread was worth it."

The hall howled with laughter.

As the night wore on, the mood softened. Some of the household and guards who still had homes in the village bid farewell, calling their goodnights as they slipped away into the cool evening.

But many lingered, unwilling to leave the warmth of the fire and the rare feeling of camaraderie.

Olivia leaned toward Tristan as the hall grew louder around them.

"I've never seen you like this," she said softly. "You look... happy."

168

Tristan gave her a crooked smile. "This is rare for me. Moments like this don't last long. That's why I hold onto them."

She touched his hand lightly. "Then let's make it last as long as we can."

He smirked. "You and that dangerous optimism."

Several families lingered at the edges of the hall—merchants, servants, and a few of the Order's own allies—people whose homes lay within the Order's stronghold, now lost in the chaos of betrayal and war.

Their faces were drawn with worry, children clinging to their mothers' skirts, unsure where they would go or what the next day would bring.

Tristan noticed.

He had been walking beside Olivia, his hand brushing hers lightly as they spoke in low tones. But when he saw the group, he stopped.

"They have nowhere to go." Olivia's voice was soft, her eyes filled with concern.

He turned, his voice carrying across the hall. "You there."

The group flinched, unsure if they were about to be scolded or ordered out.

But Tristan's tone softened. "You served the Order loyally. I will not leave you to the cold."

A murmur rippled through the group.

"Ravenshire has space enough for you all," Tristan said firmly. "It will not be easy—our stores are limited, and the land is harsh—but we will make it work."

One of the older men, his beard streaked with gray, stepped forward. "My lord... are you certain? We would not wish to impose."

Tristan's blue eyes softened. "You are not imposing. You are under my protection now."

Olivia smiled faintly, her heart swelling with pride at his words. She touched Tristan's arm. "That was kind," she said softly.

Tristan smiled, though there was a tired edge to it. "Kindness or foolishness? Time will tell."

"It's not foolish."

He glanced down at her, eyes searching. "You approve?"

"Of course." She hesitated, then teased, "I always thought you'd make a fine lord."

His smirk deepened. "Careful, Olivia. I might start believing you."

She arched a brow. "And what then?"

Tristan leaned closer, his voice dropping low. "Then you'd be stuck with me... forever."

She laughed softly. "I think I could survive that."

CHAPTER THIRTEEN

The air was crisp and heavy with the scent of pine as Tristan, Olivia, Evelyne, Aldric, and Gideon set out at dawn with their small band, moving swiftly across rugged terrain, the sound of hooves and boots crunching over frostbitten earth echoing in the silence.

Their mission was clear:

Find Kaelen.

Stop him before he could create a twisted new Order under his control.

But the journey itself would be a test—of loyalty, strength, and their fragile trust in each other.

The forest was thick with morning mist, the sunlight barely piercing through the twisted canopy above. Tristan rode at the front, his expression carved from stone, every muscle tense beneath his tunic. Olivia rode beside him, her hand occasionally drifting to the amulet at her throat—its pulse had quickened in recent days, as if urging her forward.

Behind them, Aldric kept a watchful eye on the trail, his sword never far from hand. Evelyne, cloaked in gray and silent as a shadow, rode slightly behind, her bow strung and ready. Gideon trailed the group, muttering under his breath as he scanned the trees.

"We're being followed," he finally said. "Light footsteps. No animal moves like that."

Tristan slowed his horse. "How many?"

"One, maybe two. But good. Real good."

Aldric's jaw tensed. "Kaelen's scouts?"

"Or worse," Evelyne added. "A trap."

They dismounted in a small clearing, drawing their weapons and tightening their formation. Olivia's amulet flared, a soft silver light that bathed her fingers. "It's reacting to something," she whispered.

"Kaelen?" Tristan asked, his voice low.

"No," she said, "not him. The Heart. It's close."

Suddenly, a figure stepped from the trees—hooded, gaunt, and wrapped in the faded cloak of the Order of the Silver Flame. A survivor.

The man raised a hand. "Peace. I bring word."

Tristan stepped forward, blade still drawn. "Speak quickly."

"The Heart was moved. Kaelen has taken it to the chasm below Ravenfell Keep—the ancient place of binding. He's already begun the ritual."

"The ritual?" Olivia asked.

"To corrupt it," the man replied, "and himself."

Gideon swore. "Well, that changes the game."

Tristan's gaze narrowed. "Then we ride for Ravenfell."

Olivia stepped closer to him, placing a hand on his arm.

172

He looked at her, the storm in his eyes tempered only by her presence.

Tristan rode at the front, his eyes scanning the horizon. He knew Kaelen's mind well enough to guess the paths he might take—but that didn't make the hunt any easier.

Olivia rode beside him, the amulet at her neck growing warmer as they moved east. It pulsed faintly at odd intervals, as though warning them of unseen danger—or guiding them toward it.

"It's like it can feel him," Olivia murmured, touching the gem.

Evelyne glanced back from her horse. "Or perhaps he can feel you."

Aldric growled under his breath. "Let him. I'd sooner face him in the open than let him skulk like a rat in the dark."

Gideon, bringing up the rear, smirked. "So eager for battle, Aldric. You know I prefer subtlety. Perhaps I'll find Kaelen first and slit his throat before you even draw your sword."

Aldric shot him a glare. "You'd best pray you don't get in my way, Cross."

"Gentlemen," Tristan interrupted, his voice firm but calm. "Save your blades for Kaelen."

At a small village along the way, they stopped for supplies and information.

An old monk, cloaked in tattered wool, spoke in hushed tones of Kaelen's growing forces.

"He seeks to bind the Heart to his will," the monk whispered. "To create a new Order... not of honor, but of fear and darkness."

Tristan's jaw tightened. "Then we'll stop him."

"You don't understand," the monk said, voice trembling. "The Heart amplifies what lies within. If he has it, he will become unstoppable."

Olivia's fingers brushed her own amulet. A chill ran down her spine.

Their path took them through fog-choked forests, across icy rivers, and over craggy hills where Kaelen's men could lie in wait.

They fought off an ambush one night—Kaelen's scouts sent to slow their pursuit.

Tristan led the charge, blade flashing in the moonlight. Olivia stood behind him, clutching the amulet as it glowed bright blue, sending a pulse of energy that knocked two attackers to the ground.

Evelyne's arrows flew true, and Aldric cut down anyone who got too close.

Gideon moved like a shadow, slipping behind enemy lines and dispatching foes with silent efficiency.

Afterward, as they caught their breath, Gideon knelt beside one of the fallen scouts.

"He carried this," Gideon said, tossing Tristan a scrap of parchment.

On it was a crude map—and a symbol Tristan recognized instantly.

"Kaelen is heading for the Black Spire," Tristan murmured.

"We have no time to waste," Olivia said, her voice steady but her fingers tight on the reins.

The forest was eerily quiet, the usual sounds of birdsong and rustling leaves replaced by a heavy silence that pressed against Tristan's senses.

"He can't have gone far," Evelyne whispered, her eyes scanning the shadows between the trees.

Olivia moved carefully beside Tristan, her hand resting near the hilt of the small blade he'd insisted she carry. A twig snapped.

Tristan froze. "Get behind me," he said sharply, his hand going to the sword at his hip.

Evelyne and Gideon heard it too—the soft shift of boots against earth, the faint exhale of breath.

"It's a trap," Gideon growled, already reaching for his own blade.

And then Kaelen struck.

From the undergrowth, Kaelen lunged like a predator, a dagger flashing in his hand.

Tristan pivoted just in time, his sword clashing against the blade with a metallic ring that echoed through the forest.

"Coward!" Tristan spat, forcing Kaelen back with a powerful shove.

Kaelen snarled. "You were always blind, Tristan. You don't see the game being played."

"And you were always a traitor," Tristan countered, his voice low and dangerous.

Evelyne lost an arrow, forcing Kaelen to retreat a step, but the traitor knight ducked behind a tree with startling speed.

Gideon circled around, cutting off Kaelen's escape. "I'm getting tired of cleaning up your messes, Kaelen," he called, his voice sharp with mockery.

"Then don't," Kaelen hissed, throwing a dagger toward Olivia.

Tristan moved without thinking—

His arm caught hers, yanking her aside as the blade embedded itself in the tree where she'd stood seconds before.

"Stay behind me!" he barked.

"Stop saying that!" Olivia shot back, clutching her small blade. "I'm not helpless!"

Kaelen laughed—a hollow, vicious sound. "How sweet. Tristan's little pet thinks she can fight."

Tristan's fury flared. "Say another word about her, and I'll silence you myself."

Kaelen lunged again, but this time Tristan was ready.

Their swords clashed violently, the sound of steel striking steel ringing out like a bell. Tristan pushed forward, each strike fueled by his rage and determination.

"You betrayed everything you swore to protect," Tristan snarled.

Kaelen sneered. "And yet here you are—protecting her. What would the king say if he knew the truth about your witch?"

"He already knows everything he needs to know about Olivia." That was enough.

Tristan's blade swept low, knocking Kaelen's feet out from under him. With a swift movement, he had the traitor pinned to the ground, his sword at Kaelen's throat.

"You'll never speak her name again," Tristan said, his voice a dangerous whisper.

"Tristan," Evelyne called, her voice urgent. "Don't kill him—not yet. We need answers."

For a moment, Tristan didn't move, his chest heaving with restrained fury.

Then he pulled back, keeping his sword at Kaelen's throat. "Fine. But he's your problem now."

Kaelen smiled faintly. "You've grown weak, Tristan."

"And you've grown stupid." Gideon kicked Kaelen's dagger away. "Try anything, and I'll gut you before you can blink."

As the others tied Kaelen's hands, Tristan turned to Olivia. "Are you hurt?"

She shook her head, though her heart still pounded. "No. But you—you shouldn't have thrown yourself in front of me like that."

Tristan cupped her face gently, his thumb brushing her cheek. "You are worth every risk."

"And you're impossible," Olivia whispered.

"So, you keep telling me."

* * *

Kaelen sat bound to a chair in the cold stone chamber, the torchlight flickering against his sweat-slicked brow. His tunic was torn, and a shallow cut on his cheek still bled from Tristan's earlier blow. Despite the bindings, his eyes glittered with defiance.

Tristan stood over him, arms crossed, his blue eyes sharp as steel. Olivia hovered nearby, trying to mask her unease.

"Where is the Heart?" Tristan demanded, his voice low but edged with deadly calm.

Kaelen spat at the floor. "I'll never tell you."

Tristan leaned closer, his shadow falling over the man. "You do know. And unless you want to leave this room with fewer fingers than you came in with, I suggest you speak."

Kaelen gave a bitter laugh. "You're too noble to maim a man, Lord Tristan. That's not in your nature."

Tristan's lips curled in a humorless smile. "Try me."

Olivia stepped forward, her voice steady despite her racing heart.

"Your men ambushed us in the forest. Two are dead. Where are the others?"

Kaelen smirked. "Closer than you think."

Tristan slammed his fist onto the table, the sound echoing off the stone walls.

"If they're near, they'll be dealt with. But you—Kaelen— you might yet live if you speak now."

Kaelen hesitated. A flicker of doubt crossed his face.

Tristan straightened, his voice cold. "Bind him. Lock him away."

Kaelen was taken and chained deep within the castle dungeon, refusing to speak.

* * *

Tristan stood before the heavy oak door, the torchlight flickering against the damp stone walls.

"He knows where the Heart is hidden," Evelyne whispered behind him. "But he won't speak—not even under threat."

Tristan's jaw tightened. "We must make him speak."

Kaelen smirked as they entered, even in chains, his dark eyes glittering with defiance.

"The Heart isn't yours to command, knight," Kaelen said coolly. "It belongs to a power far older than you can imagine."

"If you don't tell me where it is, I will drag the truth out of you myself."

Kaelen only chuckled. "You won't get the chance."

Tristan's eyes were fixed on Kaelen, still chained in the cell, his lips curved in a knowing smile.

"They're coming for me," Kaelen said calmly. "And they will not fail."

The torches in the dungeon flickered low, casting long shadows across the damp stone walls. Tristan stood just outside Kaelen's cell, his arms folded, his eyes locked on the prisoner.

"Where is it, Kaelen?" Tristan asked, his voice low but edged with steel. "Where is the Heart of Elander?"

Kaelen only smirked, lounging against the cold wall as though he were in a place of comfort, not captivity.

"You ask the same question every time you come, my lord," Kaelen said, voice smooth and mocking. "And yet here we are—still no answers. You ask tthe wrong questions."

Tristan's jaw tightened. He had tried reasoning, intimidation, and even offering terms, but Kaelen was too cunning—too slippery.

The sound came suddenly—a dull thud, faint but unmistakable. Tristan's head snapped up. "What was that?" he murmured.

Before he could call for his guards, a crash echoed through the corridor. The door to the dungeon bursts open, and Kaelen's men flooded in like a dark tide, weapons drawn.

"Protect the lord!" shouted one of Tristan's guards.

Steel clashed on steel as a brutal fight erupted in the narrow hall.

Tristan drew his sword, cutting down two attackers with swift, precise strikes. But there were too many. They had planned this carefully, striking at night when Ravenshire's defenses were thinnest.

"Do not let them take Kaelen!" Tristan barked.

But even as he fought, he felt the shift in the air—a trap within a trap.

Two of Kaelen's men lunged at him in unison, one slamming into his side and sending him sprawling. Tristan's sword skittered across the stones.

Before he could reach it, another blow cracked against the back of his head, and stars exploded behind his eyes. As his vision blurred, he heard Kaelen's mocking laugh.

"I told you, my lord... you ask the wrong questions."

Darkness swallowed him.

By the time more guards arrived, the dungeon was a ruin of broken iron and blood. Kaelen's cell stood open and empty.

"They've taken Lord Tristan," a guard gasped, clutching a wound in his side. "He's gone."

When word reached Olivia, her blood ran cold. "No..." she whispered, her hands trembling. "Not Tristan."

Evelyne's face hardened with determination. "We're getting him back. Whatever it takes."

CHAPTER FOURTEEN

Tristan's eyelids fluttered open to darkness and the heavy scent of damp stone.

His head pounded, and a sharp ache ran through his shoulder where the blade had struck. As he shifted, he felt the clink of iron—chains. His wrists were shackled above his head, cutting into his skin.

"Ah... so the lion still breathes." A low, mocking voice echoed through the chamber. "Did you sleep well?"

Tristan raised his head, his wrists chafed and bloody from the chains that held them above him. "I slept fine, Kaelen. I dreamed of you falling on your own sword."

Kaelen chuckled darkly, stepping closer. "You still have your tongue, I see. Perhaps I should cut it out."

Tristan smirked faintly. "Go on, then. But you'd best make sure you take my head too. Otherwise, I'll use what's left of my tongue to tell the entire court how a coward like you couldn't finish the job."

Kaelen's smile faltered. He grabbed Tristan's hair, jerking his head back.

"You mock me, even now? You're in no position to play the hero."

Tristan's voice was raw but steady. "I don't need to play the hero. I only need to keep denying you what you want."

183

Kaelen's eyes narrowed. "You'll break. They all do." He let go of Tristan. "Then you haven't met a knight of Ravenshire," Tristan growled. "We don't break. We bury bastards like you."

Kaelen's hand snapped across Tristan's face, leaving a sharp red welt.

"You're weaker than you think," Kaelen hissed. "Your body is failing. Your mind will be next."

Tristan's head lolled forward, a bead of blood on his lip. He laughed faintly. "Then you'd better hurry. I don't plan to die until I see your face on the executioner's block." Kaelen froze for half a second, then drove his fist into Tristan's stomach. Tristan grunted but refused to cry out.

Kaelen's fingers brushed the hilt of the dagger at his belt. He drew it slowly, the blade glinting in the torchlight. Tristan's fingers curled into fists as he watched him.

"You've always been so proud, Tristan. So untouchable." He pressed the flat of the blade lightly against Tristan's chest, just above his heart. "But here? You're just a man. And men bleed. Do you know how easy it would be to carve a man apart?" Kaelen's voice was low, almost amused, as though they were discussing a fine meal.

The tip of the blade touched Tristan's chest—just above the ribs—and began a slow, deliberate drag. A thin line of fire followed in its wake.

Tristan hissed through his teeth but held still.

"That's it," Kalen purred. "Be brave. Pretend it doesn't hurt."

The knife traced downward, slowly dragging over Tristan's stomach, leaving a cold line in its wake. Tristan didn't flinch.

Kaelen smirked. "Still fighting, even now. How noble."

The knife tip pressed harder. Tristan felt the sting as it broke the skin. A warm line of blood trickled down.

"This is just the beginning, knight," Kaelen whispered near his ear. "When I'm finished, you'll beg me for death."

Tristan forced a bitter laugh, his voice hoarse but steady. "You'll have to do better than that, Kaelen."

The blade carved into his skin, tracing his ribs, his abdomen, leaving shallow, stinging trails.

"You speak boldly for a man at my mercy," Kaelen said, pressing the knife point against the tender skin just above Tristan's hip.

Tristan's jaw tightened. His breath came in ragged pulls.

But his eyes—ice blue and defiant—never left Kaelen's face.

"Mercy?" Tristan spat the word like a curse. "You wouldn't know mercy if it struck you down where you stand."

The knife dug in harder, and Tristan couldn't stop the sharp hiss of pain.

Still, he smiled through clenched teeth. "Do it, then. Break me if you can. But I swear to you..." His voice dropped, cold and dangerous. "When I get free, I'll make you regret not finishing the job."

Kaelen chuckled darkly. "We'll see if you're still so defiant when the real pain begins."

And with that, the knife slid away—only for a moment— leaving Tristan's skin burning, his chest heaving with controlled fury.

The tip of the dagger slid up to Tristan's face, brushing along the line of his jaw, then resting just beneath his chin.

"Let's see how long that fire lasts." Kaelen tilted Tristan's chin upward with the blade, forcing their eyes to meet.

"If I were you," Kaelen murmured, his voice low and dangerous, "I'd start begging. But then again, you never were very smart about knowing when you're beaten."

Tristan's lips curled into a faint, defiant smile. "If you're going to kill me, do it. Otherwise, stop wasting my time."

Kaelen's grin faltered for the briefest moment, a flash of irritation breaking through his cruel amusement. He pressed the blade a fraction harder against Tristan's throat, enough to make a drop of blood well up.

"Careful, knight. Pride is a dangerous thing to cling to in a place like this."

Then, with a flick of his wrist, Kaelen withdrew the dagger and stepped back.

"No," he murmured. "Killing you now would be too merciful. I think I'll let you rot a little longer."

He circled in front of Tristan like a predator, his eyes gleaming with amusement. "Do you know why you're still alive?"

Tristan glared at him, his muscles tensing against the chains. "Because you don't have the courage to face me in a fair fight."

Kaelen chuckled darkly. "No. Because I want you to watch as I undo everything you've built. Your stronghold. The Order. And that lovely woman..."

Tristan's jaw tightened. "Don't you dare speak of her."

"Ah, Olivia, wasn't it?" Kaelen's grin widened. "So defiant. So protective. I'll enjoy breaking you... and I wonder how long she'll last before she breaks, too."

Tristan lunged forward, the chains rattling violently. "If you touch her—"

Kaelen's hand shot out, gripping Tristan's jaw painfully. "You're not in a position to make threats, knight."

He released him with a shove, sending Tristan's head slamming back against the stone wall.

"I haven't touched your precious Olivia yet," Kaelen said, smirking. "But I will... if you keep fighting."

"Rest well," Kaelen sneered. "You'll need your strength. Tomorrow, I have plans for you." And with that, Kaelen turned and strode out of the cell, the door slamming shut behind him.

The cold of the dungeon walls bit into Tristan's skin as he pressed himself against the stone, his breath ragged from exhaustion and pain. His wrists were raw from the iron shackles, and every movement sent fire lancing through his battered body.

He had to escape.

For Olivia.

For everything he still had to protect.

But Kaelen...

Kaelen wasn't finished with him yet.

* * *

Sometime later Kaelen returned. Tristan heard the sound of many boots hurrying along the corridor and a small whimpering.

This time, Kaelen didn't bring whips or blades. Just a riding crop and a young boy.

Two guards entered behind him, dragging in a young stable hand—barely more than a boy—his eyes wide with terror, his small frame shaking under the weight of Kaelen's glare.

"You were told not to feed him. Or do you think my orders don't apply to you?"

The boy swallowed hard. "I—I thought he'd starve."

"And what would that matter to you?" Kaelen's sharp green eyes narrowed. "You think him a friend? A knight worth saving?"

The boy dropped to his knees. "Please, my lord, forgive me!"

"This one tried to sneak food down to you," Kaelen said smoothly. "A touching gesture. Would you like to see what happens to those who help traitors?"

Tristan's jaw tightened. "Leave him out of this. Your quarrel is with me."

Kaelen chuckled. "Everything is with you, Lord Tristan. He suffers because of your stubbornness. How many more will you doom before you finally break?"

Kaelen turned back to the youth. "You'll never make a soldier, boy," he sneered, shaking the lad by his tunic collar. "Feeding a traitor? Shall I bring you to the whipping post, or should I just slit your thieving fingers here?"

The boy pleaded, eyes wide with fear. "Lord Tristan isn't a traitor! He's a good man—please, m'lord, I only—"

"Enough!" Kaelen spat.

Tristan pulled against his chains, fury flashing in his eyes. "Coward!" he roared.

Kaelen's eyes narrowed. "Perhaps. But even cowards win wars when knights are too noble to save themselves."

He drew back his riding crop, the handle glinting in the torchlight. "Shall we see how long that boy screams before you start begging?"

Tristan's entire body tensed. His mind screamed at him to give in, to end this, but another voice—Olivia's voice—echoed in his memory. *You are stronger than this. Don't let him break you.*

Kaelen raised the crop, slow and deliberate. "Well, Lord Tristan?"

Tristan's lips parted, but no words came. Then—

"Take me instead," Tristan said firmly, his voice calm but carrying the weight of steel beneath it.

Kaelen's lips curled into a cruel smirk.

"So, the great knight sacrifices himself for a peasant boy?" He laughed, low and bitter. "How noble. How predictable."

From where he hung, Tristan's voice rasped out, raw from thirst. "Kaelen. Touch him, and I'll take your arm the next time we meet blade to blade."

Kaelen laughed bitterly. "You're in no position to threaten, knight." Kaelen's hand shot out suddenly, gripping Tristan by the shoulder and yanking him close, hard enough to make the chains rattle violently against the wall. Pain shot through Tristan's arms and chest.

"Do you think you're a savior, de Léon?" Kaelen hissed in his ear. "You think offering yourself changes anything? That I won't enjoy watching you break?"

Kaelen shoved the boy aside, sending him tumbling to the ground.

But even in that moment, Tristan's mind worked.

If he defied Kaelen openly, the boy would suffer more for Tristan's insolence.

But if he said nothing... he'd become the coward they accused him of being.

So, he tried a different path.

"He's just a boy. Too young for politics, too young to know the cost of his loyalty. Punish me instead. Isn't that what you came for? If discipline is needed," Tristan said evenly, "then give it to me. Not him."

Kaelen's lips curled into a cruel smile. "So eager to play the hero, are we?"

"He's a child," Tristan said firmly. "The fault lies with me."

"Very well." Kaelen's smile sharpened. "If you wish to take his punishment, then you shall."

The boy's voice cracked. "Lord Tristan—no!"

Tristan didn't look at him. "Stay silent."

Kaelen paused, eyes gleaming like a predator circling its prey. "So noble. So foolish."

And then Kaelen's fist slammed into Tristan's stomach, hard enough to force the air from his lungs.

Tristan grunted but didn't fall.

"You knight bleed like any other man," Kaelen sneered.

Another blow—this time a backhand across Tristan's face, splitting his lip. Blood welled, but Tristan straightened, glaring back at Kaelen with cold defiance.

"Strike me all you like," Tristan growled. "But leave the boy out of this."

Kaelen chuckled darkly. "Oh, I intend to. But you? I'll enjoy taking you apart piece by piece. Turn him," he said to his guards.

The guards stepped forward and turned Tristan roughly, baring the broad expanse of his back, his face to the wall. He stood tall, unflinching, as Kaelen stepped forward.

The torchlight flickered, casting shadows over the scars crisscrossing his broad shoulders and down his spine— remnants of Malric's past cruelty.

Kaelen paused, tilting his head to take in the marks.

"Ah," he murmured, his tone dripping with mockery. "So Malric has already had his fun with you."

He traced the tip of the crop lightly across one of the older scars, watching Tristan's muscles tense.

"I wonder," Kaelen continued, stepping closer, his voice low and venomous, "did you cry out for mercy then too? Or are you saving that for me?"

Tristan's eyes burned with defiance as he lifted his head, his jaw tight. "You'll not hear a sound from me."

Kaelen smirked. "We'll see."

He raised the crop high—

"Ten lashes," Kaelen said. "Perhaps then you'll learn humility."

The first strike landed with a crack, the crop biting deep into Tristan's skin.

He didn't make a sound.

The second strike came harder, leaving an angry red welt across his shoulders.

The boy sobbed softly behind him.

By the fifth strike, blood welled at Tristan's back, the flesh broken in angry streaks.

Still, he stood. Silent. Unmoving. His jaw clenched tight.

The soldiers watching shifted uneasily. Some looked away. Others stared, their faces hard with respect.

Kaelen, frustrated by Tristan's lack of reaction, lashed him harder. "Say something!"

Tristan finally spoke, his voice low and dangerous. "Is that all you've got?"

Kaelen's hand faltered.

When it was done, Tristan straightened, blood dripping from his back, his breaths sharp but steady. He looked over his shoulder at the boy. "You're safe now," he said with a reassuring nod.

Kaelen spat on the ground, his satisfaction hollow.

The boy looked up at Tristan, tears still streaking his face. "Why?"

Tristan glanced down, his voice soft but steady. "Because no one should suffer because of me."

But Tristan knew the danger wasn't over. Not for the boy. Not for him.

He counted Kaelen's steps, the weight of his keys, the looseness of his manacles.

This wasn't just pain—it was opportunity.

* * *

When Kaelen left, promising to return for more, Tristan slumped forward, feigning defeat.

The guard outside laughed as Kaelen's boots retreated down the hall.

But Tristan wasn't finished.

He twisted his wrist hard, wrenching his raw flesh against the manacle. The metal bit deep, but it shifted.

Once. Twice. And then—

His hand slipped free.

He twisted his other wrist and pulled it free as well.

Tristan exhaled a shaky breath, adrenaline surging. He had to move. Now.

He staggered into the corridor, silent as a shadow despite the fire in his wounds.

Every step was agony, but he gritted his teeth and pressed on.

He could almost hear Olivia's voice in his mind. *Don't you dare give up, Tristan de Léon.*

And he wouldn't. Not now. Not ever.

The night air was sharp and cold as Tristan tore through the underbrush, his breath ragged in his chest. Behind him, the sounds of pursuit were relentless.

The crack of branches.

The hiss of Kaelen's voice.

The thundering of boots against the forest floor.

"Hunt him down!" Kaelen bellowed. "I want him alive!"

Tristan's muscles burned, but he forced himself to keep moving. No weapon. Just his speed and his wits.

He ducked under a low branch, heart hammering.

Kaelen was close. Too close.

Tristan could hear the man's harsh breathing, feel the weight of his presence pressing in on him like a wolf circling its prey.

"You can't run forever, de Léon!" Kaelen's voice echoed through the trees. "I'll drag you back in chains—or in pieces."

Tristan gritted his teeth. Running wasn't enough. He needed to think. To turn the tables.

He veered sharply to the left, plunging into a thicket of brambles. The sharp thorns clawed at his arms, but he didn't stop.

Suddenly, the sound of pursuit stopped.

Tristan's breath came fast and shallow as he pressed himself against a tree, listening.

Silence.

Too much silence.

And then—

A whisper of movement.

A shadow in the corner of his eye.

Kaelen lunged from the darkness, a dagger flashing in his hand.

Tristan dodged, but not fast enough, and the blade sliced his side under his rib.

The two men crashed to the ground, rolling in the dirt and leaves. Kaelen's dagger clattered away into the undergrowth.

Tristan struck hard, his fist connecting with Kaelen's jaw. But Kaelen was just as strong, slamming his knee into Tristan's ribs.

They grappled, a brutal, primal fight for survival.

At last, Tristan's fingers closed around a fallen branch—thick and sturdy.

He swung hard.

The branch cracked against Kaelen's head with a sickening thud.

Kaelen slumped, dazed, giving Tristan just enough time to stagger to his feet.

Tristan grabbed the dagger from the forest floor.

Now he was armed.

He didn't wait for Kaelen to recover. He ran, deeper into the woods, knowing the rest of Kaelen's men were still hunting him.

Tristan's heart pounded. The forest was dark and endless, but he knew he couldn't run forever.

If he wanted to survive, he'd have to fight.

One by one.

And this time, he'd be the hunter.

Tristan's heart pounded like a war drum in his chest.

The air thick with mist and the faint scent of blood. Twigs cracked underfoot—not his. They were following him. Stalking him. Waiting for him to break.

But Tristan was no stranger to being hunted.

Not this time.

He ducked behind the gnarled trunk of an ancient oak, his hand tightening around the hilt of his blade. The sound of hushed voices carried through the trees. Two. Maybe three men.

They thought they had him cornered.

They thought he'd run like prey.

But they were wrong. This time, Tristan would be the hunter.

The first man stepped into the clearing, scanning the shadows. A mercenary by his stance, cocky and overconfident.

Tristan struck fast, silent as a predator.

His blade flashed in the moonlight. One swift motion— one life ended.

He caught the man before he could fall, lowering him silently into the undergrowth.

Two more to go.

The second mercenary moved cautiously, his sword half-drawn. "He's here somewhere," he hissed to his companion.

Tristan's voice cut through the night like a blade. "Here."

The man spun—too slow.

Steel met steel. Sparks flew.

The clash echoed through the trees, the mercenary forcing Tristan back a step. But Tristan's eyes blazed, his movements sharp and deliberate. He fought not like a knight in a tournament, but like a man with nothing left to lose.

A swift kick. A parry. A brutal counterstrike.

The second man fell.

The final mercenary hesitated at the edge of the clearing, his face pale in the moonlight. He realized too late that he was alone.

Tristan emerged from the shadows, his blade dripping, his breath slow and controlled.

"Your choice," Tristan growled. "Run, or join them."

The man turned and bolted into the forest.

Tristan didn't follow. Not this time.

The forest fell silent again, save for the whisper of wind through the branches.

Tristan pushed the blade into the waist of his breeches, his jaw tight, his muscles coiled.

He knew this wasn't over. This was just the beginning.

If they wanted to hunt him, they'd better be ready to pay the price.

The forest was eerily quiet, save for the faint crackle of a dying fire in the distance. Shadows stretched long beneath the pale moonlight, and the air was heavy with tension.

Tristan moved like a ghost through the trees, clutching his side where Kaelen's blade had cut him earlier. Blood had dried along his side but his blue eyes burned with fierce determination.

He had escaped Kaelen's grip for now. But he knew the man wouldn't stop hunting him.

As he crouched low, scanning the tree line for movement, he caught the faintest sound—

A voice.

Familiar.

Aldric.

Tristan's jaw clenched in relief. They had come for him.

In a small clearing not far ahead, Aldric, Evelyne, Olivia, and Gideon were huddled around a dim fire. Their faces were tense, their weapons close at hand.

"We're close," Aldric murmured. "Kaelen's men can't have taken him far."

Olivia's voice was tight. "If he's hurt—"

Evelyne placed a hand on her shoulder. "He's alive. Tristan is too stubborn to die."

Gideon smirked faintly. "And if he isn't too stubborn, at least he's too damn proud."

"Quiet," Aldric hissed suddenly. He stood, hand on his sword hilt. "Someone's coming."

The group spun around as a figure stepped out of the trees—tall, broad-shouldered, with dark blond hair matted from sweat and dirt.

"Tristan," Olivia breathed.

His eyes locked onto hers, and for the briefest moment, relief flickered across his tired face.

"You found me," he rasped.

"You're bleeding," Olivia said sharply, rushing forward. "What did he do to you?"

Tristan held up a hand. "Later." His voice was calm but urgent. "Kaelen isn't far behind."

Aldric stepped forward. "We'll get you out of here. There's a river half a mile east—we can lose them there."

Gideon pulled a dagger, spinning it lazily in his hand. "Or we could stay and give Kaelen a little surprise."

Tristan's lips curved into the faintest smirk. "Tempting. But we're outnumbered."

Olivia touched his arm gently. "You can barely stand."

His hand brushed hers briefly. "I can stand."

Evelyne moved closer, her tone sharp. "Then let's move before Kaelen finds more dogs to send after us."

Shouts and the clash of steel faded behind them, but the danger was far from over.

Tristan's steps were faltering now, his breathing ragged. Blood seeped down his side where Kaelen's blade had sliced him. His back covered with welts and bruises.

"Tristan!" Olivia's voice broke as his knees buckled.

Aldric caught him just in time, throwing Tristan's arm over his shoulder. "He's losing blood."

"We need to keep moving," Olivia said, trying to sound steady, but panic knotted in her chest. "They're still out there."

Aldric's jaw tightened. "We can't outrun them—not with him like this."

But there was no choice. If they stopped now, the enemy would find them.

* * *

Meanwhile, further back in the forest, Gideon moved like a shadow.

His green eyes gleamed with mischief as he pulled a coil of rope from his satchel. "Time to slow down the bastards," he muttered.

He strung the rope low between two trees, then scattered leaves and dirt to disguise it.

Nearby, he stacked dry brush and soaked it with oil. A single spark from his flint—and flames would leap to life, cutting off the enemy's path.

"That'll buy them a little time," Gideon murmured with a smirk.

* * *

Aldric half-dragged, half-carried Tristan through the trees, Olivia keeping pace beside them.

"There!" Olivia pointed to a small, abandoned shepherd's hut.

They pushed through the door and set Tristan down gently on the floor. His face was pale, his blue eyes glassy.

"Stay with me, Tristan," Olivia whispered, pressing a hand to his cheek.

Aldric began tearing more strips of cloth for bandages. "We need to stop the bleeding."

Tristan's lips curled faintly. "You sound... worried."

"Don't you dare joke right now," Olivia snapped, though her voice trembled.

"I'm fine," Tristan rasped. "Just... tired."

"No, you're not fine," Olivia shot back. "You're bleeding all over my skirts."

His faint smile widened. "They look better that way."

"Tristan—" Olivia's voice broke. "Don't you dare leave me."

"Not planning to, love."

And then his eyes slipped closed.

* * *

The night air was thick with tension as Gideon crouched low behind a cluster of gnarled oaks, the faint crackle of firelight flickering across his sharp features.

Kaelen and his men were close. Too close.

Gideon had no intention of letting them stumble upon Tristan and Olivia. Not tonight. He had tied a thick rope across the narrow woodland path, just high enough to catch an unsuspecting rider. At the same time, he'd lit a small fire off to the side—a lure, a distraction, and a test all in one.

"Come on, you bastards," Gideon muttered under his breath, green eyes glinting in the glow. "Take the bait."

Hoofbeats sounded in the distance, muffled at first, then louder as Kaelen's men drew closer.

Gideon could hear their voices—low, murmuring.

"Light up ahead."

"Could be them."

"Fan out."

Perfect. They'd taken the bait.

The first rider didn't stand a chance. His horse surged forward, and the rope caught him square in the chest.

He was flung backward with a shout, crashing hard into the dirt. The horse screamed and bolted.

Panic spread through Kaelen's men.

"An ambush!"

"Hold your ground!"

Then Gideon struck.

He loosed a single arrow from the shadows, striking the torch one of the riders held. The flame sputtered and died, plunging the path into darkness.

"Damn it! I can't see!"

Chaos. Exactly what Gideon wanted.

Gideon pressed a hand against the rough bark of the tree he hid behind, his lips curling into a sly grin. "That should keep you busy for a while."

But he wasn't done. Not yet.

If Kaelen regrouped too fast, Tristan and Olivia wouldn't have enough time to get clear.

Gideon slipped silently through the underbrush, ready to draw them even further away. The faint glow of torchlight flickering behind him. They were getting closer—too close.

"Come on, then," he muttered under his breath, the corner of his mouth curling into a smirk. "Let's see if you're clever enough for this."

He slid behind a fallen tree, fingers working quickly to rig the snare he'd left half-prepared earlier. A thin trip line stretched across the forest floor, nearly invisible in the moonlight. The tension in the rope promised chaos if triggered.

Shouts rang out—Kaelen's men. They were almost upon him.

Gideon crouched low, his dagger drawn, the grin on his face sharpened by adrenaline.

"Right on time."

The first of Kaelen's soldiers crashed through the trees—and Gideon pulled.

A branch snapped back with violent force, sending one man sprawling into a tangle of thorns. Another slammed face-first into the dirt as the trip line yanked him off balance.

"That's two."

But Kaelen was no fool.

From the tree line, his sharp eyes caught a flicker of movement—Gideon.

"There!" Kaelen raised his hand, signaling his men to fan out. "Enough of this. I'll take him myself."

The hunter became the hunted.

Kaelen moved like a predator, silent and fast, cutting Gideon off before he could set another trap.

"You've run far enough, Cross."

Gideon froze, his smirk widening. "Kaelen. I was wondering when you'd catch up."

"You're clever," Kaelen said coldly. "But not clever enough to walk out of these woods alive."

"Care to bet on that?" Gideon quipped, his blade flashing in the moonlight.

In the shadowed forest, the air was thick with tension.

The moonlight broke through the canopy in fractured beams, illuminating flashes of steel as Gideon Cross moved like a wraith, silent and deadly. His green eyes scanned the darkness, every sense on high alert.

Somewhere out there, Kaelen was waiting.

His rival. His equal.

And tonight, only one of them would walk out alive.

A twig snapped to Gideon's left.

He didn't flinch. Instead, he darted forward, spinning behind the thick trunk of an oak as Kaelen's blade sliced through empty air where Gideon had just been standing.

"Too slow, Cross," Kaelen's smooth voice taunted from the shadows. "You've lost your edge."

"Funny," Gideon replied coolly, stepping silently across the underbrush. "I was about to say the same about you."

Kaelen's laugh was low and cold. "We'll see who's laughing when I have your head."

The clash of swords rang out as they met in a clearing.

Gideon's dagger moved in tandem with his rapier, striking in a whirlwind of precision and speed. Kaelen countered with brute force, his broadsword hacking with deadly intent.

"Still favoring two blades?" Kaelen sneered.

"Still swinging like a drunken ox?" Gideon shot back.

Kaelen lunged forward, forcing Gideon back against a tree. The mercenary twisted, deflecting the blow and raking his dagger across Kaelen's arm.

"First blood's mine."

Kaelen growled, his eyes blazing. "Not for long."

Kaelen retreated into the trees, vanishing like a phantom.

Gideon crouched low, his breath slow and controlled. He knew Kaelen's game.

"You're trying to lure me in..." he murmured under his breath. "...but I wrote the book on traps."

With a sudden pivot, Gideon doubled back, silent as death.

And there—he saw the glint of a blade.

Kaelen lunged from his hiding place—only to meet Gideon's boot in his chest.

The larger man slammed to the ground with a grunt, his sword skittering across the dirt.

Gideon pressed the tip of his dagger against Kaelen's throat. "Yield."

Kaelen smirked despite the blood on his lips. "Never."

"Good." Gideon's eyes gleamed. "I like it when they struggle."

But then— a whistle cut through the night.

Both men froze. Reinforcements. Kaelen's men.

Gideon cursed, yanking Kaelen to his feet. "Looks like we're not done yet."

Kaelen grinned darkly. "Next time, Cross. Next time, you won't walk away."

And just like that, Kaelen vanished into the darkness, leaving Gideon alone in the clearing.

"Damn it," Gideon muttered, sheathing his blades. The game wasn't over.

Not yet.

* * *

The hut smelled faintly of old woodsmoke and damp straw. Wind howled through cracks in the walls, but inside, there was a tense, fragile warmth.

Tristan lay on the rough pallet, his torso bloody, his jaw tight as Olivia pressed a damp cloth against the gash along his ribs.

"Hold still," she whispered, brushing his sweat-soaked hair from his forehead.

"I'm all right," Tristan muttered, his voice low but strained.

"Don't be stubborn." Olivia shot him a look. "You're losing blood, and I can't help you if you keep moving."

Evelyne knelt beside them, holding a basin of clean water. "She's right, brother. You'll need your strength if we're attacked again."

Aldric stood at the doorway, sword drawn, his sharp gaze scanning the tree line. "Speaking of which... I don't like this quiet. It's too still."

Tristan exhaled slowly, wincing as Olivia tightened a bandage around his torso. "Kaelen's men won't give up so easily."

The door slammed open. Wind and leaves swept in as Gideon Cross strode into the hut, his boots slick with mud.

"Well, this is cozy."

Olivia jumped, spinning toward him. "Gideon!"

Aldric raised his sword, but lowered it with a growl as he recognized him. "What are you doing here?"

Gideon smirked. "Delivering bad news, as usual."

"Then out with it," Tristan said through clenched teeth, his hand pressed against his wound.

Gideon's expression sobered. "Kaelen's men are regrouping. They've sent a hunting party this way. They're less than an hour behind me."

Evelyne cursed under her breath. "We're trapped."

"Not yet," Gideon said, his grin returning. "But we will be if we don't move."

Olivia checked Tristan's bandages. "He's in no condition to travel."

"And you're in no condition to fight off an army," Gideon shot back.

"Enough." Tristan's voice was hoarse but commanding. "We move."

"Are you mad?" Olivia protested. "You can barely stand!"

Tristan's blue eyes met hers, steady and fierce despite the pain. "I'll stand if it means keeping you safe."

* * *

Tristan's blood dripped steadily, leaving a dark trail across the forest floor.

His arm hung heavy over Olivia's shoulders, his face pale and lips pressed tight against the pain. Evelyne, on his other side, struggled under his weight but refused to let him falter.

"Keep moving," Aldric hissed from ahead, his hand gripping the hilt of his sword.

The flickering torchlight caught the sharp angles of his jaw as he scanned the trees for movement.

Behind them, Gideon's voice was low but urgent. "Kaelen's men are closing in. They're moving faster than I thought."

"Then we must move faster," Aldric growled. "Ravenshire isn't far. We just have to make it past the ridge."

211

Tristan let out a low groan, his knees nearly buckling.

"Tristan—stay with me!" Olivia's voice cracked as she tightened her hold on him.

She felt his blood soaking into the sleeve of her gown. "Don't you dare give up now."

His lips curved faintly, though his voice was a rasp. "I wouldn't dream of it, my lady."

Evelyne's jaw clenched. "You're heavier than you look, brother."

"That's because I'm full of... stubbornness," Tristan murmured weakly. "You've always said so."

Evelyne blinked back tears. "And now you'll prove me right. Stay alive, Tristan."

Aldric raised his hand suddenly, signaling for them to stop.

"What is it?" Gideon asked, his voice low.

"Movement. To the left."

Gideon's dagger was already in his hand. "Shadows or Kaelen's men?"

"Both," Aldric said grimly. "Keep them moving. I'll hold them off."

"Not alone," Gideon snapped. "We do this together."

Aldric glanced back at Olivia and Evelyne struggling to keep Tristan on his feet.

"They need time. We give it to them."

The clash of steel rang out in the cold air as Aldric and Gideon stood shoulder to shoulder, their blades flashing in the torchlight.

"Hold the line!" Aldric roared, his sword cutting down another of Kaelen's men.

Gideon smirked through the chaos, his dagger already finding its next target. "Do I look like I'm running?" he called, twisting to avoid a strike before burying his blade in the attacker's side.

More enemies poured in from the treeline, but neither man gave ground.

"They just keep coming," Gideon muttered. "Any more brilliant ideas, Aldric?"

"Aye," Aldric growled, deflecting a blow with his shield. "Fight harder."

"You're a damn poet."

Every second they held Kaelen's men at bay was another second Tristan, Olivia, and Evelyne had to make it to Ravenshire.

"We can't let them through," Aldric snarled. "If Ravenshire falls, all's lost."

"I know," Gideon said grimly. "So, we don't let them through."

* * *

Olivia's chest heaved with every step as she and Evelyne half-dragged, half-carried Tristan through the trees.

"I can walk," Tristan murmured. "Just... let me try."

"No." Olivia's voice was fierce. "You've already done enough. Let us carry you now."

"She's right," Evelyne added sharply. "For once in your life, let someone else fight for you."

Tristan's lips curved faintly. "Bossy women... the bane of my existence."

"And your salvation," Olivia shot back, her grip tightening. "Now hush."

In the distance, the walls of Ravenshire loomed like a dark promise.

But behind them, Kaelen's men shouted—closer now.

"We're almost there!" Evelyne urged.

"Almost," Olivia whispered. "Hold on, Tristan. Just a little longer."

The night was heavy with mist as Olivia and Evelyne struggled under Tristan's weight, half-dragging, half-carrying him toward the gates of Ravenshire. Each labored breath he took sent a spike of panic through Olivia's chest.

"Stay with us, Tristan," Evelyne whispered sharply, her usually calm voice tight with fear.

"I'm fine..." he rasped, though his legs faltered beneath him.

"You're bleeding out," Olivia snapped, adjusting her grip under his arm. "You're not fine. Don't you dare collapse now."

"I can walk..." Tristan muttered, but his knees buckled again, forcing Evelyne and Olivia to catch him before he hit the ground.

The gates loomed ahead, torches flickering in the fog. Ravenshire's guards stirred uneasily at the sight of their lord—wounded, pale, and leaning heavily on the two women.

"Open the gates!" Evelyne barked, her voice sharp enough to break their hesitation.

"My lady—"

"NOW!"

The gates creaked open just as Tristan's legs gave way completely. Olivia and Evelyne managed to haul him forward, staggering under his weight.

"We're almost there," Olivia whispered to him, though her own arms trembled with exhaustion. "Just hold on a little longer."

Tristan's blue eyes fluttered open for a moment, catching Olivia's gaze.

"You... shouldn't have..." he murmured, voice weak but laced with the faintest smirk.

"Don't start with me," Olivia shot back. "You're going to make it. You're going to make it because I didn't come this far just to watch you die, your stubborn fool."

The courtyard erupted into chaos.

Evelyne's voice cut through the night air like a blade: "Knights of Ravenshire—to arms! Help Sir Aldric and Sir Gideon hold the line!"

At her command, half a dozen knights surged forward, their swords gleaming in the torchlight as they joined Aldric and Gideon in the fierce melee against Kaelen's men.

Aldric's blade struck down an opponent with a roar. "Hold fast! Don't let them through!"

Gideon darted past him, quick as a shadow, knives flashing as he took down a soldier creeping toward the keep's door.

"We're outnumbered!" Gideon shouted. "But not outmatched!"

Aldric gave a grim grin, sweat streaking his face. "Aye— but we need to give them time to get Tristan inside!"

Meanwhile, inside the keep, the women had sprung into action.

"Get my brother inside!" Evelyne called, her gown swirling as she helped push the heavy door open wider.

Two stable hands and an older matron rushed forward to assist, their faces pale but determined.

"Lift him carefully!" Evelyne ordered as they hoisted Tristan's limp and bloody form.

Olivia was at his side, refusing to let go of his hand as they carried him across the threshold.

"Stay with me, Tristan," she whispered fiercely. "Don't you dare leave me now."

Outside, Kaelen's soldiers roared, pressing forward.

"Break their line!" one of their captains shouted.

But the defenders of Ravenshire refused to yield.

Aldric cut down another man and growled to Gideon, "We're buying seconds here—not minutes!"

Gideon parried a blade and snarled back, "Then let's make every second count!"

As Tristan was laid gently on a table inside, Evelyne shouted, "Pull back! We've secured the keep—fall back to the gates!"

Aldric barked the order, and with a final push, he and Gideon fell back, slamming the smaller gates closed and barring them.

The courtyard fell eerily silent except for the ragged breathing of the defenders.

* * *

Olivia bent over Tristan, her hands stained red as she pressed cloth to his wound. "He's lost so much blood," she whispered.

His face was pale, a thin sheen of sweat clinging to his skin. Blood smeared over his torso. His shoulder wound was swollen and angry-looking, his back lacerated and the long gash along his ribs oozed fresh blood.

"He hasn't had food or water in—" Olivia's voice broke.

"Thirty-six hours at least," Evelyne murmured grimly. "We'll be lucky if he hasn't taken fever."

Gideon strode in, his eyes flicking to Tristan's pale face. "We bought the time. Let's not waste it."

The Great Hall had fallen silent after the chaos, but the tension still clung to the air like smoke.

Tristan's arm was slung across Aldric's shoulder as the knight and Gideon helped him up the stairs, his weight heavy but his will unbroken. Blood seeped into his breeches, and his jaw was tight with pain.

"Don't you dare faint on me, Tristan," Aldric muttered under his breath as they rounded the corner. "You're too damned heavy to drag."

Gideon smirked darkly. "If he collapses, we'll just roll him down the hall."

"I can still hear you," Tristan growled, his voice strained but defiant.

They pushed open the door to his chambers, the firelight inside flickering in welcome. Evelyne and Olivia were already waiting.

"Lay him here," Evelyne instructed, her voice calm but edged with worry.

They eased Tristan onto the bed, his frame tense as pain shot through his side.

Olivia knelt beside him, her fingers gentle. "Oh Tristan..."

"It's not as bad as it looks," he murmured, but his voice was weaker now, betraying the truth.

"Hush," Evelyne said sharply. "You're not here to speak. You're here to heal."

"Fetch water, lots of it. Warm and cold," Evelyne commanded. "And rags."

Old Martha shuffled into the room, carrying a basin of hot water and clean linens. "Stubborn fool," she muttered, setting down her supplies. "Always charging in like a wild beast. Now lie still before I knock you senseless."

Tristan smirked faintly. "I think the pain's doing that already."

"He's dehydrated. We have to get water into him, slowly."

Martha pressed a damp cloth to Tristan's cracked lips. "Just a little, my boy. Don't choke."

Olivia pressed a damp cloth to his wound, her eyes shimmering with unshed tears. "You scared me half to death, you know that?"

He reached for her hand, squeezing it weakly. "But I'm still here."

Evelyne took the lead on cleaning the gash under his ribs, carefully wiping away the grime and dried blood.

Tristan groaned weakly, trying to move away.

"Hold him still," Evelyne barked. "If we don't clean this, he'll rot from the inside."

"Tristan, listen to me," Olivia said gently, leaning close to his ear. "You have to let us do this. I'm here. It's all right now."

His eyes fluttered open for the briefest second, the blue dulled with exhaustion, but he gave the faintest nod.

Martha began stitching the deep slice across his shoulder while Olivia cleaned the lash marks on his back. Every touch made him flinch, his body rigid with pain.

When the worst was over, Olivia eased a spoon of water to his lips.

"Small sips," she whispered. "Don't try to swallow too fast."

Evelyne prepared a thin broth and helped Olivia coax him to take a few mouthfuls.

Tristan's voice was hoarse and faint. "Enough—"

"No," Olivia said firmly. "Not enough. You're staying alive for me, do you hear?"

While the women worked, Aldric and Gideon moved to the window, their eyes fixed on the courtyard below.

Kaelen and his men were preparing to leave, their cloaks snapping in the cold wind as they mounted their horses.

"Do you think they'll strike again?" Gideon asked quietly, his usual smirk absent.

Aldric's jaw tightened. "If they do, I'll cut them down before they even cross the gate."

"So will I." Gideon's hand brushed the hilt of his dagger. "But they'll come at us smarter next time. That Kaelen doesn't look like the sort to leave grudges behind."

"Then we'll be ready," Aldric said grimly.

Back at Tristan's side Olivia leaned closer, her voice soft but fierce. "You can't keep doing this, Tristan. You're not invincible."

Tristan's lips curved faintly. "Are you sure?"

Evelyne placed a reassuring hand on Olivia's shoulder. "He's alive, and that's all that matters for now."

Old Martha huffed as she wrung out another cloth. "If he doesn't rest, he won't stay alive for long."

"You heard her," Olivia murmured, brushing his damp hair from his forehead. "Rest. Please."

Tristan closed his eyes, his hand still gripping hers. "Only because you asked."

CHAPTER FIFTEEN

While Tristan recovered from his injuries, Aldric and Gideon took charge—plotting their next move to take back the Heart of Elander.

The two men met in Tristan's solar, the heavy wooden door locked tight behind them. Tristan slept fitfully in the adjoining chamber, his wounds still fresh and his strength slow to return.

"We can't wait for him," Aldric said bluntly, pacing the floor. "Every day we hesitate is another day Kaelen's and his men could move the Heart further out of reach."

Gideon lounged in a chair, boots propped on the edge of the table, swirling a goblet of wine. "You don't need to tell me that, old friend. But rushing headlong into their trap won't do us any good either."

Aldric's eyes narrowed. "Do you have a plan, or will you just sit there drinking?"

Gideon smirked. "Oh, I have a plan." His grin was sharp, wolfish, but his green eyes gleamed with deadly purpose.

"Listen carefully, Aldric," Gideon began, swirling the wine lazily. "Because if this goes wrong, we're all dead men—or worse."

Aldric stood with his arms crossed, his expression carved from stone. "I'm listening, Gideon. The Heart of

Elander—how exactly do you plan to steal it from under Kaelen's nose?"

Gideon smirked. "Simple. I don't."

Aldric's brow furrowed. "Then what are we doing?"

"We let Kaelen think he's won."

Aldric's eyes narrowed. "Explain."

"Kaelen's arrogance is his greatest weapon—and his greatest flaw," Gideon said smoothly, pacing in front of the flickering firelight. "He believes he's the only one who understands the Heart's power, the only one who knows how to unlock it. But he's wrong."

Aldric's jaw tightened. "And you're saying you know?"

"Better than him," Gideon said with a sly grin. "I've been gathering pieces of the puzzle for years. Old manuscripts, coded letters, even a drunk monk or two with loose tongues."

He leaned closer, lowering his voice. "The Heart isn't just hidden. It's protected—by a bond only true devotion can unlock."

"So how do you intend to get it?" Aldric asked, his voice tight.

Gideon's grin widened. "By letting Kaelen lead us right to it."

Aldric said, "You're playing a dangerous game, Cross."

"Dangerous games are the only one's worth playing," Gideon shot back smoothly. "He believes the Heart is his. He'll hold it up high for the world to see—"

Gideon's grin darkened. "And that's when we take it. Right from under his greedy little nose."

Aldric growled. "And what of Tristan? Olivia?"

"They're the key," Gideon said seriously now, the smirk fading. "The Heart will respond to them. Kaelen doesn't know that yet, but we can use it."

"And if you're wrong?" Aldric pressed.

Gideon chuckled. "Then I'll die spectacularly, and you can spend the rest of your days brooding about how wrong I was."

Aldric glared at him, but there was a flicker of reluctant respect in his eyes. "Fine, Cross. But if you betray us—"

Gideon smirked. "You'll gut me yourself. Yes, yes, I've heard it all before."

"Just remember," Aldric said coldly, "this isn't a game for us. This is Tristan's life. Olivia's. And the Order of the Silver Flame."

Gideon raised his goblet in mock salute. "Which is why we're going to win. A knight and a thief," Gideon mused, draining his cup. "We'll make quite the pair."

Aldric crossed his arms with a doubtful grunt.

Gideon's grin widened. "But for now, let's get your precious artifact back before Kaelen learns how to use it."

Aldric's dark eyes narrowed. "This isn't a jest, Cross. That artifact is the key to protecting Tristan—and Olivia. You know what will happen if we don't get it away from Kaelen."

"Oh, I know." Gideon leaned back in his chair lazily, but his green eyes gleamed with sharp intelligence. "That's why we need a plan that doesn't end with us in a shallow grave." Gideon said, his tone quiet but cutting. "You're not the only one who understands its value."

Aldric nodded grimly. "The Heart reacts to the amulets. That's why Tristan and Olivia must stay close. Their bond may be the only thing keeping it dormant for the moment."

"We'll need help," Aldric admitted. "And secrecy. If word gets out, we'll be swarmed before we ever find it."

"I know a few men who'll work for coin and keep their mouths shut," Gideon offered. "But it'll cost you."

"Tristan's life is worth any cost," Aldric replied without hesitation.

Gideon gave a low whistle. "Careful, Aldric. If you keep talking like that, people will think you have a heart under all that iron."

Aldric's lips twitched faintly. "And if you keep talking, Cross, people will think you don't."

"We leave at first light," Aldric said firmly. "We have to get the Heart back as quickly as possible."

Gideon drained the last of his wine and stood. "First light, then. But you'd better pray Tristan doesn't wake and find us gone."

"Tristan trusts me," Aldric replied. "You, on the other hand..."

Gideon's grin returned. "He trusts me enough to keep me close. That's all I need."

As they stepped from the table, the candle sputtered out—leaving the room in darkness and silence. But their plan was already in motion.

* * *

It was late when the knock came.

The fire crackled low in the hearth, casting warm light over the heavy stone walls of Tristan's chamber. He lay propped against a mound of pillows. His blue eyes remained sharp despite the exhaustion in his body. "Enter," he called.

Olivia sat nearby, her hand resting gently over his, her thumb tracing circles on his skin. Evelyne stood at the window, arms crossed, tension lining her face.

The door creaked open.

Aldric stepped in first, his expression as stern as ever, his boots heavy on the floor.

Gideon leaned casually against the frame with his usual infuriating grin.

"You're awake," Aldric said, his voice low. "Good. We need to talk."

"We've been talking," Gideon said, striding in without waiting for an invitation. "And we may have something you'll want to hear."

Aldric shut the door behind them, giving Evelyne a brief nod before turning his attention to Tristan.

Tristan arched a brow. "You're not here to tell me to rest?"

Gideon chuckled. "Oh, we would— we need you alive to finish what you started."

Evelyne's head snapped toward them. "You shouldn't be burdening him with—"

Tristan's voice cut her off, steady despite his pain. "Enough. Speak."

Aldric pulled a chair closer to the bed and sat heavily. "The Heart of Elander. We have to find where Kaelen hid it. We've got a plan."

Gideon leaned against the wall, arms crossed. "We're going to recover it. But we'll need Olivia."

Olivia blinked. "Me?"

"The Heart reacts to you," Aldric explained. "You and Tristan are... connected to it in ways we don't yet understand."

Evelyne stepped forward, her voice sharp. "You want to take her out there?"

Gideon smirked faintly. "Do you have a better idea, my lady? Or shall we sit here and wait for Kaelen and his men to come knocking?"

Tristan's jaw tightened as he listened, his hand flexing against Olivia's.

"This plan... it's dangerous."

"They're all dangerous," Gideon replied easily. "But this one gives us the advantage."

For a long moment, Tristan said nothing. His gaze drifted to Olivia, her green eyes wide but unflinching.

"You'd risk yourself for this?" he asked her softly.

Olivia nodded, her fingers tightening around his. "I'd do whatever it takes to get the Heart back—to protect you."

Tristan exhaled slowly, his voice deep and steady despite the storm in his chest. "Then I go too."

Aldric shook his head. "You're not ready."

"I don't care," Tristan growled. "You're not taking her anywhere without me."

Evelyne placed a hand on his shoulder. "Tristan—if you go in your condition, you'll be dead weight. Let them prepare. Let Olivia and I help them."

His jaw worked as though he wanted to argue, but finally he leaned back against the pillows, his blue eyes still burning with defiance. "Fine. But the moment I can stand—I ride with you."

Gideon's smirk returned. "Knew you'd say that."

* * *

Later that night, when Tristan and Olivia were alone, Olivia sat by the small fire in their chamber, staring at the amulet glowing faintly in her palm.

A sudden heat radiated from it—followed by a cold shiver that seeped deep into her bones.

And then it came.

A vision.

She saw the Heart's Flame—a once brilliant fire, now flickering weakly in a sea of shadows.

The flames sputtered as if struggling to stay alive. A dark force circled it, smothering its light little by little.

A voice whispered in her mind. "If the Heart dies... so too does the bond."

Olivia gasped, clutching the amulet as tears pricked her eyes.

She felt Tristan's arms around her in an instant. "Olivia? What did you see?"

"The Heart..." she whispered. "It's fading."

"Then we'll save it. Whatever it takes," Tristan whispered. His voice was steady, but she could feel the fear beneath it.

They both knew the Heart was more than magic—it was their link, their protector. And if it failed, all would be lost.

CHAPTER SIXTEEN

The night was heavy with tension as Aldric, Gideon, and Olivia slipped from the castle gates under the cover of darkness. The moon hung low, its pale light flickering through the branches like watchful eyes.

The Heart of Elander—They had no choice but to find it. Olivia's amulet pulsed, seeming to lead them deeper into the forest, toward the ruins of an old abbey, guarded by more than just time.

"So," Gideon whispered as they guided their horses along a narrow trail, "this little jaunt into the wilds—will we find glory, gold, or our heads on pikes?"

Aldric scowled. "If you're going to complain the entire way, I can arrange the last one."

Olivia tried not to laugh. "Do you two always bicker like this?"

Gideon shot her a grin. "Oh, no. Usually I'm much worse."

Aldric muttered under his breath, "Why did I agree to bring him along?"

As they neared the abbey ruins, the trees thickened, the air turning colder. Olivia's amulet began to hum faintly against her chest, a sign they were close.

"We're not alone," Aldric warned, his hand on his sword.

Shadows moved between the trees—bandits hired by Kaelen, no doubt.

"We don't have time for this," Gideon murmured, already drawing a dagger. "Want me to do this the loud way or the quiet way?"

Aldric frowned. "The quiet way, for once."

"You wound me," Gideon said, smirking as he slipped into the trees.

While Aldric guarded her, Olivia pressed her hand to the amulet. The closer they came, the warmer it grew, pulsing like a heartbeat.

"It's guiding us," she whispered.

Aldric nodded. "Then trust it. And stay behind me."

Moments later, Gideon reappeared, his tunic smudged with dirt but otherwise unscathed.

"Bandits are... sleeping now," he said with a wicked grin.

Aldric raised a brow. "Sleeping?"

"More or less."

"I don't want to know."

The abbey loomed before them—its crumbling stone walls draped in ivy, the air thick with an eerie stillness.

"This is it," Olivia murmured.

"Then let's find your Heart and get out," Aldric said, his tone sharp. "Before Kaelen finds us first."

"What's the worst that could happen?" Gideon asked with a smirk.

Aldric shot him a glare. "Stop saying things like that."

The old stone hall was cold and silent, the air thick with the scent of dust and something older... ancient.

Olivia's amulet pulsed faintly against her skin, glowing softly in the dim light as if urging her forward.

"We're close," she whispered, her breath visible in the chill.

"Close doesn't mean safe," Aldric murmured, his hand resting on the hilt of his sword. His eyes scanned the shadows, every muscle in his body tense.

Gideon followed behind, his usual smirk absent. "So this is where Kaelen hid it... I should've known."

"You know him?" Olivia asked, glancing back.

"Not well," Gideon replied, his voice low. "But a thief knows another thief. Kaelen didn't just hide things—he made sure no one else could find them."

The amulet's glow brightened as Olivia reached a crumbling stone wall. "It's here."

Aldric stepped forward, pressing his hand against the stones. "There's no door."

"Maybe not for you," Gideon said, kneeling to inspect the cracks. "But Kaelen loves his traps."

He pulled a dagger and ran the flat of the blade along the mortar, listening carefully. There—a hollow sound.

"Here," Gideon murmured. "Help me."

Together, Aldric and Gideon pushed against the stone. Slowly, with a groan of ancient mechanisms, a section of the wall shifted inward, revealing a narrow, winding passage.

The amulet in Olivia's hand flared, its light now strong and steady.

The air was heavier here, the walls lined with faded carvings.

"These are Kaelen's marks," Gideon whispered. "He left them as warnings."

Olivia traced one with her fingers—a circle within a circle, crossed with jagged lines.

"What do they mean?" she asked.

"That we should tread carefully," Aldric said grimly.

As they moved deeper, the glow of Olivia's amulet began to pulse faster, the light spilling across the stone floor.

"It's leading us straight to it," Olivia breathed.

"Or straight into a trap," Gideon muttered.

At the end of the passage stood a small stone pedestal. And there, resting in its center, was a crystalline orb, glowing faintly with a soft, inner light.

"The Heart..." Olivia whispered. She stepped forward, but Aldric's hand shot out, stopping her.

"Wait."

Gideon crouched, scanning the ground. "Kaelen wouldn't have left it unguarded."

"Traps?" Olivia asked.

"Always."

But her amulet's light grew so strong now it was almost blinding.

The air grew colder as Olivia stepped into the ancient stone corridor, the flickering torchlight keeping the oppressive darkness at bay. Each step echoed too loudly in the silence, and she clutched the amulet in her hand until her knuckles turned white.

The air felt... wrong.

It was as if the shadows themselves pressed against her skin, whispering in a language she didn't understand.

The amulet's surface burned hot in her palm, pulsing faintly like a heartbeat.

A faint sound caught her attention—like the scratch of nails on stone.

She froze. "Tristan...?" she whispered, though she knew he wasn't there.

The sound grew louder.

A voice hissed in her ear. "You do not belong here..."

Olivia spun, but there was no one behind her.

The torch flickered violently, then went out.

In the darkness, glowing runes began to appear on the walls—red as fresh blood.

The amulet grew hotter, and as Olivia raised it, a sudden gust of wind swept down the corridor, carrying with it the faint sound of laughter.

"Kaelen..." she murmured.

Suddenly, the runes flared brighter, and a figure materialized in front of her—a man draped in dark robes, his face hidden beneath a hood. His eyes glowed faintly red as he stepped forward, feet not quite touching the ground.

"You seek the Heart?" His voice was a low growl, like gravel scraping together.

Olivia's breath caught in her throat.

"It does not belong to you."

"And yet..." Olivia whispered, forcing her voice steady, "I'm here."

Kaelen raised a hand, and the air grew heavy. "If you want it... prove yourself."

The floor beneath her began to crack, stone splintering as black smoke poured through.

"What do you fear most, Olivia?" Kaelen hissed. "Shall I show you?"

The amulet burned like fire now. A voice—not Kaelen's—whispered in her mind: "Walk forward. Do not falter."

Olivia clutched it tightly and stepped into the swirling smoke.

Instantly, images assaulted her—Tristan, chained and bloodied; Evelyne screaming her name; flames consuming the world around her.

"This is your fate," Kaelen's voice echoed. "Turn back now... or be destroyed."

Olivia pressed the amulet to her chest, its light flaring outward in a brilliant golden glow.

"No." Her voice cracked but held firm. "You will not stop me."

Kaelen's figure let out an unearthly shriek as cracks spiderwebbed across the runes. The corridor shook violently, stones tumbling from above.

Olivia raised the amulet higher, its light flooding the darkness.

And then—silence.

Kaelen's figure dissolved into black mist, and the runes faded.

The air cleared. The corridor was whole again, as if nothing had happened.

Footsteps approached... and paused right outside the door.

Olivia's heart raced.

A chill. A whisper. A presence pressing at the edges of her mind.

"You cannot save him..."

She turned around, her breath catching in her throat.

The room was dark, but the faint outline of a figure lingered near the wall.

"You'll only bring ruin," the voice murmured, soft and cold like wind through a graveyard.

"Kaelen..." Olivia whispered.

The figure tilted its head, its eyes glowing faintly in the shadows. "He will fall, and you will watch."

"No," she whispered fiercely, clutching the amulet at her throat. "I won't let you."

A low, hollow laugh. "It has already begun."

And then—The figure dissolved into mist, leaving the room icy cold.

The moon hung low, pale and cold as Olivia wandered the dim corridors alone. The stone walls seemed to press inward, carrying a chill that had nothing to do with the night air. She clutched the amulet at her neck—it pulsed faintly, as though warning her.

"Olivia..."

The voice was little more than a whisper. Soft. Deceptive. Her breath hitched as the shadows at the end of the hall shifted, swirling like smoke.

237

Kaelen emerged from the darkness.

His figure wasn't solid—a phantom draped in shadows, his eyes like twin coals smoldering in an ashen face. The air grew heavier, and Olivia's pulse raced.

"Why do you fight it?" Kaelen murmured, stepping closer, though his boots made no sound on the stones. "You wear his amulet, yet you still don't understand, do you? It binds you as much as it binds him."

Olivia stumbled back, clutching the amulet tighter. "Stay away."

Kaelen tilted his head, almost pitying. "You're seeking answers, aren't you? But what will you do when you learn the truth? Will you still cling to him then?"

The torches on the wall flickered violently, their flames dancing as if caught in an unseen wind. The shadows deepened.

"What truth?" Olivia demanded, though her voice trembled.

Kaelen's mouth curved into a slow, cruel smile.

"The amulet chose him for a reason. But it didn't choose you."

"You're lying."

"Am I?" Kaelen's form shifted, becoming taller, darker, less human. "You think you've come here to save him... but tell me, Olivia—are you so sure you're not the one who needs saving?" He reached out for her.

Olivia tore herself from Kaelen's grasp, her heart pounding in her chest. His fingers slipped from her arm like icy tendrils, but his voice followed her as if carried on the air itself.

"You can run, Olivia," Kaelen murmured, his eyes glinting with an otherworldly fire. "But the threads of fate have already wrapped around you."

A strange pressure filled her head. Images flashed in her mind—too quick, too vivid to make sense of.

Tristan, kneeling in blood-soaked earth, his hand outstretched.

A tower crumbling into the sea.

The amulets—glowing like fire in the dark.

Her own reflection in a mirror... but her eyes were not her own.

And then Kaelen's whisper, deep and cold:

"Two paths lie before you, Olivia. One where you save him... and one where you destroy him."

A hand gripped her shoulder, snapping her back to reality.

"Olivia!" It was Aldric's voice—sharp, steady. "We have to move!"

Gideon was already pulling her down a side corridor, his dagger drawn. "Whatever he told you, forget it for now. He won't be the last thing trying to twist your mind."

Olivia's breath came in ragged gasps. "He... he showed me something."

Aldric frowned, his hand on her arm. "What did you see?"

But Olivia shook her head. "I... I don't know. It didn't make sense."

Gideon's eyes narrowed. "Visions never do—until it's too late."

As Aldric, Olivia, and Gideon dart out of the darkened abbey, the cold night air hit them like a slap. Their boots crunched over gravel, cloaks whipping around their legs as they sprinted toward the woods beyond.

Behind them, a sharp command echoed—Kaelen's voice.

"Stop them! Do not let them escape!"

Torches flared to life in the abbey courtyard as Kaelen's men gave chase, their armor clattering, boots pounding against the earth.

Olivia glanced back over her shoulder, her heart hammering in her chest.

"They're gaining on us!"

Aldric's jaw was set. "Keep moving. Don't look back!"

Gideon muttered under his breath, a dagger already in his hand. "This is why I hate abbeys."

Kaelen himself stepped into the courtyard, long dark robes flaring like wings, his voice low but carrying across the night.

"Bring me the woman alive. Kill the rest if you must."

Olivia's blood ran cold.

They reached the tree line just as arrows whistled through the air.

One struck a tree just inches from Olivia's shoulder, sending splinters flying.

Aldric yanked her forward. "Faster! We'll lose them in the woods!"

Gideon glanced back, his grin sharp even in the chaos. "I'll slow them down."

"Don't you dare," Aldric growled.

"Relax," Gideon said, tossing a small vial over his shoulder. It hit the ground and erupted in a sudden flash of light and smoke, startling Kaelen's men.

"Let's see them run through that."

The night was thick with mist as Aldric, Gideon, and Olivia fled through the narrow forest path, the sound of pounding hooves echoing behind them.

Kaelen and his men were gaining ground. Their war cries cut through the darkness like blades, sending shivers down Olivia's spine.

"Faster!" Aldric barked, his hand gripping the reins as his horse darted around a fallen tree.

"I am going faster," Gideon shot back from behind, his tone still maddeningly calm despite the danger. "Perhaps you should have picked better terrain for a chase, knight."

Olivia's heart raced. Her fingers clenched tightly to her reins. "Where are we even going?!"

"Away from Kaelen," Aldric growled. "That should suffice!"

But the sound of arrows slicing through the air silenced them all.

An arrow grazed Gideon's cloak, tearing the fabric.

"Cheeky bastards," Gideon muttered, twisting in his saddle to hurl a dagger at one of their pursuers. A cry of pain followed, and a rider fell.

"Less talk, more riding!" Aldric snapped. "We need to reach the river!"

Behind them, Kaelen's voice roared. "Don't let them escape! Bring me the girl alive—kill the rest!"

Olivia's stomach twisted. Her hands ached from clutching the reins, her hair whipping across her face in the cold wind.

"Why does he want me alive?!" she shouted over the sound of galloping hooves.

"Because you're valuable!" Gideon called back. "Try not to think about it too much."

Aldric glanced back, his face grim. "The river's up ahead. We can lose them in the current—if we make it that far."

Olivia's horse stumbled for half a heartbeat, and she let out a cry. Gideon was instantly at her side, steadying her mount.

"Focus, lass! You fall now, and Kaelen will have you before you can blink."

"I am focused!" she shot back, her voice tight with fear and determination.

At last, the roar of water filled their ears. The river.

Aldric didn't slow. "We cross here. Hold on tight!"

"You're insane!" Olivia cried.

"You'll thank me later!" Aldric shouted back.

One by one, they urged their horses into the rushing water. The current was strong, icy cold as it clawed at their boots and saddles.

Kaelen's men skidded to a halt at the riverbank, hesitating.

"Cowards! After them!" Kaelen bellowed.

But even he hesitated as he watched Aldric, Gideon, and Olivia disappear into the mist rising from the water.

They emerged, soaked and breathless, on the far bank.

Olivia slid from her horse, her legs shaking. "You... you're mad."

Aldric smirked, his dark hair plastered to his forehead. "Alive, aren't you?"

Gideon chuckled, wringing out his cloak. "Admit it, Olivia. You're having fun."

"Fun?" she glared at him. "I nearly drowned!"

"Nearly," Gideon said, his grin widening. "Not quite."

The air was tense, thick with the sound of distant hoofbeats echoing in the dark forest.

Kaelen was relentless.

His men swept the woods with ruthless efficiency, torches blazing as they moved in a wide arc. "Find them," Kaelen barked. "Leave no stone unturned. If she escapes again, you'll wish the enemy's sword had taken you first."

He wanted Olivia alive.

But Aldric and Gideon? He wasn't as particular.

* * *

The trio ducked into a narrow ravine, their breath coming in shallow gasps.

"We can't keep running forever," Gideon muttered, his voice low but sharp. "Kaelen's not a man who gives up."

Aldric turned to him, eyes like steel. "We don't need forever. We need a plan."

Olivia pressed a hand over her racing heart, the amulet at her neck pulsing with faint warmth. "He's close. I can feel it."

Aldric glanced around, scanning the dark forest. "There's an old hunting lodge a mile north. If we can reach it, we might hold him off long enough for reinforcements to arrive."

"Or for him to box us in," Gideon countered.

"Do you have a better idea?" Aldric snapped.

"I never said I did." Gideon's smirk was grim. "I just hope you're better at defending a position than running from one."

"Quiet," Olivia whispered sharply. "We're losing time."

The hunting lodge was a rugged stone structure, small but sturdy, built long ago for royal hunts. It sat nestled in a clearing, surrounded by towering pines and a narrow stream.

"We don't have much time," Aldric said. "Get inside. Bar the doors."

Olivia hesitated. "And you?"

"I'll set traps," Gideon said. "They'll regret following us this far."

She nodded, her heart pounding, and disappeared into the lodge as Gideon moved swiftly, his boots crunching over frosted leaves.

He worked methodically—placing snares near the tree line, preparing buckets of oil near the entrance, and checking his bowstring.

Inside the lodge Olivia lit the hearth, the orange glow spreading warmth and light through the small room.

She found a hunting knife in a drawer and gripped it tight. Her hands trembled, but her jaw was set. "I won't let them take me alive," she whispered to herself.

A loud knock made her jump.

It was Gideon, pushing through the door. His hair was windswept, his cloak dusted with frost. "It's done," he said. "We're ready."

"How many do you think are coming?" Olivia asked.

"Too many," Aldric replied, sliding his sword from its sheath to check the edge. "But if we're clever, we might thin their numbers before they reach us."

Olivia touched the amulet around her neck. It was warm again—thrumming faintly. "Maybe it can help us."

Outside—shadows approached. The sound of hoofbeats grew louder. Torches flickered in the distance as Kaelen and his men closed in.

Aldric stepped into the doorway, his silhouette outlined by firelight. "Let them come," he murmured. "They'll find more than they bargained for."

The tension inside the hunting lodge was thick as smoke.

The dim light of the fire flickered over Aldric's hardened face as he peered out the door, hand resting on the hilt of his sword. Across the room, Olivia knelt beside Gideon, who was quietly laying out a series of small traps and tripwires on the floor—his usual cocky grin replaced with sharp focus.

"They're close," Aldric murmured.

Gideon didn't look up as his nimble fingers tightened a snare. "Good. Let's make them feel it too."

Olivia glanced between the two men. "How many are there?"

"Kaelen doesn't move with fewer than a dozen," Aldric replied grimly. "We're outnumbered."

Gideon smirked. "We're not outsmarted."

He set the last tripwire, hiding it beneath a rug, and rose to his feet. "By the time Kaelen's men realize what's happening, they'll be choking on their own mistakes."

In the forest beyond, Kaelen's men moved like shadows between the trees.

Kaelen raised a hand, signaling for silence.

"They're here," one of his scouts whispered.

Kaelen's lips curled into a predatory smile. "Good. We take the girl alive. Kill the rest."

Olivia tightened her grip on the small dagger Gideon had handed her. "What happens when they breach the door?"

"We don't let them get that far," Aldric said flatly.

Gideon chuckled low in his throat. "And if they do, they'll be limping out with fewer teeth."

He leaned closer to Olivia, his green eyes gleaming mischievously. "If we get out of this, remind me to teach you how to set one of these traps. You'd be dangerous."

Olivia smirked despite herself. "And if we don't get out of this?"

"Then I'll haunt Kaelen personally."

A sharp snap and a scream cut through the night.

"What was that?!" one of Kaelen's men shouted as a spiked snare clamped onto his leg, dragging him into the underbrush.

Gideon grinned, peering out the window. "One down."

Aldric grunted. "Don't get cocky."

Aldric's hand tightened around the hilt of his sword. "We hold here," he said firmly, planting his feet like a rooted oak. "We retreat now, and they'll run us down."

Gideon smirked, though his eyes stayed sharp. "I was hoping you'd say that. I'd hate to run and miss all the fun."

He flipped his dagger in his hand, light catching the edge. "Besides, the lady here fights well enough. Don't you, Olivia?"

Olivia's fingers brushed the amulet at her neck before wrapping around the hilt of her small blade. Her pulse thrummed, but her eyes were steady. "I'll do what I must."

The first of Kaelen's soldiers came at the hut—five, then six, then more, blades drawn and eyes glinting with anticipation.

"There they are!" one barked.

Aldric's jaw tightened. "Shields up. Don't let them break the line."

Gideon grinned, stepping forward just enough to whisper, "Try not to die too fast. I hate fighting alone."

Aldric shot him a sharp look. "You don't fight alone. Not today."

Olivia exhaled, planting her feet beside them. "Then we hold."

The front of the hut was chaos.

Screams echoed off stone walls as blood stained the ground. The clash of steel rang out in every direction, firelight flickering across terrified faces and fallen bodies.

Aldric stood at the center, his sword dripping red, his stance wide and unyielding. His armor was dented, his breath coming hard, but his eyes burned with determination.

"Hold the line!" he roared, cutting down an enemy soldier who had broken through.

To his left, Gideon moved like a shadow. Where Aldric was force, Gideon was precision—daggers flashing, his movements so quick they were almost a blur. He ducked under a blade, drove his dagger upward, and sent a man crumpling to the ground.

"We can't keep this up forever!" Gideon shouted, his voice laced with a grin despite the blood on his face. "Any grand strategies, Aldric?"

"Don't die," Aldric growled back. "That's the strategy."

Olivia stood behind them, her hair wild, her dress torn, but her grip on the dagger was firm.

She had not been trained like them, but desperation had a way of sharpening instincts.

An enemy lunged for her, and she stepped aside, slashing out. The blade connected, and the man fell.

Her stomach churned, but she swallowed the fear.

"They just keep coming!" she cried.

"And we keep sending them to the grave," Gideon said grimly, pulling his blade free from another foe.

Suddenly, a horn sounded in the distance.

Both friend and foe hesitated.

"Reinforcements?" Olivia asked, her voice tight with hope.

Aldric's eyes narrowed. "Or a worse nightmare."

The attackers surged forward again.

"We hold this ground!" Aldric shouted. "We don't give them one step more!"

Gideon glanced at Olivia. "Think you can handle another round, my lady?"

Her jaw tightened. "I have to."

"That's the spirit." Gideon smirked, then turned and hurled a dagger, catching another man between the eyes.

"For Tristan," Aldric growled, raising his sword. "We fight for him."

"And for us," Olivia said, her voice steady now. "We fight for us."

The wind clawed at the rotted shutters of the old hunting lodge as Aldric slid the iron bolt across the door. Dust hung thick in the air, stirred by their ragged breaths. Olivia crouched near the hearth, clutching her knife and a rusted poker like a sword. Gideon knelt at the window, peering through a crack in the boards.

Gideon whispered, his voice tight. "Kaelen's banner... a black raven."

Footsteps crunched on the frost-bitten leaves outside. A man barked a sharp command. Hounds snarled in the distance.

Aldric drew his dagger. "We hold this line."

Olivia shook her head. "We may have to run."

The sound of Kaelen's voice slashed through the cold. Calm. Mocking. "Give me the lady... and I'll let the others live."

Aldric met Olivia's eyes — a flicker of steel beneath the fear. "We don't surrender. We don't break."

Outside, boots began to circle the lodge. One man struck the door with the flat of his sword.

Aldric leaned close to Olivia, voice low. "If it comes to it... you run. Gideon and I will buy you what time we can."

Olivia's grip tightened. "I'm not leaving you."

Gideon slid his sword free. "Then we make them bleed for every step."

The wind fell silent.

The door shuddered. Kaelen watched the crooked lodge from the shadows beneath the trees, his gloved hands resting lightly on the hilt of his sword. The place reeked of desperation — a hunter's shack fit for cowards and cornered prey. His men fanned out at his silent signal, steel whispering from scabbards.

Fools. Did they think rotting walls would stop me?

A hound snarled at the scent of blood. Kaelen smirked. They were close.

He strode forward, boots sinking into the damp moss. "Give me the lady," he called, voice smooth as ice, "and I'll let the others live."

Silence answered. Predictable. He heard them shifting inside — scraping furniture, bolting doors. The sharp, shallow breaths of the hunted.

Cowards always hesitate before dying.

He gave the order with a flick of his fingers. Men encircled the lodge, blades drawn. One slammed the door with the flat of his sword — a little warning.

Kaelen stepped closer. "You have until I count to three."

He listened. Waited. The air inside was thick with fear. He could almost taste it.

"One."

He imagined Aldric stiffening — *the loyal lapdog.* Gideon gripping his sword with trembling hands. And the lady... *Olivia. Would she plead? Would she beg?*

"Two."

Still nothing.

He let a cold smile curve his lips. "Three."

He nodded once. The battering ram struck the door. Wood cracked — and Kaelen intended to savor every moment before the walls fell.

The first slam cracked the doorframe. The second blew the door inward. Kaelen's men surged forward with a roar— steel flashing, boots hammering the floorboards.

Kaelen hung back in the threshold, watching. The smart men let their soldiers rush first. Aldric met them head-on, driving a dagger into the throat of the first man through the door. Gideon was there a heartbeat later, sword carving a brutal arc.

Two of Kaelen's men fell before they crossed the threshold.

Kaelen's lip curled. *So. They have teeth after all.*

He drew his sword, the polished steel black against the snow light. He stepped inside.

The fight was raw, close — bodies grappling in the choking dust. Aldric slammed a man against the hearth, cracking skull against stone. Gideon locked swords with another, sweat flying.

Kaelen moved through it like a shadow.

Then he saw her.

Olivia stood by the far wall, eyes wide, clutching that ridiculous poker like a weapon. Her hair tumbled loose, face pale—but her hands didn't shake. Not yet.

Their eyes locked.

Kaelen felt a slow, dark satisfaction curl in his chest. *There you are.*

He stalked toward her, boots scraping blood across the floorboards.

"Run," Aldric snarled behind him—shouting at her.

But Kaelen was faster.

He caught her wrist in a gloved hand, twisting the poker from her grip. It clattered to the floor. "No more running," he whispered.

And for one heartbeat—just one—he thought she might scream.

But Olivia met his eyes and slammed her knee into his ribs. Hard.

Kaelen staggered back with a snarl, Olivia's knife scraping his arm.

So... not a damsel after all.

His grin sharpened. "Good," he said softly. "I do so hate when they don't fight back."

The sharp bloom of pain from Olivia's knee faded as Kaelen caught her arm again, harder this time. He wrenched her against him, steel sliding to her throat.

Around them, the fight raged — Gideon cursing, Aldric roaring — but Kaelen let it all blur into background noise. He could feel her heartbeat, fast against his grip.

"You'll come with me," he murmured at her ear, "or I'll start with them."

She glared at him, lips parted in something between a snarl and a breathless curse. *Brave. Stupid.*

Aldric surged forward — but Kaelen dragged Olivia between them like a shield. "Move," Kaelen warned, "and I'll cut her deep enough she'll wear the scar for life."

Aldric froze. Gideon hesitated.

Kaelen leaned closer to her. "You wanted to play hero?" His breath ghosted her cheek. "Let's see how far you're willing to go."

He hauled her backward, toward the open door. His men closed in, blades at the ready. One tried to seize Gideon — the sound of steel and bone rang out as Gideon fought him off.

255

Kaelen didn't care. The others could die. The girl was the prize.

The cold air hit them as he dragged her over the threshold, the wind lifting her hair like a banner. She twisted once, a sharp, desperate move — nails scraping his wrist.

Kaelen slammed her hard against the doorframe. Not enough to break her — just enough to take the fight out.

Her breath hitched. But she didn't scream.

His mouth curled in something dark. "Good girl."

Behind them, Aldric's shout echoed — Gideon's blade struck something hard — and still Kaelen smiled.

Let them fight. Let them bleed.

Because tonight, the lady was his.

Kaelen's grip never loosened as he dragged Olivia across the frozen clearing. His men fell in step, flanking them with drawn swords, eyes darting toward the lodge where Aldric and Gideon still fought like cornered wolves.

The horse waited, black and restless, steam curling from its nostrils. Kaelen hauled Olivia forward.

"Mount," he ordered.

She jerked against him, planting her feet in the frozen ground. "I'd rather die."

Kaelen slammed her back against the saddle, pinning her with one hand. "That can be arranged."

She glared up at him, chest rising fast. But he saw it—the flicker of fear behind her defiance. The tremble she tried to hide.

Kaelen leaned closer. "You'll come with me... or I'll let my men have you first."

Her eyes flashed with pure hatred.

Kaelen smirked. There it was. Hate was easier to mold than fear. Hate made people reckless.

He seized her arm and shoved her foot into the stirrup. She struggled—clawed at his coat—but he lifted her like she weighed nothing.

"Get her up!" he barked at a soldier.

One of his men caught her waist and tried to hoist her. Olivia lashed out—elbow to the man's face. He cursed, staggering back.

Kaelen's temper snapped. He yanked her forward by the collar of her coat and slammed her against the saddle horn.

"You'll ride," he hissed, "or I'll break your legs and drag you behind me."

The words hung in the cold, ugly and real.

For the first time, Olivia went still.

Kaelen gave her a thin, satisfied smile. He reached for the reins—

And that's when the arrow struck the ground inches from his boot.

Kaelen froze. His head snapped up.

From the shadows of the trees... Tristan stepped forward. Bow in hand. Expression carved from stone.

"Let her go," Tristan said, his voice low and dangerous. "Now."

Kaelen's head turned slowly toward the voice.

Tristan stood at the edge of the trees, bow raised, another arrow already nocked. His eyes—*those damned silver-flame eyes*—burned with a quiet, deadly calm.

Kaelen felt his grip on Olivia tighten before he realized it.

Of course. Of course, Tristan would crawl out of the shadows like some righteous spirit.

Kaelen bared his teeth in a sharp smile. "You should've stayed dead."

Tristan didn't move. "Let her go."

Kaelen's mind raced — calculating distance, his men's positions, the half-drawn bow. He could put Olivia on the horse, use her as a shield, make a run for it—

Another arrow slammed into the ground at his other boot.

"Now," Tristan said, voice like ice splitting stone.

Kaelen felt the stares of his men shifting — waiting. Watching. *Even the damned horse seemed to sense the change in the air.*

And for one blistering heartbeat... Kaelen hesitated.

But then his rage coiled tight in his chest.

He shoved Olivia toward his nearest soldier and drew his sword in the same breath. "Kill him!"

The arrow struck one of Kaelen's men. It buried itself in the soldier's throat before the man could even shove Olivia aside.

Kaelen spun. "Form up!"

But Tristan was already moving — a blur of black and silver crashing through Kaelen's line like a hammer. He dropped the bow, drawing steel in one smooth motion.

The first soldier lunged. Tristan's sword opened him from shoulder to hip.

The second didn't even have time to scream.

Kaelen's men broke formation, some rushing Tristan, some hesitating — *fools! Always fools!*

Kaelen surged forward, catching Olivia by the arm again, yanking her back toward the horse. He saw her twist, saw the flash of metal in her hand—

She drove a knife into his forearm.

Kaelen hissed, fury igniting white-hot. He struck her across the face with the back of his hand, sending her sprawling.

He didn't see the next arrow until it tore past his ear.

Kaelen spun in time to catch Tristan's sword on his own. The impact jolted up his arms, rattling bone.

"Should've killed you myself," Kaelen snarled.

Tristan's eyes were dead calm. "You'll wish you had."

Kaelen struck again—hard, brutal. The clash of swords rang across the clearing.

Tristan met every blow with cold, practiced precision, forcing Kaelen back step by step. The kind of skill Kaelen's men whispered about when they thought he couldn't hear. The kind of skill Kaelen hated.

Around them, his soldiers fell—one after another. Gideon cut down two by the lodge. Aldric slammed a man's head into a tree trunk with a savage roar.

Kaelen fought harder. Desperation licked at the edge of his rage. *No! This isn't how it ends!*

He drove Tristan back with a flurry of strikes—but Tristan didn't falter. His sword caught Kaelen's across the guard—and with a brutal twist, ripped it from Kaelen's hand.

Kaelen staggered.

And Tristan's blade kissed his throat.

For the first time that night... Kaelen froze.

Tristan's voice dropped, low and lethal. "Touch her again... and I'll make sure you don't leave this forest breathing."

The clearing fell silent.

Kaelen stared into those silver-flame eyes—fury boiling beneath his skin. But beneath that... the first whisper of something colder.

Fear.

Kaelen held Tristan's gaze, his mind racing. He could feel the bite of the sword at his throat, the sharp burn of his own blood trickling down his arm.

He forced a slow smirk. "You won't kill me."

Tristan's blade pressed a fraction deeper. "Try me."

And in that heartbeat—Kaelen moved.

His free hand shot toward his belt dagger, a flash of steel aimed straight for Tristan's gut—

Tristan caught his wrist mid-strike.

The bones in Kaelen's arm ground together with a sickening crack as Tristan twisted. Kaelen snarled—then gasped when Tristan wrenched the dagger from his grip and drove the hilt of his sword straight into Kaelen's ribs.

Pain exploded in his chest. Kaelen dropped to one knee, the breath ripped from his lungs.

But Tristan wasn't done.

He stepped in, grabbed Kaelen by the collar, and slammed him face-first into the frozen earth.

Hard.

The world spun. Kaelen tasted blood and dirt.

Tristan's boot pinned him down, blade still at his neck. "I said... don't touch her again."

Kaelen clawed at the ground, gasping. "You... don't have the guts..."

Tristan leaned lower, voice like gravel. "Next time, I don't leave you breathing."

And then—he was gone.

Kaelen lifted his head in time to see Tristan turn his back on him... and walk toward Olivia.

Kaelen lay in the dirt, fury coiling in his gut, breath shallow, ribs screaming—

But alive.

For now.

Kaelen's face was twisted with rage and humiliation. His attempt to kidnap Olivia had failed—spectacularly. He had underestimated Tristan, and now he was paying the price.

Kaelen spat to the side, blood streaking his lip. "This isn't over, Tristan."

"It is tonight," Tristan said coldly.

Kaelen's glare shifted to Olivia, who stood by Tristan.

"You'll regret this, girl," he hissed, his voice venomous. "I'll see you both ruined."

Tristan's jaw clenched. "Say her name again, and I'll cut out your tongue."

Kaelen's smirk returned, bitter and vengeful. "You may have won this fight, knight, but the game isn't finished. Next time, I won't be so careless."

Tristan kicked Kaelen's sword across the dirt. "Next time, you won't leave alive."

Kaelen staggered to his feet, clutching his wounded arm. "Enjoy your victory, Tristan. It's the last you'll have."

And with that, he disappeared into the shadows of the forest, leaving only the promise of revenge in his wake.

Olivia exhaled shakily as Tristan turned back to her.

"Are you, all right?" His voice softened, though the edge of battle still clung to it.

She nodded, but her eyes flicked to the darkness where Kaelen had vanished. "He'll be back."

Tristan sheathed his blade, stepping closer to her. "Then we'll be ready."

He brushed his fingers against her cheek, his gaze steady. "I won't let anyone take you from me, Olivia. Not him. Not anyone."

She reached for his hand, gripping it tightly. "And I won't let you face him alone."

For a moment, the world was quiet around them—save for the promise of danger lingering in Kaelen's parting words.

The clearing had gone quiet once more. The echo of Kaelen and his men's departure lingered like a faint shadow.

Tristan stood tall despite the wound still aching in his side, one hand resting casually on the hilt of his sword. Olivia was at his side, her brow furrowed in equal parts worry and irritation.

The snap of twigs behind them drew their attention. Aldric and Gideon stepped out from the tree line, their cloaks swirling around them like trailing shadows.

"By the saints, Tristan—" Aldric's voice was low and sharp. "What in the devil are you doing out here? We left you in your bed!"

Tristan smirked faintly. "Beds are for the wounded. I'm only a little inconvenienced."

Aldric crossed his arms, his jaw tightening. "You were half dead this morning."

"Half dead, but whole now," Tristan replied smoothly, though Olivia could see the faint sheen of sweat on his brow.

Gideon chuckled, stepping closer with a cocky grin. "I should've known you wouldn't stay put. I told Aldric you were as stubborn as a warhorse."

"And yet you still sound surprised to find me standing," Tristan said dryly.

Olivia's hands went to her hips. "Tristan de Léon, you are impossible."

Tristan turned to her, his blue eyes glinting with amusement. "So you keep saying."

She huffed, brushing a stray curl behind her ear. "You should be resting. If that wound tears open—"

"Then you'll patch me up again." His tone softened. "You always do."

Olivia's glare faltered just slightly, her lips twitching with reluctant affection.

Aldric stepped closer, his voice dropping. "You tracked Kaelen and his men alone?"

Tristan's smirk faded, replaced with a steely resolve. "No. I tracked them with purpose."

Gideon raised a brow. "And how, pray tell, did you find us? You're not exactly light on your feet with that injury."

Tristan's lips curved into a knowing smile. "The amulet."

Olivia blinked. "It led you here?"

Tristan nodded. "It pulses when I'm near you. When you're in danger, it's as if it pulls me forward."

Olivia's hand drifted to the amulet around her neck, her heart pounding. "It... brought you to me."

"Always." Tristan's voice was quiet, but the weight of his promise settled over them like a warm cloak.

"How romantic," Gideon said with a mock sigh. "I almost feel bad for interrupting."

Tristan shot him a sharp look. "Almost?"

Gideon grinned. "Almost."

Aldric shook his head with a long-suffering sigh. "You'll be the death of us all, Tristan."

"Better me than her." Tristan's voice was calm, but unshakable. "And you'd do the same."

Aldric fell silent, conceding the point. "Let's go home," he said,

CHAPTER SEVENTEEN

In the morning after a good rest, the four of them gathered in the solar, a fire crackling low in the hearth. Outside, the wind howled against the stone walls, but within, the air was thick with tension.

Tristan leaned over the table, his hands braced against the wood as he studied the map spread before them.

"The abbey lies here," he said, tracing the route with a gloved finger. "It's in ruins, but that's where Kaelen has hidden the Heart. Kaelen's influence will make it more dangerous than any battlefield."

Olivia shivered, the amulet around her neck warm against her skin. "It's calling to us," she whispered. "Even now, I can feel it."

Gideon, lounging casually in a chair, swirled his goblet of wine. "Let's not pretend this will be a simple walk in the woods. Kaelen's evil seeps through that place like rot through an apple. He draws power from the Heart—and he'll know the moment we set foot near it."

Tristan's jaw tightened. "Then we will be swift. We take only who we trust, we move under cover of darkness, and we get out before Kaelen has time to rally his forces."

"Or before the Heart turns on you," Gideon muttered.

Olivia shot him a glare. "You think we should leave it in his hands? How long before Kaelen uses its power to destroy the rest of the realm?"

Gideon smirked. "Oh, I don't doubt we need it. I'm just saying—don't get yourself killed over it. Or worse, possessed."

Aldric nodded grimly. "The abbey was said to be a place of holy power. If Kaelen has corrupted it, then the Heart may already be twisted too."

Tristan reached for Olivia's hand, gripping it firmly. "We have no choice. If Kaelen has even a fraction of the Heart's power, there will be no stopping him."

Olivia met his gaze, her resolve hardening. "Then we go together."

"Together," Tristan agreed.

Gideon drained his goblet and rose, flashing them a wolfish grin. "Well then, my lord and lady, let's plan this little suicide mission properly. I do enjoy a challenge."

Aldric sighed. "Challenge or not, we'll need every ounce of skill and luck to make it out alive."

And so, they began to plot—unaware that even now, Kaelen felt their pull on the Heart and was preparing for their arrival.

* * *

Evelyne leaned against the heavy oak door, her arms crossed as she listened to Tristan and Olivia and the others whispering in the dim glow of the candlelight.

"You're serious about this?" Evelyne's voice was low, though her sharp eyes betrayed her unease.

Tristan nodded. "We don't have a choice. The answers are at the abbey. If the amulets are to be understood—and if we're to stay one step ahead of Kaelen—we must go."

Olivia glanced at Evelyne. "Come with us. We could use you."

But Evelyne shook her head firmly. "No." Her voice was steady, but her jaw tightened. "You'll be moving fast, drawing attention. Someone must remain here to temper suspicion at court. If I vanish with you, Kaelen will know you're up to something."

Tristan frowned. "You'll be in danger staying."

Evelyne offered him a small smile. "I can handle a den of vipers, brother. You forget who taught you to watch for poison."

Tristan's lips twitched, but the worry in his blue eyes lingered. "Very well."

"We'll ride at first light. The abbey lies to the east, through the Blackwood."

Olivia traced her finger over the winding path. "The Blackwood?"

"Dense forest," Tristan replied. "Few dare travel it anymore, but it will keep us hidden."

Gideon appeared in the doorway with his usual roguish grin. "Sounds like fun. Shall I pack the wine and a deck of cards?"

Tristan arched a brow. "You're not coming."

"Oh, I think I am." Gideon sauntered in. "You'll need someone to sniff out trouble before it bites."

Tristan gave him a withering glare, but Olivia smirked. "He has a point."

Evelyne groaned. "You're all mad."

* * *

The next morning, the air was crisp as Tristan, Olivia, Aldric and Gideon led their horses through the misty courtyard, boots quiet against the cobblestones. The soft clinking of bridles and the low rumble of hooves filled the air as Tristan swung easily into his saddle, his eyes scanning the gates ahead. Olivia adjusted her gloves, trying to quiet the butterflies in her stomach.

"Keep to the shadows," Tristan murmured. "If anyone asks, we're out on a hunt."

Gideon muttered under his breath, "A hunt for trouble, more like."

Evelyne stood at the castle gates, her cloak drawn tightly around her shoulders.

Aldric approached her. "Evelyne," he said in that steady, low voice of his.

She turned, her brow arching slightly. "Yes?"

Without another word, he reached out and cupped the back of her neck, pulling her to him for a firm, lingering kiss. The world seemed to pause for a heartbeat—Evelyne stiffened in surprise before melting just slightly into him, her hand resting on his arm.

When he finally pulled back, a rare smirk curved his lips. "For luck," he murmured. "And because I've been thinking about that all morning."

Evelyne blinked at him, trying to hide the faint flush creeping up her neck.

"You're shameless," she said softly. But there was no real bite in her tone.

Aldric's grin widened. "Only with you."

Tristan cleared his throat from atop his horse, his voice dry but amused. "If you're finished making the rest of us uncomfortable, Aldric..."

Aldric chuckled and strode back to his horse, mounting with effortless ease.

Evelyne shook her head with a faint smile, whispering to herself, "Reckless man..."

As the group rode out together, there was a different energy in the air—a little lighter, even with the danger ahead.

"Return alive." Her voice was soft but carried a command Tristan and Aldric couldn't ignore.

He inclined his head. "You have my word."

Evelyne's gaze shifted to Olivia. "And yours, lady?"

Olivia nodded. "We'll bring him back."

Evelyne smirked faintly. "Good. I'd hate to see the court without its favorite scandal."

* * *

The early afternoon sun streamed through the thinning clouds as Tristan, Olivia, Aldric, and Gideon rode side by side, the sound of hooves thumping against the dirt road that wound through rolling fields and woodlands.

"Do you always ride this stiffly?" Gideon called over to Olivia, his tone rich with amusement as he leaned lazily in his saddle.

Olivia shot him a glare. "I've only recently learned, in case you've forgotten. And I think I'm doing rather well."

"For someone who nearly fell off last time, I suppose so," Gideon teased with a smirk.

"She's doing perfectly fine," Tristan cut in firmly, though the faintest curve of a smile touched his lips. "Not everyone was born in a saddle like you, Cross."

"True," Gideon said with a mock bow from his horse, "but I'd wager I still ride better than you."

"Careful," Aldric warned, though his deep voice rumbled with humor. "You're not half as charming as you think you are, Gideon."

"But twice as handsome," Gideon quipped.

"Debatable," Olivia muttered under her breath, earning a soft chuckle from Tristan.

"So, my lady," Gideon continued with a sly grin, "shall we wager on who arrives first at the abbey? I say Aldric and I will leave you two in the dust."

Olivia raised a brow. "You think you can outpace Tristan?"

Tristan turned slightly in his saddle, giving Gideon a sharp, confident smirk. "Try it and see."

"Oh no," Aldric interjected, his voice even and calm as always, "I'm not joining this foolishness. If you and Gideon want to race, do it without me."

"You spoil all my fun, Aldric," Gideon sighed dramatically. "But very well—Tristan, a race then? Unless you're afraid Olivia will weigh you down."

Olivia gasped in mock offense. "Weigh him down?" She turned to Tristan, her eyes sparkling. "Show him, Tristan. I'd like to see his face when we pass him."

Tristan smirked, leaning close enough that Olivia could feel his breath. "Hold tight, then."

In a flash, Tristan's horse surged forward. Gideon yelped in surprise before urging his own mount after them, spurring it hard.

"You cheat, de Léon!" Gideon roared with laughter as dust flew up around them.

Olivia laughed so hard she nearly lost her grip. "Faster, Tristan!"

"As my lady commands," Tristan growled, his grin widening as his horse ate up the distance.

Behind them, Gideon howled with outrage. "You'll pay for this, I swear!"

Aldric's deep voice rumbled behind them like thunder. "Idiots, all of you."

By the time they reached the abbey, Tristan's horse slowed to a steady trot, Olivia's laughter still echoing across the courtyard.

"You should've seen Gideon's face," she said between gasps. "I think he might still be choking on our dust."

Tristan chuckled low in his throat. "Satisfying, wasn't it?"

"It was perfect," she admitted, her smile softening as her eyes met his.

Behind them, Gideon finally arrived, brushing dirt off his sleeve with exaggerated care. "Enjoy your little victory, my lord. Next time, I'll leave you both in the dirt."

"You'll need a faster horse," Tristan replied smoothly.

Aldric dismounted quietly, shaking his head. "You'll draw attention with your antics. Try to remember we're here for a reason."

Tristan gave him a small nod. "I know."

But as he glanced at Olivia, still smiling in the golden light, he couldn't help but think...*perhaps a little laughter was worth the risk.*

* * *

The bones of the old abbey rose black against a bruised sky, arches broken like the ribs of some fallen beast. Ivy strangled what was left of the cloister walls, and wind hissed through the empty window frames, a mournful sound that prickled Olivia's skin.

Tristan stood a few paces ahead, lantern in hand. His sword was strapped to his hip, but his hand hovered near the hilt. His eyes—sharpened by nights in darker places—swept the shadows between the columns.

The great wooden doors groaned as Tristan pushed them open. Inside, the air was cool and damp, heavy with the scent of moss and old stone.

Candles—long burned down to nubs—lined the walls, and fractured sunlight poured through cracked stained glass, painting the floor in shards of muted color.

"This place..." Olivia murmured, her voice almost reverent. "It feels alive."

Tristan's jaw tightened. "Or haunted."

The amulets they wore seemed to hum in unison, guiding them down the aisle, past crumbling pews and broken statues.

"This way," Tristan said. "It's pulling us forward."

They moved cautiously, their footsteps echoing in the nave.

They reached the chancel where the altar had once been—now a jagged slab split by time. Moss grew thick in the cracks. Olivia pressed her palm to the cold stone, eyes scanning the wall.

"There's a seam," she breathed. "Gideon found it yesterday." Somewhere deeper within lay the Heart of Elander—the crystal of legend said to awaken powers long forgotten.

Tristan knelt beside her, running a gloved hand along the faint line barely visible in the dust. "Here," he said. "Help me." His mouth tightened. "If it's still here... we'll need leverage."

Together they strained, pushing against the stone, breath catching—until with a low groan, the wall shifted a hand's breadth.

A rush of cold, damp air coiled up from the dark inside. Tristan held the lantern out, revealing a narrow, winding passage.

A sudden chill filled the air. The ground beneath them trembled, and a whisper curled through the shadows:

"Only those who are pure of heart may take the Heart of Elander."

Olivia's breath caught. "Did you hear that?"

Tristan's hand shot out to steady her. "Aye. And I don't think it was the wind."

They exchanged a look—equal parts fear and determination.

"Stay behind me," Tristan said gruffly. "If there's a test... it'll come for me first. Ready?" he asked, voice low.

Olivia nodded, heart hammering.

Tristan heaved the door open enough for them to pass. A staircase spiraled into blackness.

And below... a faint pulsing light, as if something in the depths stirred with a heartbeat of its own.

The staircase groaned beneath their steps, slick with damp. Tristan moved first, lantern raised, Olivia close behind. The air grew colder with every descent, until even their breath hung pale in the gloom.

At the base of the stairs, the crypt opened into a round chamber ringed with crumbling stonework. Faded carvings circled the walls—knots and runes long forgotten.

In the center stood a pedestal. And atop it... nothing.

Olivia's heart sank. "It should be here—It's gone—"

Tristan's hand rested on the hilt of his sword, his eyes scanning the shadows. "Then why do I feel as though we're not alone?"

Then the shadows shifted. A sudden rush of cold swept through the room, extinguishing the candles with a hiss. The shadows deepened, swirling like smoke until a faint, spectral figure emerged near the empty pedestal.

It was a woman's spirit—tall, robed in tattered grey, her form translucent, her eyes glowing with sorrow. She did not walk so much as drift, silent across the floor.

Tristan's hand went to his sword. The spirit lifted a pale hand—fingers long, almost skeletal—and spoke in a voice like wind through hollow halls.

"Who seeks the Heart of Elander?"

The weight of its words pressed against Olivia's chest.

Tristan answered, firm but steady. "I do. Tristan de Léon of Ravenshire. Knight of the Silver Flame."

The spirit's head tilted, as if studying him. "The Flame... flickers in you. And the one beside you?"

Olivia stepped forward, voice clear though her heart thundered. "I am Olivia. His wife."

A silence fell—long, heavy.

The spirit's face twisted with anguish. "Another... has already claimed it. One whose soul is steeped in darkness," the spirit whispered. "The Heart is no longer whole. Its power is unbalanced."

Olivia stepped forward, gripping her amulet as it pulsed faintly against her chest. "What does that mean?"

"It means the Heart's power will corrupt the unworthy." The spirit's voice grew sharper. "If it is not reclaimed... it will bring ruin to this world."

Tristan's hand shot out to steady Olivia as the chamber seemed to shudder around them.

The spirit's eyes darkened. "You know him already. The one who seeks to bind you both in chains of fire. Beware... the Heart calls to him."

Tristan and Olivia exchanged a sharp glance—they both knew the answer.

"Kaelen," Olivia whispered.

The spirit began to fade, her voice distant now. "Hurry... before it is too late..."

And then the chamber fell silent again, leaving only the sound of their breathing in the cold, still air. As the oppressive chill lifted, a hollow sound swept through the room—a sound that sent shivers crawling down Olivia's spine.

Kaelen's laugh. Twisted, mocking, and full of malice. It rippled through the air like a phantom breeze, curling around them even as the faint glow of the amulets dimmed.

"Did you hear that?" Olivia whispered, clutching Tristan's arm.

Tristan's blue eyes narrowed, his hand tightening around the hilt of his sword. "I heard."

The laughter faded slowly, like smoke dispersing in the wind, but its venom lingered.

Kaelen wasn't gone. Not truly.

They had to find The Heart now.

Kaelen's corruption was spreading like a poison through the land, and worse... the Heart itself was calling out—its power twisting and warping as Kaelen drew closer to unlocking its full strength.

CHAPTER EIGHTEEN

Tristan stood at the window of his chambers, fists clenched tight on the cold stone ledge.

"The Heart is in Kaelen's hands…" he said, his voice low and tight, "it will not only destroy him—it will destroy everything. We have to find the Heart before that happens."

Olivia stepped closer, placing her hand gently on his arm.

Tristan turned to face her, his eyes dark with determination.

"This journey won't be safe, Olivia. There will be no room for mistakes."

"There never was," she replied, her voice steady.

* * *

While they made plans, strange omens rippled across the land:

Crops rotted in the fields overnight.

Animals fled into the forests in terror.

The sky grew heavy with an unnatural red glow at dusk.

Kaelen had already begun tapping into the Heart's magic—his eyes said to glow faintly like coals. Each use of its power twisted him further, but he didn't care.

"When I master the Heart," Kaelen murmured to himself, "no king, no knight, and no woman will stand against me."

Kaelen sat in the dim glow of his chamber, the Heart of Elander pulsing faintly in his grasp. At first, it had felt like a gift—an ancient artifact whispering secrets of power and destiny. But now?

Now it felt alive.

And it spoke only to him.

At first, the whispers were soft.

A gentle coaxing: "You deserve more... You could rule them all..."

Kaelen resisted. He had been a knight once. An honorable man. But the long nights of solitude, the weight of betrayal, and the thirst for retribution had left cracks in his armor.

The Heart seeped into those cracks like poison.

And with every pulse of its crimson light, he felt stronger. Faster. Sharper.

But the strength came at a price.

His temper flared more easily now. His dreams were twisted visions of fire and conquest. He began to see enemies everywhere—even in those who still swore loyalty to him.

One evening, Kaelen stood before a mirror.

His reflection seemed... different.

His once-clear eyes had darkened to a stormy gray, flecks of deep red swirling in the irises when the Heart pulsed in his hand.

His veins stood out faintly on his forearms, almost glowing in the dim light.

"They will never understand you," the Heart whispered. "But they will kneel. Make them kneel."

Kaelen clenched his jaw, torn between his old self and this new, powerful voice.

"You don't need them. You don't need anyone."

When one of his lieutenants questioned the growing power of the Heart, Kaelen silenced him. Permanently.

The strike had been too fast—too brutal. The man hadn't even drawn his blade before Kaelen's hand was around his throat, crushing it effortlessly.

The room had gone silent.

"Is there anyone else who doubts me?" Kaelen asked, his voice low and calm.

No one spoke.

But in their eyes, he saw it.

Fear.

And...he liked it.

* * *

Kaelen stood in his darkened chamber, the firelight casting sharp shadows across his face. His fingers traced the edge of his wine goblet, though the wine itself had gone untouched.

He could feel it.

The amulets. Their presence burned like a thorn in his mind, an itch he could not ignore.

The seer's warnings haunted him still—that these two would change the course of fate itself.

"Two amulets," Kaelen muttered under his breath. "Two fools bound together by power they cannot control."

Kaelen had once thought to destroy Tristan through betrayal, through lies whispered into the king's ear.

But now?

Now he realized Tristan and Olivia were more than mere enemies—they were a threat to everything he had built.

"If I don't stop them now..." he whispered, gripping the edge of the table until his knuckles whitened, "...there will be nothing left for me to rule."

The torchlight flickered across Kaelen's sharp features as he paced the cold stone floor of his chambers.

Malric had failed. Marlowe had been outmaneuvered. And Tristan? Somehow, that cursed knight still lived.

Kaelen's lips curled into a sneer. "Fools, all of them."

Where brute force and courtly schemes had failed, Kaelen would succeed. His attacks weren't loud, weren't showy—they were like poison in a cup. Subtle. Undeniable. Deadly.

A hooded figure stepped into the room, kneeling in front of him. "You summoned me, my lord?"

Kaelen's voice was low, deliberate. "The time has come to remove Tristan de Léon. And this time, there will be no chance for him to fight back."

The spy nodded. "Shall I strike at him directly?"

Kaelen shook his head. "No. His strength lies in his allies. Break them first. Start with the girl."

"Lady Olivia?"

Kaelen's eyes gleamed. "She's the key. Take her, and Tristan will lose his reason. He'll come for her—and walk straight into the trap."

"And the knight's sister?" the spy asked cautiously. "Evelyne is no fool."

Kaelen smirked. "Then we keep her busy. And distract Aldric and Gideon.

Kaelen's fingers traced the edge of a dagger resting on his desk. "This time," he murmured, "there will be no escape for Tristan and his little witch."

Kaelen summoned his most loyal spies and mercenaries—men who owed him their lives and their coin. He didn't trust them anymore, but he knew they feared him.

Outside his window, the wind howled like a beast, carrying his quiet vow into the night.

* * *

Ravenshire was unusually quiet that night. The moonlight streamed through high windows, casting long shadows across the stone corridors.

Kaelen moved like a phantom, his black cloak blending into the darkness.

This was his moment. Plotting, bribery, and whispers had built to this. Tonight, Olivia would be in his hands—and Tristan would crumble.

* * *

As Aldric patrolled the western halls, the sharp scent of smoke caught his attention. He broke into a run, finding a small fire crackling in the armory. Sparks leapt from a stack of oiled rags, licking at the wooden racks of practice swords.

"Damn it!" Aldric barked, grabbing a water barrel and dousing the flames.

But it wasn't just a fire. It was bait.

As Aldric worked, he failed to notice the two cloaked figures slipping past behind him.

* * *

Gideon lounged in the lower hall, keeping watch as usual, when a young page approached.

"Sir... someone's asking for you."

"At this hour?" Gideon narrowed his eyes.

"They said it's about your... debts."

Gideon swore under his breath. If someone had tracked his old life to the castle, it could jeopardize everything. He followed the page down into the wine cellars, the shadows thick around him.

But no one was there.

By the time he realized the ruse, it was already too late.

* * *

Evelyne heard it as she returned to her chambers—a sharp cry echoing from a servant's quarters.

She hurried toward the sound, hand on the dagger hidden in her skirts.

A young maid stumbled out, clutching her arm. "My lady, please—it's my brother—he's fallen down the stairs. He needs help."

Evelyne hesitated only a moment before following the girl down the narrow steps toward the servants' wing.

But the moment she descended, two cloaked figures barred the way back.

* * *

Meanwhile, Olivia sat near the window of her chamber, the cool night air brushing her face.

Tristan was making his rounds. Gideon and Aldric were patrolling. Evelyne was checking on the kitchens.

And she was alone.

She didn't hear the door open. She didn't see the shadow move behind her.

But she felt the cloth press over her mouth.

"Stay still, my lady," a low voice hissed. "And you might live."

Her heart pounded. The amulet beneath her gown pulsed violently, hot against her skin. She struggled, but strong arms pinned her tight.

Kaelen stepped out of the darkness, his smile sharp. "Time to end this."

* * *

Tristan strode into the east wing, his boots echoing on the stone floor.

But something felt wrong.

The guards were missing.

The hall was too quiet.

And then—he saw the overturned chair in his chamber. The flutter of Olivia's blue shawl on the floor.

His blood ran cold. "Olivia," he whispered.

The sound of clattering hooves echoed into the night as Kaelen's horse disappeared beyond the castle gates, Olivia's muffled cry fading with the distance.

Tristan burst through the hall doors, rage burning in his chest.

"Olivia!" he roared, but she was already gone.

He sprinted for the stables. His boots pounded against the cobblestones, his heart racing with fury and fear.

The stable boy barely had time to react before Tristan yanked open the stall door.

"Valour!" he growled, swinging onto his massive black warhorse's back.

He didn't bother with a saddle. There wasn't time.

"Out of the way!" Tristan shouted as he kicked open the stable doors, spurring Valour into a dead run.

The stallion screamed and charged forward, hooves striking sparks off the stone.

The cold night air whipped against Tristan's face as he rode hard through the gates.

In the distance, he caught sight of Kaelen's horse—a dark shape moving fast under the pale moonlight.

"I swear by God, Kaelen—if you harm her, I'll gut you where you stand!" Tristan snarled into the wind.

The air was thick with the scent of pine and damp earth as Tristan urged his horse forward, branches clawing at his tunic.

Ahead, he could see Kaelen's dark figure slipping through the trees, Olivia slung over his shoulder like a sack of grain.

"Kaelen!" Tristan roared, his voice carrying like thunder through the woods. "Put her down!"

But Kaelen only laughed, spurring his mount faster.

Suddenly, the forest seemed to come alive around Tristan.

A sharp whistle cut through the air, and his horse reared violently as a rope snared his legs, sending Tristan crashing to the ground.

Before he could rise, a dozen armed men emerged from the undergrowth, blades and cudgels glinting in the dim light, their faces grim.

"Now, Lord Tristan," their leader said with a cruel grin, "this is where your chase ends."

Tristan rolled to his feet, his hand already on his sword. He swung his blade, cutting down the first attacker with ruthless precision. "If you want me dead, you'll have to do better than this," he growled, his blue eyes blazing.

Meanwhile, Olivia kicked and writhed against Kaelen's grip.

"Tristan will kill you for this!" she hissed, her fingers clawing at his arm.

Kaelen smirked. "Not if my men kill him first."

He glanced over his shoulder, catching sight of Tristan felling another attacker. His smirk faltered. "Though he is making them work for it."

Two men lunged forward, but Tristan moved like lightning, parrying their strikes and sending one sprawling with a vicious backhand.

As two more men charged, Tristan caught one by the wrist, twisting viciously until the man's sword clattered to the ground.

"I don't have time for this," Tristan snarled.

With a roar, he pushed through the circle of enemies, his blade flashing like silver lightning.

"Surround him!" the leader barked. "Don't let him reach Kaelen!"

There were too many.

Two came at him from behind. He spun, parrying one strike and elbowing the other in the jaw, but the numbers were overwhelming.

Just as he broke free—an arrow whistled past, grazing his shoulder.

Tristan staggered.

Kaelen grinned. "That's more like it, boys! Keep him busy!"

Three more crashed into him, dragging him down with ropes and brute strength.

A hard blow to the back of his head sent him to his knees.

Tristan's hands were bound tightly behind his back. Blood dripped from his shoulder as Kaelen's men hauled him to his feet.

Tristan struggled, but the ropes cut deeper into his wrists as two men dragged him away.

CHAPTER NINETEEN

The fire roared in the hearth, casting long shadows across the ancient stone walls. The air was thick with the scent of smoke, iron, and the faint tang of spilled wine.

Kaelen's boots echoed on the flagstones as he strode in, his grip iron-tight around Olivia's arm.

"Let go of me!" Olivia spat, struggling against him, but Kaelen only smirked.

"So much fire," he drawled. "No wonder he's so bewitched by you."

The heavy doors slammed open again, and two of Kaelen's men dragged Tristan in, shoving him to his knees.

Tristan's eyes burned like blue steel, his hair damp with sweat and his tunic streaked with dirt and blood.

"If you've harmed her, Kaelen—" His voice was low and dangerous, each word coiled like a viper ready to strike.

Kaelen chuckled darkly. "You're in no position to make threats, de Léon."

He circled Tristan, his fingers still gripping Olivia's arm as if to taunt him.

"You've been quite the thorn in my side," Kaelen continued. "Your king favors you, your soldiers follow you, and even my dear ally Malric couldn't break you."

Tristan's jaw clenched. "Release her. Now."

Kaelen laughed, tugging Olivia closer to him. "She's a fine prize. I can see why you've risked everything for her."

"Kaelen—don't," Olivia hissed, but he only scoffed.

"Perhaps I should keep her here. A lady as lovely as this... deserves better than a disgraced knight."

Tristan surged forward, but Kaelen's men gripped his shoulders hard, forcing him back to his knees.

"Easy," Kaelen sneered. "You're in my hall, on my land. One wrong move, and I'll have your head on a pike."

"Then do it," Tristan growled. "But I swear by every god and saint, if you hurt her—"

Kaelen's smile faltered for a fraction of a second. He saw it in Tristan's eyes—cold, unyielding fury.

This wasn't a man who would break. This was a man who would burn the world down before letting Olivia be taken from him.

The torchlight flickered along the cold stone walls of Kaelen's hall. The air was heavy with the scent of smoke and sweat.

Tristan knelt on the flagstones, his wrists bound tightly behind his back, shoulders straining against the ropes. Blood trickled from a split in his lip, but his eyes never left Kaelen.

Kaelen stood above him, smug, his gloved hand gripping Olivia's arm with possessive force. She struggled, but his hold was firm—though not as unyielding as his voice.

"Look at you, de Léon," Kaelen drawled, circling Tristan like a wolf savoring its prey. "The great knight, brought low. You're not so fearsome now, are you?"

Tristan's jaw tightened. "You'll regret this."

Kaelen smirked. "Will I?" He turned slightly to Olivia, his dark eyes glinting with malice. "She's quite something, isn't she? The way she fights me, even knowing she has no chance. I almost admire it."

Olivia wrenched at his grip, her voice sharp. "Let me go."

Kaelen's grip loosened slightly as he chuckled, but he didn't release her.

"I could let you go... but why would I want to do that?" he murmured, brushing a stray curl from her face. "Your knight here would just come charging after you again." SEP SEP

Tristan surged against his bonds, muscles straining. "I will end you, Kaelen."

Kaelen crouched down to Tristan's level, smirking. "Such fire. And yet, here you are—on your knees, completely at my mercy."

Olivia's voice trembled with anger. "You're a coward, Kaelen. Let him stand and fight you like a man."

Kaelen laughed low in his throat. "Why should I? This is so much more satisfying."

The flickering torchlight cast jagged shadows across the cold stone walls.

Tristan knelt on the ground, his hands bound tightly behind his back, shoulders heaving from fury. A crimson gash ran across his shoulder where the arrow had struck, and blood had soaked into the black tunic clinging to his chest.

Kaelen stood above him, his hand gripping Olivia's arm as though she were a prize to be paraded. He jerked Olivia closer, forcing her to stand just within Tristan's line of sight. "Does it burn, knowing you cannot save her?"

Olivia struggled in his grasp, her hair tumbling loose as she tried to wrench free. "Let him go, Kaelen!"

Kaelen laughed. "Oh no, my dear. I've waited too long for this moment. Shall we hear him, the mighty Tristan, begging me to spare you?"

"You've already lost," Tristan growled, his voice hoarse but unbroken. "You think you're in control, Kaelen, but this will be your ruin."

Kaelen crouched in front of him, bringing his face dangerously close. "And yet it is you kneeling at my feet, isn't it?"

Kaelen scoffed, standing up. "Perhaps I'll keep her," he whispered mockingly, brushing a lock of Olivia's hair from her face. "She'll make a lovely trophy."

Kaelen's taunts cut like a blade. Tristan's blue eyes flashed with fury.

"You look less like a knight and more like a dog cowering at my feet, Tristan," Kaelen sneered, circling him.

"Let her go," he said, his voice low and deadly, "or I swear by every god and king in this land, I'll tear you apart."

Olivia's eyes darted to Tristan—desperate, terrified—not for herself, but for him.

Kaelen smirked. "Big words from a broken man."

"Leave her out of this," Tristan growled, his voice hoarse but steady. "This is between you and me."

Kaelen's smirk widened. "Oh, but where's the fun in that?"

He gripped Olivia's chin roughly and forced her to look at Tristan.

"Watch, knight. Watch as your lady bends to me."

Olivia struggled, her voice cracking. "Don't touch me—"

"Kiss me," Kaelen commanded darkly.

Olivia froze. Her heart pounded, her stomach turning. But Kaelen's grip on her arm tightened like a vice.

"Do it, or I slit his throat right here."

Tristan's chest heaved, every muscle in his body straining against the ropes. *If she refused she would watch him die. He couldn't help her if he were dead...* "Olivia..." Tristan whispered. He knew the pain she felt. "Please, Kaelen. Leave her alone."

But Kaelen's dagger pressed against Tristan's throat, a thin line of blood forming. "Do it."

Tears stung Olivia's eyes. She leaned forward stiffly and pressed her lips to Kaelen's, her entire body shaking with revulsion.

Tristan roared, his voice echoing in the chamber. "Kaelen! I'll kill you for this!"

Kaelen broke the kiss and threw his head back in laughter. "Oh, I do hope you try, Tristan. It will make your death all the sweeter."

But even as he spoke, Tristan's fingers flexed against the ropes. He had been working them loose, ignoring the pain as the fibers cut into his skin. He needed one chance—one mistake from Kaelen.

And Olivia saw it.

Her eyes flicked to Tristan's hands, then back to Kaelen. "You're a coward," she spat at Kaelen suddenly, her voice steady.

Kaelen's head snapped toward her. "What did you say?"

"You heard me. You've always been a coward. That's why you need ropes and blades and threats. Because you know you could never face Tristan fairly."

Kaelen's smirk faltered for the briefest moment. Just long enough.

With a roar, Tristan ripped his hands free, the ropes snapping. Blood dripped from his wrists where the cords had bitten deep, but he didn't hesitate.

He lunged, tackling Kaelen to the ground in a blur of motion.

Olivia stumbled back, gasping as the two men hit the stone floor with a crash.

Kaelen slashed wildly with his blade, but Tristan was faster, fueled by rage and desperation.

He caught Kaelen's wrist, forcing the dagger from his grasp.

The two men crashed against the long table, splintering a bench beneath their weight.

Kaelen swung, but Tristan caught his arm and twisted, forcing him down.

"This ends now," Tristan growled, slamming his fist into Kaelen's jaw.

Kaelen's guards rushed forward. Two seized Tristan's arms, wrenching him off their lord, while another stepped between them with a drawn sword.

Tristan struggled, his muscles straining against their grips. "Let go of me!"

Kaelen staggered to his feet, wiping blood from his split lip. "Hold him. You brought this on yourself, Tristan," Kaelen spat. "Take him to the cells and have your fun with him."

As the guards began to drag Tristan down the corridor, Kaelen turned his full attention to Olivia.

"I will not forget this, Kaelen!" Tristan said low, his voice like a growl.

"Oh, I expect you won't," Kaelen replied. "And as for you, my lady..." he murmured, stepping closer, his voice dropping to a silken purr. "You're coming with me." Before Olivia could react, Kaelen's hand shot out and gripped her wrist.

"Unhand me!" Olivia shouted, struggling against his iron grip.

Kaelen's grin widened. "To my chambers. And I don't want to be disturbed."

Two guards exchanged glances.

"Sir, is this wise—" one began, but Kaelen cut him off with a sharp glare.

"Did I ask for your counsel?"

"N-no, my lord."

Kaelen began to pull Olivia down the hall, her heels scraping against the stone.

"Tristan!" Olivia screamed.

Tristan surged against his captors, his voice like a roar. "Kaelen! Hurt her and I will kill you!"

But the heavy doors slammed shut between them, the sound echoing like a death knell.

CHAPTER TWENTY

Meanwhile, Valour—Tristan's loyal warhorse—galloped through the forest like a phantom.

Reaching the gates of Ravenshire, the stallion whinnied wildly, hooves striking the earth in a frenzy.

A guard recognized the beast instantly. "That's Lord Tristan's horse!"

Aldric, Evelyne, and Gideon rushed to the gates, alarm in their faces.

"Where's Tristan?" Evelyne demanded, her voice tight.

Aldric's expression darkened. "Something's happened."

Gideon's smirk faded. "I'll wager Kaelen has him. And Olivia too."

Aldric's hand went to his sword hilt. "We ride at first light."

Evelyne's eyes blazed with determination. "No. We ride now."

* * *

Kaelen's expression was cold, a predator's gleam in his eyes as he shoved open the door to his chamber, the wood slamming into the stone wall with a deafening crack.

With a forceful pull, Kaelen yanked Olivia inside and kicked the door shut behind them. He slid the latch into place.

He pushed her hard, and she stumbled, falling backward onto his bed. The mattress sagged beneath her weight, the scent of leather and smoke filling her nose.

Kaelen's smile was slow and wolfish as he leaned back against the carved bedpost. "I thought you'd make this easier for yourself," he drawled, tossing aside his leather gloves. "But I've always admired a little fire in my prey."

"I'm not your prey." Olivia's voice was slow but steady.

Kaelen laughed, stepping toward her with predatory grace. "You're in my room, alone. No Tristan to save you this time. You should surrender, little dove."

"Never."

Olivia squared her shoulders as Kaelen loomed over her in his richly appointed chamber.

His smile was lacivious, his hand reaching for her arm. "You'll learn your place, my lady," he sneered, his voice dripping with false charm.

But Olivia had had enough. "Don't touch me."

Kaelen's brows shot up in amusement. "And if I do? What will you do? Call for your knight in shining armor?"

Olivia's eyes narrowed. "No. I'll handle you myself."

Kaelen reached for her again, but Olivia moved first—a sharp, precise kick to his ribs that knocked the air from his lungs.

"You little—" he growled, doubling over.

Before he could recover, Olivia jumped up and grabbed the ornate wine decanter from the table and hurled its contents straight into his face.

The red liquid splattered down his tunic as he stumbled back, shouting. "You'll pay for that—"

But Olivia didn't wait. She kicked the chair toward him, forcing him off balance.

Kaelen slipped on the spilled wine, crashing hard onto the marble floor.

His smirk faltered as Olivia stepped forward. She held a heavy candlestick like a weapon.

The flickering light from the hearth cast shadows across her face, turning her eyes into hard, glittering embers.

"I said don't touch me." Her voice was steady, but there was fire beneath it—the fire of someone pushed too far.

Kaelen hesitated, his confidence wavering for the first time. "You wouldn't dare—"

Olivia tightened her grip. "Try me."

The weight of the candlestick didn't matter. It felt like power in her hands. Her knuckles were white, her muscles tight, but her heart was hammering so hard she thought he might hear it.

Kaelen's eyes darted to the door, then back to the improvised weapon. He took a step back, his bravado cracking. "You don't know what you're doing."

Olivia's voice dropped to a cold whisper. "I know enough. Take one more step, and you'll find out just how much."

For a moment, silence hung between them. The only sound was the crackle of the fire.

Kaelen grinned, catching her wrist before the heavy brass candlestick could connect with his head.

"Tsk, tsk, my lady," he purred, his grip tightening just enough to make Olivia's pulse quicken. "You almost singed my hair."

Olivia glared, twisting in his hold. "Let me go!"

"Oh, but you were doing so well," Kaelen mocked, effortlessly wrenching the candlestick from her hand and setting it on the table behind him. "I rather like a woman with spirit."

She spat the words like venom. "You won't win this."

Kaelen leaned in close, his dark eyes glittering. "You're in my grasp already. That's a sort of victory, wouldn't you say?"

Her fingers tightened around the hilt of the dagger she had hidden in her skirt—one of Tristan's blades, its weight reassuring.

Steel flashed in the dim light of the chamber as Olivia slashed upward, forcing Kaelen to twist aside. His smirk faltered for only a heartbeat before he recovered, drawing his own blade in one smooth motion.

"So, Tristan's been teaching you tricks," he snarled, his voice dropping its mockery. "Let's see if you've learned enough."

Kaelen struck first, a vicious downward slash aimed for her shoulder. Olivia ducked, the blade slicing through the air so close she felt the rush of wind on her cheek. She pivoted and kicked out, her boot catching him in the shin.

He grunted, stumbling back a step. "Bitch—"

Olivia didn't wait. She struck again, aiming for his side. But Kaelen was faster now, his blade meeting hers with a shower of sparks.

"You're good," he hissed, driving her backward with a flurry of strikes. "But you're still not fast enough."

Her back hit the wall with a painful thud, but Olivia gritted her teeth and ducked under his next swing. She rolled across the floor, coming up on her knees and throwing her dagger.

Kaelen's eyes widened as the blade flew toward him.

At the last second, he swatted it aside—but not before Olivia charged him head-on.

She slammed into him with all her weight, and they tumbled onto the bed in a tangle of limbs.

Kaelen cursed, grabbing for her wrists. "You're going to regret—"

Olivia twisted violently, breaking free. She scrambled over him, grabbing for his discarded dagger on the bedside table.

Kaelen grabbed her ankle and yanked her back. She hit the floor hard, her breath rushing out in a sharp gasp. He wrested the dagger from her hand.

"Enough games!" he roared, towering over her with his blade raised high.

Olivia's hand darted to the amulet at her neck—it pulsed with a sudden heat, and Kaelen's blade froze mid-swing.

"What—what is this?!" Kaelen's voice cracked in panic.

The amulet's glow burst outward in a flash of light, momentarily blinding him.

Olivia didn't hesitate. She surged up and drove Tristan's smaller blade—the one she'd kept hidden in her sleeve—straight into Kaelen's side.

He let out a strangled cry, stumbling backward and dropping his weapon.

Kaelen clutched his side, his eyes wide with disbelief as blood seeped between his fingers.

"You—" He tried to speak, but Olivia cut him off.

"Stay down, or I'll make sure you never get up." Her voice was like steel, her stance steady.

Kaelen sneered through his pain. "Tristan... has made you dangerous. But you'll never—"

"Get out of my way."

Olivia stepped past him, her heart pounding but her grip on her blade unshaken.

For the first time, she felt it—not just fear, but power. Her power.

* * *

The stone corridors of Kaelen's keep were cold and damp, the air heavy with the scent of mildew and old iron. Torches flickered along the walls, their light barely reaching the shadows where Aldric, Gideon, and Evelyne moved like ghosts.

Gideon crouched low by a heavy iron door, his deft fingers working on the lock. "This is too quiet," Aldric muttered, his hand resting on the hilt of his sword. "I don't like it."

Evelyne's eyes darted around the corridor. "Quiet means we have time. Don't waste it."

With a soft click, Gideon pushed the door open. "And they said I was only good for lying and stealing," he murmured with a grin.

"You are," Aldric growled. "Now move."

The three slipped inside, entering the winding stairway that led down to the dungeon below.

The stone corridor stretched ahead like the throat of some ancient beast—narrow, cold, damp. Evelyne pressed her back to the wall, her breath shallow as a guard's boots echoed past the iron-barred stairwell behind them.

Aldric signaled with two fingers, then moved forward swiftly. Gideon brought up the rear, dagger in hand, his usual cocky grin replaced by grim focus.

"I count three more turns until the lower cells," he whispered. "If Kaelen's keeping Tristan out of sight, he'll be there."

Evelyne nodded. "And if they've touched a hair on his head—"

"They have," Aldric said grimly. "I heard the guards laughing about it."

They rounded another corner, ducking as another patrol passed. A torch guttered in its sconce on the wall, barely lighting their path. When they reached the heavy wooden door at the end of the corridor, Gideon stepped forward, kneeling at the lock.

"I'll have it open in seconds."

"Don't jinx it," Aldric muttered, glancing back the way they came.

A quiet click. Gideon grinned. "Ladies and knights first."

Evelyne pushed the door open—and froze.

Inside the cell Tristan stirred, his face bruised and one eye nearly swollen shut, as the cell door creaked open. He groaned, trying to push himself up. Torchlight flickered on the stone walls, and the familiar voices made his heart jolt.

"Tristan," Aldric's voice was low and urgent. "We're here."

Evelyne rushed to his side, dropping to her knees beside him. "Gods, what have they done to you..."

"It's nothing," Tristan told her.

Gideon crouched at the door, keeping watch. "We don't have much time. Can you walk?"

Tristan looked up, his voice hoarse. "Where... where's Olivia?"

A heavy silence followed.

Evelyne's hand tightened on his arm. "We don't know yet. We haven't seen her. We feared the worst. That's why we're here."

Tristan's jaw clenched, blood on his split lip. "I have to find her."

"You will," Aldric said firmly, slipping an arm under his shoulders. "But first, we get you out of here before they come back for more."

Tristan nodded, the pain momentarily forgotten.

Meanwhile...

Olivia's feet pounded the stone steps as she raced down a parallel corridor. She didn't know how she'd escaped the guards—just that one moment, the amulet had pulsed, and the next, she'd found herself through a hidden archway behind a tapestry. Her gown was torn, her hair wild, but she didn't care.

"Tristan," she whispered under her breath. "Please be alive."

She turned a corner—then halted, heart pounding.

Voices. Boots. Coming closer. She ducked into an alcove, pressed her back against the cold stone, and held her breath.

As the guards passed, she could hear Kaelen's voice echoing down the hall.

"Find her. She couldn't have gotten far. I want her dragged back, screaming if she must."

Olivia's hand clutched the amulet. It burned like fire.

"Lead me to him," she whispered—and followed the pull.

* * *

Torches bobbed in the gloom, illuminating the narrow corridor as Aldric and Gideon half-carried, half-dragged Tristan between them. His feet stumbling—but he was alive.

"Keep going!" Gideon hissed, glancing over his shoulder. "I don't care if you have to carry him the rest of the way—We have to move faster. Kaelen's men are on us."

Aldric gritted his teeth. "He's heavier than a mule and twice as stubborn."

Then a new sound echoed from the stairwell—soft footfalls, urgent.

"Wait!" came a voice.

Olivia.

She emerged into the torchlight, eyes wide with frantic hope. The moment she saw him—half-carried by his comrades—she ran.

"Tristan!" she cried.

He stirred at the sound of her voice, his head lifting slightly, mouth parting to speak "Liv..." he rasped.

She threw her arms around him. "I'm here. I'm here."

Tristan cupped her cheek. "Did he hurt you?"

"No," she said, shaking her head. "But I hurt him."

Tristan smiled. "That's my girl."

Gideon nodded toward the tunnel entrance. "We have to move—now."

Behind them, the sound of shouts and clanging armor grew louder. From behind, the alarm bell tolled—a shrill warning that their escape had been discovered. Kaelen's men had discovered the empty cell.

Aldric drew his sword. "I'll hold them if I have to—get him out!"

They fled into the tunnels as the fortress exploded in chaos behind them.

"We're almost there," Gideon whispered urgently, peering around the next corner. "Horses are just beyond that gate."

They burst into the open air of the lower courtyard, where the horses were waiting. Hooves stamped nervously, sensing the urgency.

Behind them, Kaelen's guards erupted from the castle entrance. Shouts rang out. Arrows hissed through the air.

"There are only three horses," Aldric said

"I ride with Aldric," Tristan rasped. "I can hold on."

"No," Olivia objected. "You're hurt—"

"I can manage," he insisted.

Evelyne pulled Olivia toward another mount. "Come on—ride with me."

Gideon swung into his saddle, already scanning the courtyard walls for shadows moving in the torchlight. "We've got maybe two minutes before they find us. Let's go!"

Tristan climbed onto Aldric's horse with a grimace, his grip tight around his friend's waist as they thundered out into the forest, hooves striking sparks against the stone. Olivia and Evelyne followed, their horse galloping hard through the open gate. Gideon brought up the rear. "Ride!"

And they were already gone—riding into the night, the stars overhead, and freedom within reach... if only they could stay ahead of the storm now chasing them.

Behind them, Kaelen's fury echoed through the trees. "Find them! Bring me the knight's corpse and the girl alive!"

But the group vanished into the dark woods, the amulets around Tristan's and Olivia's necks pulsing faintly—guiding them toward safety, and whatever destiny still awaited them.

The horses thundered forward into the darkness, hooves pounding like war drums as they fled into the wild night.

* * *

That evening back at Ravenshire, after the tension of the escape, Tristan, Olivia, Evelyne, Aldric, and Gideon retreated to the small chambers they'd claimed as a private refuge. The fire crackled low in the hearth, casting flickering shadows on the stone walls, and the mood was quieter—still laced with tension, but finally private.

Tristan reclined in a carved chair with one leg extended, a goblet of wine in hand, his tunic open at the throat. Olivia sat close by, curled beside him, her eyes fixed on the fire. Evelyne leaned against the window ledge, sipping from a silver cup. Gideon sat cross-legged on a rug, flipping a dagger over and over in one hand. Aldric stood at the fire, one arm resting on the mantle.

"We can't wait any longer," Tristan finally said, his voice low. "The Heart of Elander *must* be reclaimed. If it stays in Kaelen's grasp it will destroy everything."

Olivia nodded slowly. "And to get it, I think we need the Order."

Evelyne frowned. "Scattered as they are, can we even find them?"

Gideon chuckled darkly. "Some don't want to be found. Others are nursing old wounds. But I know where a few of them are. If I start tonight, I can reach one by week's end."

Tristan turned his gaze to him. "Start with Sir Dalen. If he still wears the sigil, he'll answer."

"We'll need their trust," Evelyne added. "And proof. The amulets alone might not be enough."

Aldric finally spoke. "We bring them the truth. About the prophecy. About Kaelen. About what's coming."

Olivia looked down at the amulet around her neck, which had begun to glow faintly again—warmer now, pulsing as if listening. "Then we ride soon. But we do this smart. Quietly. Before Kaelen knows we're coming."

Tristan reached over and squeezed her hand. "We'll gather them, Liv. One by one. And we will take back what was stolen."

Outside, the wind picked up, brushing leaves against the windows. Inside, the five of them sat in a protective circle of loyalty, firelight, and hope. The battle was not over.

But tonight, they would rest—and tomorrow, the hunt for the Order of the Silver Flame would begin.

CHAPTER TWENTY-ONE

Deep beneath the crumbling catacombs of the old abbey of the Silver Flame, where the scent of earth and magic clung thick in the air, Tristan stood before the flickering torchlight, surrounded by the last loyal members of the Order. Their faces were grim but resolute—men and women sworn to protect the ancient truths.

"We ride before dawn," Tristan declared, gripping the hilt of his sword. "Kaelen has twisted the Heart of Elander to his will. But it still listens to us. It remembers its purpose—and so do we."

Evelyne nodded sharply, her eyes burning with fierce determination. "He thinks he's won. He hasn't counted on the fire that still burns in our blood."

Aldric slammed his fist into his palm. "Then we storm the vaults beneath the black citadel. We take back what's ours."

Olivia stepped forward, the amulet around her neck glowing faintly in response. "The Heart is reacting. It knows we're coming."

Together, they drew their swords and renewed their oaths—flames flickering behind them as the Order itself was reborn in that moment.

* * *

The wind pulled at their cloaks as the riders crossed the moor, the ruined spires of the Order of the Silver Flame rising in the distance like broken fingers clawing at the sky. The sun was low, casting long shadows that flickered over the golden grass. Ravens wheeled above them, their cries sharp and ominous.

Tristan rode at the front, his expression carved from stone. Olivia rode beside him, her face pale beneath her hood, her hand steady on the reins. Her gaze never left him.

Behind them Aldric rode silently, his eyes flicking constantly to the others as if calculating their worth. He hadn't spoken much since rejoining the Flame — not after what happened at the stronghold.

Evelyne's white cloak billowed behind her like wings as her mare moved with unnatural grace through the forest. She whispered something to the wind again — ancient words from the Flame's oldest rites, or perhaps to steady her own heart. Her fingers brushed the hilt of her dagger, her trust stretched thin.

Gideon, brought up the rear, rode hunched in the saddle, crossbow slung over one shoulder. He caught Tristan's glance and gave the faintest nod. He had stood by Tristan at the trial at court. He would do so again.

And around them — the remaining Silver Flame. Fifteen riders. Some still loyal, some uncertain. One or two perhaps only biding their time.

"The Heart won't give itself up," Aldric finally said. "Kaelen has it. He will use it."

"He already is," Evelyne replied softly, eyes forward. "The land is wilting. The birds don't sing here anymore."

Tristan didn't answer. He was listening — to the silence between hoofbeats, to the uneasy breath of the earth. To the questions he dared ask aloud:

Would they follow him when the time came? Would they turn on him? Would he have to fight them too?

Olivia reached across the space between their horses and touched his hand — just briefly.

"We'll face him together," she whispered.

He met her eyes. "Together."

Then the bell in the ruined tower began to toll — once, twice — a deep, hollow sound that echoed across the moor.

The Heart was calling.

* * *

When evening fell they stopped to camp for the night. The fire crackled, throwing shadows across tired faces. The scent of ash and damp moss clung to their cloaks. The looming silhouette of the Black Spire sat on the horizon, a black thorn against the stars.

Gideon hunched near the fire, sharpening a blade that barely needed it.

Evelyne stared into the flames, quiet but watchful.

Aldric leaned against a stone, arms crossed.

317

Olivia sat beside Tristan, her hand resting lightly over his. The others—ten remaining members of the Order—spread out, tense and wary.

Then, Thorne, a wiry man with silver in his beard, broke the silence and spoke. "You expect us to trust him? After what happened in the Hollow Vale? The Order nearly fractured—and now he's leading us?"

"If you've something to say, say it to me. Not around me," Tristan said.

Thorne snorted. "Fine. You shouldn't be here. You're the Flame's chosen, they say—yet Kaelen walked away with the Heart. And we burned for it."

"He didn't let Kaelen take the Heart. We all saw what it did to the Flame. You think that was cowardice? It nearly killed him," Evelyne said sharply.

"Enough," Aldric said. "We all carry our wounds. We can tally up the past or we can focus on tomorrow. Because if we fail, none of this matter."

Gideon didn't look up. "You speak like a man who believes in redemption."

"I speak like a man who's buried too many friends."

Silence.

Then Liora, the youngest of the Order spoke up. "I saw what Kaelen did in Oakhurst. The villagers twisted... crying out with mouths that didn't belong to them. He's not who he was. Whatever the Heart is, it's changing him."

318

Tristan was grim. "It's not just changing him. It's using him."

"Then we'd best hope your flame is real, Tristan. Because if it's not, we're walking into the dark with a blind man," Thorne said bitterly.

"You're not walking into the dark. Not while he's breathing," Olivia said firmly.

Tristan looked around. "I don't expect your trust. Just your steel. You'll have mine."

A long moment passed. Somewhere in the trees, an owl called. The fire hissed.

"We should sleep in shifts. Kaelen won't wait. Neither should we."

One by one, they settled, uneasy and scattered, but still there. Still together—for now.

And the Black Spire watched.

* * *

Most of the Order had drifted into a restless silence. Only the wind stirred, catching in the trees like whispered warnings.

Tristan rose and stepped away from the fire, restless. He walked the edge of the camp, eyes fixed on the Spire's silhouette in the distance. Behind him, Thorne watched with narrowing eyes.

"Tell me someone else sees it. The way he walks, the way he looks at that tower. Like he's tethered to it," Thorne said low, to the others.

"You're imagining things."

"Am I? Maybe Kaelen isn't the only one the Heart touched."

Tristan froze. Without turning he said, "Say what you mean."

Thorne stood. "Fine. I think we're walking into a trap— and you're the lure."

"Gods, Thorne—" Evelyne gasped.

"No, Evelyne. No more blind faith. First Marlowe, now Kaelen—and both were once called brother. How long before we find his name burned into the same page?"

Tristan turned, slowly, his jaw set. "I bled for this Order. I was flogged by Malric, nearly executed because of Marlowe's lies. You think I'd betray you for —what?"

"I think men break, Tristan. Even the ones who say all the right words. Maybe especially them."

Olivia rose. "Enough!"

"Do you even know what he is anymore, Olivia?" Thorne asked. "Has it ever occurred to you that the Flame chose him because it's broken too?"

Tristan stepped forward—fast. Too fast. "If you have a quarrel, draw your blade. Or keep your damn mouth shut."

Thorne stared him down. His hand twitched near the hilt of his sword.

Aldric stepped between them."Stand down. Both of you."

"Save the fight for tomorrow," Gideon said. "Or I swear I'll knock you both senseless and tie you to trees."

"Please... don't make us choose sides," Leora begged.

Thorne finally backed off, shaking his head. "I'll fight beside him. But I won't turn my back."

"That makes two of us," Tristan said softly. He walked back to the fire and sat beside Olivia. She didn't speak, only reached for his hand. He took it.

Around them, the camp settled again. But the quiet that followed wasn't peace.

It was the kind of silence that always comes before blood.

* * *

Most of the camp slept. A few embers still glowed in the fire pit. The wind had quieted, and in its place came a hush, thick and solemn.

Tristan stood at the edge of the woods alone, his back to the camp. He was staring at the Black Spire, fists clenched. His breath came hard, as if he were wrestling something unseen.

Olivia approached quietly, wrapping her cloak tighter around her. "You didn't sleep."

Tristan didn't turn. "How could I? I'm walking into battle with men who'd rather gut me than follow me."

"And still they follow. That means something."

He didn't answer.

Olivia stepped beside him. "Kaelen twisted the Heart to his will. But you—you resisted it. That wasn't weakness. It was proof you're not like him."

"What if it isn't over? What if I falter? What if Thorne's right?"

"You wouldn't be afraid of it if you'd already fallen."

A long pause.

Then, far above them, clouds shifted. Moonlight spilled through the canopy, lighting the clearing in pale silver.

And there — like a flicker — the flame on the pendant Tristan wore at his neck gave a faint, golden glow. Not fire, exactly... but warmth. Like a breath.

Tristan looked down at it. His fingers brushed the metal. He hadn't felt it stir since the Heart was stolen.

Tristan's voice was barely audible. "...Did you see that?"

"I did."

"Was it...?"

"Providence," Olivia whispered. She reached out and placed her hand over his heart. "Whatever darkness waits in that tower, you won't face it alone."

He closed his eyes. For the first time that night, the burden on his shoulders seemed to ease.

Somewhere in the trees, a lone bird called — a high, mournful sound, then silence.

And in that silence, Tristan whispered a prayer he hadn't spoken since he was a boy.

"O Flame eternal, burn in me—

Not to consume, but to refine.

Where my strength ends, let yours begin.

Where my fear lives, strike light within.

Guide my hand, guard my soul,

And if I fall, let me fall in truth.

I am not worthy, but I am willing.

Make that enough."

He finished it barely above a whisper, as if afraid the wind would carry it away before the words were finished.

Olivia said nothing. But she didn't need to. Her hand stayed over his chest, feeling the pulse of something warm and steady beneath.

"I never told you when it first happened," Tristan said.

"The Flame?"

He nodded.

"I was fifteen. Just a boy, pretending I was already a man. The others had gone before me. Most got nothing. A few claimed they felt something. I didn't expect anything at all."

He paused as his voice caught just a little. "I remember kneeling. I didn't feel holy. I was angry, bruised, and tired of being told I had to earn something I didn't understand."

"And then?" Olivia asked quietly.

Tristan lifted his head and gazed out in front of him. "I told it—demanded it—to do something. I said, 'If you're real, prove it.' Not exactly the prayer they teach in the books."

Olivia smiled."But that sounds exactly like you."

Tristan smirked. "The flame moved. Not wild. Just... leaned toward me, like it was listening. The heat didn't burn. It felt like someone putting a hand on my shoulder. And I felt this... knowing. That I wasn't alone. That I was seen."

He swallowed hard. "It wasn't thunder or light. It was just... quiet, and sure. And in that moment, I believed. For the first time in my life, I believed something bigger than me might actually care if I stood or fell."

Olivia reaches for his hand. "It does care. It always did. You were never chosen because you were perfect, Tristan. You were chosen because you kept standing back up."

He turned to her, his eyes searching hers in the dim light. "I was afraid to tell anyone. Afraid it would fade if I said it aloud."

"It didn't fade. You just forgot for a while what it felt like," Olivia said gently.

She rested her forehead to his. "But you remember now. And tomorrow, when we face Kaelen—you'll remember it again."

A breath between them. Steady. Shared.

And in the dark, the pendant at Tristan's neck pulses faintly once more — not with fire, but with promise.

* * *

Kaelen, in his obsidian tower, felt the tremor. His corrupted version of the Heart flickered in his palm. He sneered, "Come then, Tristan. Let the last of your kind fall."

But the Heart pulsed again—once, twice. And Kaelen's smirk faltered.

* * *

Pale light slipped over the horizon, washing the trees and stones in cold gold. Mist curled low around the forest floor. Birds did not sing. Even nature held its breath.

The fire was down to its last embers. One by one, the warriors of the Silver Flame rose from their blankets, cloaks, and quiet prayers.

Gideon was the first to strap on his blade.

Evelyne laced her boots in silence. Her braid was tighter than it was last night.

325

Aldric sharpened his spear-point without speaking.

Liora held her hand over the small pendant cross she wore, eyes closed, lips moving in a prayer.

Thorne stood apart. Watching. Always watching.

Members of the Order stood in a wide circle, hoods lowered, eyes turned toward Tristan. He stepped forward, his amulet resting against his chest — the faintest warmth still humming from it.

He stood at the center of the ring, shoulders squared. His tunic bore the emblem of the Silver Flame, once scorched away, now restored—stitched anew by Olivia's own hand. Behind him stood Gideon, grim-faced and silent. To his left, Aldric, pale with worry. Evelyne stood on his right, her hand on the hilt of her blade.

"We cannot delay any longer," Tristan began, his voice carrying. "Kaelen Veyne has taken the Heart of Elander—and with it, the last of the Flame's mercy."

Murmurs rippled among the gathered.

"He was one of us," said Thorne, eyes narrowed. "You vouched for him once, Tristan. And Marlowe before him. What if your judgment fails again?"

A muscle jumped in Tristan's jaw. "I have failed. I let my trust blind me. But Kaelen is no longer the man we knew. The Heart has twisted him. I saw it in his eyes—the corruption

326

has taken root. We are not dealing with a misguided brother. We are facing something far worse."

Evelyne stepped forward, voice steady. "You've all felt the silence in the Flame. The flickers of doubt. This is not just about Kaelen. If he keeps the Heart, the Flame itself will die. And with it—every vow we ever took."

Then Gideon spoke, his voice gravel and thunder. "I've seen what happens when the Heart falls into the wrong hands. Wars. Plagues. False kings with fire in their veins and death in their wake. If you want history to repeat itself, then stay behind. But if you believe in what we swore—ride with us."

One by one, they looked to Tristan. For all his youth, for all the torment he had endured—he stood unflinching. The silver fire in his soul, dimmed but not extinguished.

Tristan drew his sword. The steel gleamed in the torchlight, bearing the sacred mark of the Flame etched into the hilt.

"I won't promise we'll all return," he said. "But I swear this—Kaelen will not use the Heart to destroy what we are. Not while I still breathe."

Sir Hugh exhaled. "Then may the Flame judge us all." He stepped forward—and dropped to one knee.

A moment later, others followed. Aldric. Evelyne. Gideon. One after another, the Order knelt around Tristan in a circle of solemn fire.

Tristan bowed his head. "So be it," he whispered. "We ride."

Silence fell, heavy as lead.

Tristan surveyed the group. "We move together. No one rides ahead. No one stays behind."

Thorne said, "If we find Kaelen, we strike fast."

Tristan shook his head. "If we find Kaelen, I face him first."

A murmur of protest rippled through the group.

"Don't be noble, Tristan," Evelyne said.

"I'm not. I'm responsible."

After a pause, Gideon said, "Then don't die. We're too close now."

"Let him do what must be done. If the Flame speaks through him, we follow," Aldric said quietly.

There was a long silence. Then Olivia mounted her horse and looked down at them all. "This ends today. We take back the Heart... or we don't come back at all."

They began the march.

Through the forest, where the trees grew twisted and the air grew thin. The closer they got to the Spire, the darker the sky became — as if the sun itself hesitated to shine too near.

The air was thick with the scent of pine, steel, and anticipation. A heavy mist clung to the ground as Tristan and his men gathered beneath the ridge, the looming walls of Kaelen's fortress silhouetted in the pale light of dawn.

The Black Spire rose ahead, jagged and wrong, as if grown from bone and obsidian. At its base, blackened ruins and broken statues littered the path.

Tristan's voice was low, resolute. "We go in swift, silent, and together. Aldric, flank right with the second unit. Gideon, take the lower pass and be ready to break their line from within." He turned to Evelyne, who stood armed and ready in dark leather. "Keep the archers covered. Signal once the gate is breached."

They nodded.

Tristan dismounted first. The others followed.

They stood at the foot of the broken stone stairway. No guards. No traps. Only a wide, open doorway — like a mouth waiting to swallow them whole.

"Why does it feel like it's been waiting for us?" Liora whispered.

Tristan answered low and steady, "Because it has."

Together, the last of the Order climbed the stairs — into the black mouth of the Spire, toward the Heart... and whatever Kaelen had become.

* * *

A sharp battle cry pierced the air.

The battle had begun.

Arrows rained down in silence before the fortress erupted in chaos. The first explosion—Gideon's doing—shattered the east gate, sending debris and shouts spiraled into the sky.

Tristan charged forward, sword raised, his black and silver cloak trailing like smoke. Beside him, Aldric fought with a roar, cutting down Kaelen's guards two at a time.

The fortress yard was a blur of flashing steel and screams. Evelyne's arrows whistled overhead, striking true as she covered their advance. Gideon emerged from a shadowed corridor, bloodied blade in hand.

"They know we're here now," he shouted. "Kaelen's sending the rest."

They pushed through a phalanx of armored men. Tristan fought like a man possessed—his sword met Kaelen's dark-robed guards with brutal precision, every strike fueled by memory and vengeance.

As they reached the stairs, a surge of dark energy pulsed through the stone—Kaelen had felt them. The wind howled through the shattered stones, the air thick with unease. Light filtered in through cracks in the ceiling, casting eerie shafts of light across the broken altar where the confrontation would begin.

Tristan stepped forward, his sword drawn low at his side. His breath misted in the air. He could feel the pulse of the Heart of Elander—not from his amulet, but from somewhere deeper in the earth, twisted and wrong.

From the shadows, Kaelen emerged, his hand ablaze with unnatural fire. No longer the man Tristan once knew, Kaelen's eyes burned with a silver fire. His fingers crackled with dark energy, tendrils of corrupted magic flickering through the air around him like smoke and lightning. His obsidian amulet hung from a chain at his throat, pulsing red.

"You came, just as I wanted," Kaelen said, his voice no longer fully human. It was layered, fractured—like whispers echoing through a cave.

Tristan stepped closer, lifting his blade. "Aye," he said grimly. "Now face me," he growled. "I came for the Heart. What have you done with it?"

Kaelen smirked. "I've awakened it. Unlike you, I don't fear its power. I embrace it. And now it listens to me."

He raised his hand. The stones beneath Tristan's feet trembled. A sudden force slammed into him, sending him crashing into the pillar behind him. Pain exploded through his shoulder, but Tristan pushed to his feet.

"You think you can twist the Heart to your will?" Tristan spat. "It was never meant to be used like this."

"Oh, but it responds to me," Kaelen said with a cruel smile. "Want to see?"

He flung both hands forward—and the darkness came alive. The air crackled with tension inside the Black Spire, where Kaelen's corrupted magic pulsed like a living thing.

A wall of force slammed into Tristan, bending the very air. His sword was ripped from his hand and flung across the room with a screech of steel. Wind howled through the broken stonework as Kaelen stepped forward, eyes blazing with unnatural light, energy swirling around his body. But before Kaelen could strike—

Olivia.

She emerged from behind, ducking low beneath a curling tendril of magic and skidding across the floor. In her hands—Tristan's sword. Her eyes met his, wide but filled with fire. "Take it," she gasped, pressing the hilt into his hand.

The moment his fingers closed around it, the amulet at his throat blazed white-hot. Magic pulsed from it like a heartbeat—strong, defiant, ancient.

Tristan rose, drawing Olivia behind him with one protective arm. His sword flashed, now glowing with the same fierce light as the amulet.

Kaelen hesitated, the power suddenly faltering.

Behind them, Gideon darted through shadows, searching for a weak point in Kaelen's defense. Aldric stood with his blade ready at the edge of the chamber. Evelyne whispered a protective spell under her breath, eyes never leaving her brother and Olivia.

The Silver Flame, what remained of the old order, gathered their strength—ready to make their final stand.

Kaelen laughed, low and bitter. "So be it. You've chosen your doom—now face it."

But Tristan didn't flinch. "Not doom," he said, sword raised. "Destiny."

"You were always the favored one," Kaelen hissed. "The noble knight. The chosen. But I've seen the truth. I've heard what the Heart whispers in the deep. And now, I'll show you what happens when fate is rewritten."

Tristan stood his ground, defiant. "You're sick with it. The Heart wasn't made for control. It was made for balance."

"And balance must be broken," Kaelen snarled, his eyes glowing brighter.

Suddenly, the ground cracked open behind Kaelen— flames licking at the stone.

The earth trembled beneath their feet as the chasm widened—Kaelen teetered on the edge, his cloak whipping in the rising heat. Flames burst upward, licking at the stone like hungry serpents, illuminating his face with a hellish glow.

Tristan shielded Olivia with one arm, sword still raised, the amulet at his throat glowing fiercely in response to the chaos.

Kaelen laughed, the sound twisted and unnatural. "You think this is the end?" he spat, voice echoing over the roar. "The Heart answers to me now!"

"No," Tristan growled, stepping forward. "It never answered to power. Only to purpose."

Kaelen lunged—but the ground gave way beneath him and he disappeared.

The Heart, hidden within the chasm, screamed in Tristan's mind. A cry of ancient pain. And Tristan understood:

If Kaelen succeeded, the world would unravel.

Everyone rallied around Tristan and Olivia after Kaelen vanished into the chasm—cheers echoed, torches lit the darkened sky, and for a brief moment, hope shone bright across the battered faces of their allies. But in Tristan's heart, there was no peace.

He stood at the edge of the broken stone, staring into the void where Kaelen had fallen. The amulet at his chest pulsed faintly, no longer glowing as it had in the final moments before Kaelen disappeared. Beside him, Olivia placed a hand gently on his arm.

"He's gone," she whispered.

Tristan's jaw tensed. "No. Not destroyed."

He turned to her, blue eyes clouded with a haunted intensity. "The Heart is still out there. I can feel it." He touched the center of his chest. "This... this isn't over."

Behind them, Aldric and Evelyne exchanged glances. Gideon crouched by the chasm, peering into the depths with narrowed eyes. "No body," he muttered grimly. "No peace."

"What do we do now?" Evelyne asked, voice steady but tight with worry.

"We regroup," Tristan said, straightening. "We rest. But we don't relax. Kaelen may be wounded, but he still has allies—and he still has the Heart. We must find it."

He walked over to the wall and grabbed a torch. As Tristan peered into the darkness of the chasm, his breath caught.

The torch in his hand flickered, casting long shadows across the slick stone walls. For a moment, it looked as though the abyss below held nothing but an endless void—but then, he saw it: a winding staircase carved directly into the rock, spiraling downward into the depths.

"Olivia," he said, voice hushed but urgent. "There's a way down."

She stepped closer, her eyes widening. "You're certain?"

He nodded. "Look there—just past the ledge. It's narrow, but it holds."

Olivia took a careful step forward, her own torch held aloft. "Who would build something like this?"

Tristan's jaw tightened. "Someone who didn't want to be followed easily."

The air grew colder as they stood on the edge, the chasm breathing up a damp chill. The amulets they both wore began to hum faintly, responding to something ancient that stirred in the dark.

"We have to go," Tristan said, voice low. "The Heart, it's down there."

When Tristan declared that they would descend into the abyss to face Kaelen and recover the Heart of Elander, the room fell into a breathless silence. The shadows of torchlight flickered across stone walls, casting the grim resolve on his face into something nearly mythic. His voice, though calm, bore the weight of fate itself.

Evelyne was the first to break the silence. "Then I go with you," she said fiercely, her blue eyes unwavering. "You are my brother, and if the abyss must be faced, then it shall not swallow you alone."

Olivia looked at the swirling abyss below and back to him, her trust unwavering. "Let's go find it."

Aldric nodded once, his tone steady but resolute. "I swore an oath to follow you, no matter the path. Even if that path leads beneath the earth into darkness, I will not turn back."

Gideon gave a low whistle and leaned back against the wall, a crooked grin tugging at his lips. "Well, I've stolen from nobles, broken into fortresses, and dodged death more times than I can count. Why not add venturing into a cursed chasm to the list? Besides..." He sobered slightly. "If Kaelen truly has the Heart, we don't have a choice."

Sir Hugh gripped the hilt of his sword and said, "If the Flame was ever meant to mean something—it's now. We burn brightest in the dark."

Tristan's gaze swept over each of them, pride rising like a tide in his chest. These were not just followers—they were family, bound by loyalty and love.

"Then we descend together," he said, voice low with emotion. "Not as pawns in his game—but as fire, as light. We end this, together."

Thorne crossed his arms and gave them a hard look, his scar catching the firelight as it tugged with his frown.

"You lot have gone mad," he muttered. "Chasing a cursed legend into a chasm like it's a tavern game. You do know people don't come out of places like that, aye?"

Tristan met his gaze without flinching. "We have no choice. Kaelen has the Heart. If we don't go after him, he'll use it to destroy everything."

Thorne exhaled through his nose, shaking his head. "Well then, you'd better come out alive, Lord Tristan. All of you. Because if you don't, I swear I'll find a way to drag your bones back out myself just to yell at you."

Gideon smirked. "That's the warmest sendoff I've ever heard from Thorne. Must mean he likes us."

Thorne grunted and tossed Tristan a small leather pouch. "Tonic. For the pain. You'll need it when your pride gets bruised."

Tristan gave a grateful nod. "Thank you, Thorne."

As they turned to descend into the darkness, Thorne muttered to himself, "Madmen and their magic. Saints preserve us all." But he stood watch at the chasm's edge long after they'd gone.

The stone passage twisted downward, slick with moisture and lit only by the dim, flickering glow of Olivia's torch. Her hand trembled slightly—not from fear, but anticipation. Beside her, Tristan's sword was drawn, the steel gleaming faintly with a strange iridescent shimmer. The amulet around his neck pulsed with warmth, reacting to something deep below.

"We're close," Olivia whispered, the air thick with an ancient energy that seemed to hum through the walls themselves.

Tristan nodded. "I can feel it. He's down there. And the Heart."

A sudden gust of cold wind rose from the abyss below, carrying with it a sound—something between a whisper and a scream. Olivia stopped, her breath catching.

"That's him."

Kaelen's voice echoed up from the darkness. "You should not have come."

Tristan's eyes narrowed. "He knows we're here."

They pressed on, descending a final crumbling stair into a massive cavern veined with glowing crystal. At its center stood Kaelen, his once-regal armor corrupted and darkened by the Heart's twisted influence. His eyes blazed with a feverish light, and before him on a stone pedestal hovered the Heart of Elander, glowing blood-red.

Olivia gasped. "It's changed."

Kaelen turned, smiling coldly. "Of course, it has. You brought it to life. Your bond, your love, your defiance—it feeds it. And now, I will use it to tear your souls apart."

Tristan stepped forward, sword raised. "You'll do no such thing."

Kaelen snarled. With a flick of his hand, dark tendrils of energy lashed out. Tristan blocked one with his sword, but another caught him across the ribs, flinging him backward. The others stood back.

"Tristan!" Olivia shouted, rushing to his side. She held the amulet tightly. "We end this—together."

Behind them, Kaelen paused mid-step, his hand clenching around his dark crystal. He felt the surge.

Deep beneath the earth Kaelen raised the Heart of Elander high above his head, its eerie crimson glow pulsing like a living thing in his palm. The cavern shuddered with a low, tremulous rumble, as if the very earth sensed the wrongness of what he was attempting.

Tristan gritted his teeth. "You don't understand what you hold. It was never meant for you."

Kaelen's face twisted with fury. "I am power! I command the Heart!"

Olivia stood behind Tristan, her amulet glowing silver in response. "You don't command it. You corrupt it. And it won't let you."

The amulet flared in Olivia's hand. Kaelen recoiled.

"No! That power—"

Tristan rose slowly, blood on his cheek, his free hand closing over Olivia's. The twin amulets burned white-hot between them, and the fractured Heart began to vibrate violently.

"I think," Tristan said through gritted teeth, "you've underestimated what love truly is."

The Heart flared suddenly, blindingly bright. Kaelen stumbled. He looked at the crystal in horror as its light turned against him—burning hot, searing through his skin. Cracks spiderwebbed along his arm as the power surged uncontrollably, no longer answering his will.

"No!" Kaelen screamed. "It's mine!"

The Heart pulsed once—twice—and then unleashed a blinding eruption of energy that engulfed Kaelen's body. The scream that followed was not just of pain, but of despair and madness, echoing through the vast stone cavern.

In the aftermath, there was only silence. The Heart hovered in the air, pulsing now with a soft, warm light.

And then it spoke—not in words, but in ancient feeling. A voice of memory. Of purpose.

Echoes of past and future flooded their minds: kings and warriors long dead... seers who had guarded its secret... a fire that could cleanse or consume.

And then a truth: "Only in unity can you command me. Only in devotion shall I obey."

The Heart settled, glowing with soft, golden fire. The amulets, still humming, had changed—no longer simple talismans, but extensions of a force far greater.

Tristan stepped forward and caught it, breathing heavily. "It has chosen," he whispered.

Olivia reached for his hand. "And so have we."

Together, they turned away from the ashes and the ruin Kaelen left behind—rising from the depths, guided by the true power of the Heart, now restored.

The chamber pulsed with a strange hum, a rhythm that seemed to echo not only through the air but within their bones. Olivia's hand gripped Tristan's, their joined fingers trembling as they stepped closer, the two amulets blazed in unison, golden and silver light merging into a swirling storm of brilliance. The ground trembled. Wind spiraled from nowhere, sending dust and old leaves skittering through the chamber. The runes on the floor ignited with a searing light.

Tristan stepped forward, eyes wide. "Olivia... it's bound to us now."

She swallowed, breathless. "And we to it."

* * *

It was over.

The fires of vengeance had been extinguished, the blade of treachery broken. Marlowe and Kaelen—swept away by the very darkness they had tried to harness. The Heart of Elander pulsed no longer with chaotic energy but with a quiet, steady glow—peaceful at last.

The Order of the Silver Flame was restored.

Tristan, bearing the scars of war and the mark of a leader reborn, stood before its ancient altar, Olivia at his side. She held the restored Heart of Elander, no longer a source of mystery, but of meaning—a symbol of everything they had fought for. Together, they placed it back where it belonged, deep beneath the stone floors of the sacred hall, watched over by those who had once sworn oaths in fire and blood.

The ritual began—Tristan placed his amulet beside the Heart, and Olivia did the same. The two halves resonated with the crystal core, causing it to glow brighter.

Now, those oaths were renewed. —each member affirming their role in protecting the Heart, even unto death. Tristan and Olivia were officially bound to its legacy.

Evelyne stepped forward, flame in hand, and relit the brazier. Aldric raised his sword. Gideon, leaning lazily in a shadowed alcove, gave a nod of approval—his loyalty, ever subtle, carved in deeds rather than words.

A new prophecy was revealed—inscribed on the walls, now glowing with light. It speaks of a fire that will either purify or consume the world... and named Tristan as "The Pyre Lord."

* * *

Ravenshire, once a battered stronghold, began to live again. Olivia worked side by side with healers, bringing modern knowledge in careful measures. Children laughed in the halls again. The people no longer whispered of witches and curses, but of strength and hope.

Tristan laughed more now.

He teased Olivia in the courtyard, challenged her to spar with dulled blades, and stole moments in the kitchens where they'd sneak wine like thieves and kiss like lovers. He had learned how fragile peace could be—and how precious.

And every evening, as the sun dipped behind the hills, they would walk hand in hand across the ramparts, the wind brushing past them like memory. No longer haunted by the past. No longer chased by destiny.

Now they shaped it.

Together.

* * *

Years Later...

The autumn sun cast a golden haze over the rolling hills beyond Ravenshire. The trees had begun to turn, their brilliant leaves drifting gently to the ground. From a high window in the keep, Olivia stood, her arms wrapped around herself as she looked out over the land that had become her home.

Laughter rang out from the courtyard below.

She smiled and stepped back as the door opened behind her.

"You'll miss the chaos if you linger up here," came Tristan's familiar voice. His hair had grown a touch more silver at the temples, but his eyes—those piercing blue eyes—still burned with that same fierce light. He stepped into the chamber, and Olivia turned to meet him.

"They've roped Gideon into playing the villain again," he added with a chuckle. "Three of them armed with wooden swords. He's pretending to beg for mercy."

Olivia laughed softly. "He loves it. He just doesn't want anyone to know."

Tristan wrapped his arms around her from behind, pulling her close. She leaned into him, resting her head on his shoulder.

"Can you believe it's been ten years?" she whispered.

"I can. Every moment burned into my memory." His hand found hers, their fingers intertwining.

Below, their children—two boys and a girl—dashed about in the courtyard, wooden swords clacking, Evelyne

344

calling after them to stop before someone got hurt, and Gideon dramatically collapsing into a haystack.

"Do you ever miss the adventure?" she asked.

He kissed her temple. "Not for a second. I had enough adventure for five lifetimes. This"—his hand swept toward the window—"is the life I dreamed of. The one you gave me."

"And you gave me everything," Olivia murmured.

They stood there, wrapped in quiet contentment, as the breeze stirred the curtains and the voices of their children echoed through the keep. Somewhere in the chamber, the amulets rested, now dormant. Their purpose fulfilled.

But just for a moment, as the sun dipped below the hills, they shimmered faintly—one last eternal echo—before falling still once more.

EPILOGUE

The soft glow of a table lamp illuminated the corner of Morgan's living room. She sat curled on the couch, the ancient, leather-bound book open across her lap. Its parchment pages crackled softly as she turned them, revealing the next passage written in elegant, old-fashioned script that shimmered faintly with a golden hue.

Aaron entered from the kitchen with two mugs of tea and handed one to her before settling beside her, his shoulder brushing hers. "Where were we?" he asked, glancing at the open page.

Morgan grinned. "Just in time for some mischief. It looks like Tristan and Olivia snuck into the castle kitchens."

Aaron raised a brow. "Let me guess—more swordplay or... forbidden desserts?"

Morgan laughed and began to read aloud:

"The keep stood proud against the fading twilight, its towers brushed with gold from the setting sun. Children's laughter rang through the courtyard—two boys with their father's spirit and their mother's courage, and a golden-haired girl whose laugh could light the darkest hall.

Sir Tristan, now older, with flecks of silver at his temples, stood in the archway beside Olivia. Her gown brushed

346

the stone floor as she leaned into him, their hands entwined. Peace had long since settled over Ravenshire, but he never took a single day of it for granted.

They had fought for this—against time, betrayal, and fate itself. Together.

Inside, Evelyne guided the children's studies while Aldric and Gideon argued cheerfully over a game of strategy. The amulets were sealed away in the crypts below the chapel, watched over by the Order of the Silver Flame. Their power was no longer needed—but their legacy would never be forgotten.

Olivia looked at Tristan and smiled. 'Do you ever think about the beginning?'

'Every day,' he said, brushing a kiss to her forehead. 'You were the light in the dark, Olivia. You always will be.'"

Morgan closed the book gently, her throat tight. Across the page, the final lines glowed faintly:

"Their story was not lost to time. It lived in whispers, in stone, in memory. And for those who dared to believe… it lived on."

Aaron put his arm around her shoulders. "Think it was real?"

She smiled. "I think love like that leaves echoes," Morgan said softly. "Eternal ones."

Morgan glanced at the next page. Something shimmered at the top—a new passage that hadn't been there before. Her heart pounded.

"Oh my God," she whispered. "It's still being written…"

www.ingramcontent.com/pod-product-compliance
Lightning Source LLC
Chambersburg PA
CBHW060354260626
47160CB00006B/2304